UNFORGETTABLE

R.E. LOTEN

To Denis
Happy reading!

CONTENTS

CASTLE PRIORY PRESS

First published in Great Britain in 2022 by Castle Priory Press, Brightlingsea

978-1-7398867-0-7

For Shirley, who was the first to read this.

PROLOGUE

I'll always remember the first day I saw *her*; the woman who made me, at least temporarily, forget that I had been married to the woman I loved for ten wonderful years. She was reading a book and I think that's what caught my attention to be honest. Such a large book in the hands of so slight a person. The solemn looking tome looked out of place in such a vibrant setting, out of context with both its surroundings and its owner.

She lifted her head and blinked, as dazed by the sun as I was by her. Our eyes met and a brief half smile flashed across her face in acknowledgement of the contact; for that moment I was lost. Lost to myself, lost to every sense of moral propriety I had ever held dear; lost to my wife; lost to everything save HER.

I
OLIVIA 1997

At the age of eighteen, I had been deemed mature enough to begin making my own life choices. Fulfilling every cliché going, I cast off the guiding hand of my parents, declared myself an independent, free spirit and selected a university that was far enough from home to allow me to demonstrate this.

I was going to be a new person. Until now, I'd been quite insular in my outlook on life – in some ways I was fairly streetwise, but in others I'd been told I was hopelessly naïve. Unlike many of my peers, I didn't leave behind me a string of abandoned girlfriends. My parents were quite old-fashioned and I guess some of their views rubbed off on me. I wasn't interested in one night stands – if I'm being perfectly honest, I was more interested in women in a theoretical way. Frankly, the reality of them scared me. I'd been brought up to be respectful of them – love was something to be cherished, not a fleeting physical act. The girls I'd known however, viewed themselves differently – they didn't necessarily want to be looked after and my female classmates had set about re-educating me to some extent.

I knew I was a work in progress, but I was optimistic about this chance for a fresh start. I would consider the well-meant advice they'd given me and attempt to put it into practice. No one in Exeter knew the old me and I was determined that my new personality would be a success.

It wasn't that I disliked my home city (or my family) so much that I had to move away, or even that I particularly wanted to prove I could be a different person. It was simply a logical and calculated choice to study at the best university for my course. Exeter had an outstanding reputation. Its distance from home and the subsequent feeling of independence, were nothing more than an added bonus.

Consequently, I found myself standing outside a crumbling manor house, its cream paint peeling and flaking away to reveal the brickwork beneath. It seemed a fitting and slightly depressing reminder of the house's faded stature: from grand home of the at least rich, if not famous, to an accommodation block for a hotchpotch of students, some of whom would have been more likely to be found in the servants' quarters in the house's heyday.

Not that it wasn't attractive in its own way; it certainly had character and the grounds were beautiful – a rolling landscape of wide paths and lush gardens. At the bottom of the garden sat thickly foliaged plants that would – as we later discovered - give you a nasty looking rash if you so much as breathed too heavily near them.

Unfortunately, none of this mattered to me, not only because I knew nothing of plants and had little to no appreciation of the beauty that surrounded the house, but also because, as I was soon informed, I was not to be housed in it. The property had been gifted to the university on the proviso that no male students were to be allowed to reside in the main house. Modern equality laws being what they were, the university had, in its wisdom, decided that this stipulation was not really practical and got around the clause by housing male students in what had at one time been the stables and the Lodge House. Thus, the hall could still be mixed accommodation. It was to the latter building – now referred to as 'Westgarth', or more colloquially, 'the Garth' – that I was assigned. With a handful of other, equally disgruntled looking young men, I made my way there, dragging almost all my worldly possessions behind me along the uneven gravelled path. My battered old case bounced madly behind me, its wheels – damaged on a recent family holiday to France – squeaking maniacally as though the very notion of turning was torturous to them.

Having been shown to my room by the Deputy Hall Warden (a tall, miserable-looking PhD student, who informed us in a surly voice, that his name was Reece and he sincerely hoped we would not cause him any trouble this year) I paused for a moment, my hand on the door handle. I was suddenly unwilling to open it and meet the person who would be my room-mate for the next year. Having been part of the same group of friends from my early teens, the idea of now having to make new ones was a little alarming. I'm not normally given to these moments of introspection so it came as a nasty shock to find I was actually quite nervous.

Mentally giving myself a shake, I took a deep breath, in part just to assure myself I could, then pushed the handle down and the door open. The cold metal froze the ready smile to my face as I determined to make the best of whatever was on the other side. I was glad I'd taken those moments to steady myself because my first impressions were not positive ones. My room-mate was an anxious looking boy with a thin, pinched face. He barely lifted his eyes from his book when I entered the room, rheumy blue eyes behind thick lenses completing the unprepossessing features. I forced myself to speak.

'Hi, I'm Tom.'

'Hello,' he muttered. 'Peter.'

I appeared to be of little interest to him, so I crossed the room and dumped my case on the bed. Then, under the guise of arranging my own possessions, I surreptitiously observed him as he sat hunched over the desk.

The light from the functional white desk lamp spilled over its surface, illuminating the gathering gloom of the late September afternoon and casting a hunchbacked shadow onto the wall behind it. Spidery handwriting already filled several of the pages that were strewn across the desk and the text in the book was highlighted with scribbled notes crammed into both margins. I was reminded of an illustration I'd seen of Doctor Frankenstein at work creating his monster and smiled at how fanciful I was becoming. I imagined that somehow, the mere fact of having arrived in this hall of learning meant I was suddenly filled to the brim with new and exciting knowledge. I had a new and improved understanding of the world around me. I was now truly, indeed, a *student*: full of the same feelings of hope and optimism that had swept the country a few months earlier. The General Election had seen the first change of government for eighteen years. The new Prime Minister had swept to power on a tidal wave of support from people disillusioned with years of grey, uninspiring leadership. With his appointment, the Houses of Parliament seemed to be infused with sudden, spectacular colour. 'Things Can Only Get Better' reflected my parents' sense of buoyancy after years of floating rudderless, along a narrow blue river on which the wealthy sailed. The same wealthy who ignored those who fell off the ship and drowned under negative equity, unemployment and a whirlpool of debt. My parents were excited at the thought of change. I'd seen the new wave of women MPs greeted with joy by female friends who felt they were finally being given a voice in the halls of power. Only now did I fully understand that thrill, that sense of something have arrived, of being at the start of a brave new world. My daydream ground to a halt with this cliché and my smile became wry as I realised that perhaps there was still some work to be done on my burgeoning intellect.

I abandoned the pretence of unpacking properly and simply threw everything higgledy-piggledy into drawers, almost revelling in the gratuitous abandonment I'd not been allowed to indulge in at home. I took another look at Peter and braced myself to make another overture of friendship.

'You look like you're working hard already.'

It wasn't the most original thing I could have said and it was more in the way of being a statement than a question, but he obviously felt it couldn't be ignored so it served its purpose.

'I wanted to get a head start. I need to work my socks off if I want to get a good degree.'

His voice was thin and reedy and suited the rest of him. He could have sounded pompous, or as though he had a chip on his shoulder – and I did feel a faint flicker of guilt for being one of those people who could get away with doing little work and still walk away with good results – but he didn't. It had been said as a simple statement of fact and that made me warm to him, just a bit.

'I'm going to head over to the main house,' I said, 'Go and mingle a bit.'

Again, I felt the inadequacy of my own conversation, but he took the implied offer and to my surprise, turned the lamp off and followed me back through the grounds to the building at their centre.

The walk, although brief, provided me with an opportunity to take more notice of my surroundings, as I was no longer preoccupied by a suitcase hovering on the brink of imminent collapse. To my untutored eye, there wasn't much in the gardens to inspire deeper thought and I felt a sudden yearning for home. Devon was pretty enough, I suppose, but it had little to appeal to an adolescent who was a city boy to his core. The rolling landscape held no great attraction to one whose ideal view was the city of London from Tower Bridge: a sprawling cityscape where you were jostled impatiently should you ever have the temerity to attempt a moment to stop and appreciate the sights around you. It was a city impregnated with history but obsessively focused on the immediate; intimately aware of its heritage but insistent on living in the now. London, with its safety net of anonymity, where you could *be* whoever you wanted, *do* whatever you liked and no-one would even give you the satisfaction of a second glance. After all, who were you to warrant one? We've seen it all before, their indifference shouted at you. You were no-one special, just another living dot on a landscape so diverse, it believed itself to be un-shockable. It was totally at odds with this area of the country and I felt the difference in my heart with a sudden longing for the hard pavements and grimy air of the capital. The fresh air here was suffocating. The gruff tones and lost letters that belied the caring heart within my home city had been replaced by the softer sounds of the West Country. Its gently modulated tones were accompanied by kind-eyed looks that spoke of a genuine desire to know you better. Gone was the frenetic pace of life that screamed in your ear, telling you that like a child late for a school trip, you'd get left behind if you paused to take a breath and savour the moment. A much calmer, quieter voice took its place, reminding you to look around. It didn't want you to miss the red-orange smoulder of the sunset that illuminated fields full of grazing sheep, the glow of the dying day setting the white wool afire.

It should have made me feel more relaxed, but it didn't. I still felt like that child: I hadn't quite given up hope that something, or someone, would come along and rescue me, but was experiencing the dawning misery that I was the proverbial fish out of water here. This was not my home territory and I would have to fight to keep my standing. I wanted to have my intellect recognised, to prove I deserved to be here. I needed reassurance that being rejected from Cambridge did not signify the end of my dreams – this was the beginning of a new and different, but equally exciting future. My Cambridge failure had left me feeling as though my life had ended before it had even begun. I'd been so focused on the path I'd set out for myself that I failed to anticipate that just occasionally, life cannot be planned. The world doesn't read the script you've written for yourself and its author sometimes decides your character must travel a different path.

In this latter area at least, I knew I would not be alone. During my brief wait in the hall prior to being assigned to my room, I had overheard part of a whispered conversation.

'Of *course* you can do this, sweetheart. Oxford just wasn't meant to be; you're *more* than clever enough to be here.'

'I *am* good enough,' I told myself.

Maybe if I told myself often enough, I would begin to believe it.

These musings occupied me until I became aware that the sharp crunching underfoot had changed to the silence of the tarmac, melted into submission beneath the many feet that had trodden its well-worn surface. This change signalled we had almost reached the back of the house and it drew me out of my funk and focused me back in the present. I turned to Peter with a rueful grin as I pushed the door open and prayed he'd not said anything important while my thoughts had been wandering. As my mum would have no doubt reminded me, had she not already been on her way back eastwards; he may not have been destined to become my best friend, but he'd done nothing to deserve my rudeness, however inadvertent it may have been.

That started me thinking about home once again and I slammed the gate on that particular avenue of thought, not wanting to lose myself for a second time in memories of home. It was tempting to meander down that road, but however comforting those contemplations might have been, I needed to be here, now. The two hundred and fifty miles that separated me from everything I knew could have been a whole world away for all the good that thinking about it would do me. Home was safe and this was scary, but scary was good. Scary got the adrenaline going and kept me on my toes. Scary meant I was pushing the boundaries and making myself a better person. This was a challenge I was ready for, one I fully intended to face head on and overcome. I *would* seek out the people who I'd spend the next year living with, I *would* make friends and I *would* be a success. This was the mantra I repeated to myself through the library and the laundry room, along the corridor and out into the main entrance hall. Earlier, it had been full of freshers, dragging bags and saying their goodbyes to parents, some of whom were embarrassingly tearful. Now it was eerily quiet and gave the impression it was mourning its lost occupants. I spared little thought for its faded grandeur; gave even less thought to how many scenes of grieved departing it had been witness to and considered only how its emptiness reflected the way I felt. I hesitated, immobilised by a nauseating wave of anxiety and it wasn't until Peter stumbled over the raised edge of the rug and knocked into me, that I summoned up the courage to face the door to the Common Room.

I took a deep breath and pushed against the heavy oak fire door, unconsciously rubbing my fingers over the rough surface of the gnarled and knotted wood for good luck, in much the same way I realised, as my mum would have done.

The resistance from the door seemed to sympathise with my reluctance to enter the room. It was as though it sensed, in its aged wisdom, my need for those extra few seconds to prepare myself for this initial encounter. Then, suddenly, I was in the middle of the madness.

Names and faces flew at me from every direction, verbal assaults that engulfed me until I barely remembered my own name. I introduced Peter along with myself, knowing instinctively that left to his own devices, he would fade into nothingness. He obviously didn't understand the importance of first meetings and he would be written off before he'd even begun if I didn't help him out. My sense of responsibility towards him was however, at war with the equally pressing desire to not be associated with him, as though his oddness would somehow be transferred to me and we would forever be known as 'the weirdos from Room Three'.

Eventually, the tumult ceased and I found myself ensconced in the middle of a small group of boys, chatting about our respective tastes in music. Peter had drifted somewhere to the periphery of the room and was being shepherded by some of the Year Two and Three students who had chosen to stay in halls for a second year. My companions, it seemed, were housed in the stable block, the only mixed residence and I felt a slight twinge of resentment as already I could tell that this was where most of the fun would be happening. These were my kind of people; all from the South and up for having a laugh while they studied.

It wasn't that I had anything against people from the North, I just hadn't met many of them and those I had come across, had not made a good impression. There was one in particular who stood out in my memory; a fat man from Manchester whom I had encountered when on a family holiday in Majorca. The resort had been all-inclusive and the vast majority of patrons had not taken this to extremes. This man, however, was the exception and I remembered him vividly. The sight of his monkey-like stomach – complete with thick dark hair curling obscenely around itself – protruding over skimpy Union Jack speedos, had imprinted itself indelibly on my seven year old brain. He had marched up to the bar and ordered seven pints of lager, all for himself. The poor, harassed barman tried to explain that the hotel's rules were such that he was not allowed to serve more than four pints to one person, but monstrous Manchester man didn't care.

'If it's all-inclusive I can have as many pints as I want.'

In vain, the barman pointed out that while Sir's assertion was quite correct, he still wasn't allowed more than four in any one trip to the bar. *If, however,* the patient voice continued in a rather weary tone, *Sir would like to take four now, he could come back later for another three, should he still require them.* It took some little time for this maths to penetrate the primordial brain and be confirmed, but eventually, he subsided and waddled back to where his equally corpulent wife sprawled on a sunbed. She was bedecked in a loud floral swimsuit and screeched at him that he was a selfish pig, who had forgotten her Campari and soda. On hearing her voice, my father remarked that he was no longer surprised Manchester Man wanted seven pints.

'I'm only surprised he doesn't need more,' Mum said drily.

Thus far, this had been my main encounter with people from the other end of the country and so it was understandable I think, that I viewed them almost as a breed apart, as somehow 'not quite the same' as the people I knew.

The door to the Common Room opened again and drew my attention away from an evaluation of Radiohead's latest release. Two girls entered, each forming a striking contrast to the other. The leader was tall and slender, almost to the point of thinness with an angular face, high pointed cheekbones and a dark pixie crop that would have looked boyish on almost anyone else but suited her. She couldn't have been described as pretty, even by her friends, but she was intimidatingly confident, her gaze sweeping over us all, coolly assessing. I got the distinct feeling she was judging who would be worthy of her friendship, should they be lucky enough to have it bestowed upon them. The gaze fell on me and her face took on a calculating gleam that terrified me, before it was instantly masked and replaced by an expression which might have looked friendly, had I not seen the look that preceded it. Instead, it looked predatory.

Juxtaposed, was the girl who stood slightly behind her. Her position, half-hidden behind the ice queen, mirrored their contrasting introductions to the room. Soft waves of blond hair framed a round face that smiled gently, almost asking permission to be liked. Her demeanour was far meeker than her compatriot's, but the way she held her head up and kept her back ramrod straight made me admire her. It was clear she was nervous but had girded herself to go through the ordeal and do it properly. I sympathised with both her feelings and her determination to overcome them. How could I not, when they so closely matched my own? I also admired her. I kept my insecurities tightly locked away, masked by an air of false confidence, whereas she was brave enough to acknowledge them openly.

Her eyes darted around the room just as the dark eyes of the other girl had done, but the blue contemplation was less calculating and more in the way of searching for a friendly face. I felt her gaze fall on me and I gave her an encouraging grin. When I received a tentative one in return, her eyes creasing at the corners with the uplift of her mouth, I felt a jolt of electricity run through me and a current pulsed the length of my body.

Turning slightly, the taller girl murmured something to her and they made their way through the tightly packed chairs to where we sat.

'Hi, I'm Zoe,' dark hair said, dropping languidly into the

chair she had pulled up next to mine. 'No umlaut,' she continued, looking directly at me, leaving me wondering if she had somehow divined that German was a major part of my degree and if this was a bizarre attempt at flirtation.

Her friend perched awkwardly on the arm of the chair, as there were no others that weren't already occupied and I had to resist the urge to jump up and offer her mine. Whether this was through a misplaced sense of chivalry however, or merely a desire to remove myself from the proximity of Zoe's intimidating presence and strong perfume, I wasn't entirely sure.

'I'm Olivia,' she introduced herself, 'but everyone calls me Livvy.'

Her smile was bright, but her eyes retained their anxious look and I knew, even then, that she would always be 'Olivia' to me. I didn't want to be everyone to her. I wanted to be everything. Until this point in my life girls were something I'd only been hypothetically interested in and I didn't have the words to describe how I felt. There was one, but it was ridiculous to even think of using it. I barely knew the girl, for heaven's sake! How could I even consider using that word? All I knew for certain was that I would willingly endure Zoe's overblown overtures if it meant that I could be in close proximity to Olivia, who turned out to be Zoe's roommate.

The following day I met her again as we queued to collect our student union cards and as we chatted comfortably about everything and nothing, I was able to take more notice of her without the ever present Zoe distracting me. I now saw that Olivia too was slim, though unlike Zoe, there was the hint of curves to be discovered beneath the all-consuming jumper she wore and I found myself speculating what it would be like to run my hand over the slope between her waist and hip.

Her perfume was light and sweet and it was driving me crazy, filling my lungs until I needed her presence just to draw breath. Her eyes, that I had noted down as blue, were in actuality, almost grey in hue, but I couldn't allow myself to examine them too closely, for fear she would see the truth in mine and refuse to ever speak to me again. I kept my fists clenched deep within the pockets of my jacket in case my hands decided on impulse to respond to those thoughts. I was under no illusion what her response would be should they attempt to make a move and I was determined not to blow this by being too eager. Small she may have been, but there was an air of impenetrability about her that assured a person that unwelcome advances would be dealt with swiftly and painfully.

This in itself was another problem; her size that is, not the other stuff (that would only be a problem if I was an idiot, which I had no intention of being). I'm not the tallest of people, but she was just the right height to fit under my chin if I drew her in close. She would fit so perfectly into my embrace that I would find it hard not to risk trying it out if I spent much longer alone in her company.

Thus, the appearance of Zoe – when she inevitably turned up – was for once, as much of a relief as it was an exasperation. The flirting started the moment she arrived; coy glances, a light touch on my arm, affected giggles at comments that were not particularly witty or erudite. I'm not the most observant of people, particularly when it comes to members of the opposite sex, but this was akin to being flattened by an overenthusiastic steamroller.

After bearing up under the first five minutes of this onslaught, I sneaked a glance at Olivia, hoping to see even the slightest hint of jealousy play across her delicate features, but there was nothing. Not even a sign that she had noticed the furious flirting going on in front of her. It wasn't possible she was unaware of it; this stuff was being picked up by satellites and beamed to relationship counsellors as an exemplar of how *not* to attract a man. The most obvious answer was that she *had* seen it and didn't care, but this was an unpalatable option that I did not, *could* not allow for and so I dismissed it instantly. Or at least, I tried to. Somewhere in my subconscious it lurked, a malingering, malignant presence that constantly questioned, 'What if she *doesn't* feel the same? You don't expect her to have been hit by the same sucker punch as you, but what if there is literally *nothing* there?'

Try as I might, I couldn't find the mute button to turn the damned thing off and it continued to niggle away at me, spoiling the remainder of our time together, so it was with less reluctance than I might have expected that I said goodbye when we finally reached the front of the queue and went our separate ways.

Later that evening, I found myself at The Lemon Grove (or Lemmy, as it was more usually referred to) for the traditional Fresher's Party, designed to allow a person to meet their fellow students in a less formal setting than the vast lecture halls we were destined to spend most of our days in. In reality of course, as it was the campus nightclub, it only provided an opportunity for us all to get very drunk without too much impact on our wallets. Most of the people you met and befriended on these occasions you either didn't recognise the next time you met, or you pretended you didn't. Friendships and romantic entanglements formed under the auspices of alcohol were not necessarily the ones you wanted to cultivate when the harsh, eye-opening strip lights came on at the end of the evening.

That night though, I had an ulterior motive. I knew the girls were going to be there, as I'd gleaned as much from amid the flotsam of Zoe's chatter earlier that afternoon and I was hoping to use the cover of the crowded dance floor to try to manoeuvre Olivia away from her room-mate and begin working on giving her a good impression of myself. I had not dared to envisage a successful outcome to my attempt (the evil little devil in my head had been too vocal to allow for that possibility) but I was optimistic about the prospect of at least spending a bit more time with her. If I was fortunate enough to have the evening end with her in my arms on the dance floor, then who was I to question the workings of the fates? I *had* to believe they were on my side and that ultimately, Olivia would end up where she belonged. With me.

By the time I returned to my room in the early hours of the morning however, I was considerably less sanguine about matters. The night had been an unmitigated disaster in every way imaginable. It hadn't taken long after our arrival for me to realise I had grossly underestimated the difficulties of even finding Olivia among the gyrating crush of bodies that crammed the surface of the club's not inconsiderable dance floor. I had thought my best chance of success might be at the bar, but its length and the depth of bodies pressed against it meant I could have stood at it all night and still missed seeing her if she'd been waiting for service at its opposite end. I had also failed to factor in the cumulative effects of six or seven pints of lager on my bladder and my sensibilities.

On my third or fourth trip back from the gents, I was set upon by my fellow Thomas Hall students and dragged, laughingly protesting, onto the dance floor. For a moment, I thought that perhaps my luck had turned, as I was pulled towards a group of students among whom Olivia numbered. Her pale blue skirt was short, showing enough of her tanned legs to entice and her darker top fitted closely to her body, confirming my earlier observation that there were definite curves to be discovered. My rising excitement was quelled however as no sooner had my heart leapt nervously into my throat, than it plummeted into my Doc Martens, when I saw that yet again, where Olivia went, Zoe invariably followed. The black trousers she wore were so tight I couldn't help but wonder how she was managing to move without splitting them. Above these, was a black, sleeveless crop top that I assumed was designed to draw attention to her flat stomach. I gave it only a cursory glance before my eyes were drawn back to Olivia.

Earlier that day I had described Zoe in my head, as an overenthusiastic steam roller, but the sober Zoe of the morning had nothing on the vodka-fuelled Zoe of the evening. The girl was like a firework, spinning capriciously out of control with no thought for the safety of herself or anyone else. She fizzed from one person to another, flitting alarmingly from hysterical, Joker-esque laughter, to grinding up against a rather startled looking undergraduate from our hall. Far from not knowing where to put his hands, he knew only too clearly where he did *not* want to put them. From this she moved on to sobbing noisily on Olivia's shoulder. She had drunk far too much (*yes*) and made a complete tit of herself (*also yes*); that nobody would ever want to speak to her again (*unlikely, given that most of them are probably too drunk themselves to remember much about the evening*) and why did none of the boys want to dance with her? (*a – we value our eyes too much to get close to your flailing arms and b – frankly, you terrify us*)

Olivia led her off to the toilets, murmuring consoling words into the snot-bubbled wreckage, presumably to try to sober Zoe up and make her look presentable again. She was a far cry from the poised picture she had presented at the start of the night when the girls had walked past my window on their way to the bus stop.

Meanwhile, I was persuaded to dance. Now, I know that in some circles it's considered elegant and humble to falsely decry your abilities in a particular area, but when I say I can't dance, it's no false modesty that compels me. I have zero sense of rhythm or timing, two commodities I am reliably informed, which are essential for dancing. Nothing in my life had prepared me for the undiscerning panic and awkwardness that descended on me the first time I stepped onto a dancefloor and nothing since had done anything to dispel that sensation. However, my blood alcohol level was now high enough for me to quell the warning voice that tried to tell me that this was not a good idea and so it began.

Thankfully, this was an age before the advent of the mobile phone and social media, so no footage exists of my attempts to execute moves that were beyond my capabilities, even when I was in full control of my body. However, years later, when Olivia and I were discussing our first impressions of each other, she confessed that her main memory of that particular night (Zoe related recollections aside) had been of witnessing my ill-advised foray on her return from the toilets and thinking 'Hmm, that's an 'interesting' approach to dance' to herself. According to her, I appeared to be dancing to an entirely different tune to the rest of the room, so out of touch was I with the beat of the music. In an attempt to describe it to me in the absence of any visual record, she likened it to watching a frog in a blender. This seemed to me to be a particularly macabre image, but I was assured that such had been the awfulness of it, the simile was an apt one.

Needless to say, this incident did nothing to enhance my chances with Olivia, who on her reappearance, informed us that she was taking Zoe home. The rest of the evening passed me by in an alcohol infused haze of disappointment, which followed me back to the hall, culminating in what I fool-heartedly hoped might be a fortuitous meeting.

As I dragged my weary feet towards the Lodge, I met Olivia coming the other way, still dressed in her blue ensemble from the club, but with a brightly patterned wool scarf wrapped protectively around her shoulders. I smiled and tried to initiate a conversation, but she turned tired eyes on me and gave me a wayworn glance where only the very corners of her lips turned upwards. Laying a gentle hand on my arm, she stemmed the flow of speech.

'Sorry, Tom, I'm exhausted. Zoe's only just stopped

throwing up and fallen asleep. I only came out to get some fresh air and clear the smell of sick from my nose before I go to bed. I'll see you tomorrow.'

She looked genuinely disappointed as she stood there, soft tendrils of hair hanging down, her slim hand pale against the dark suede of my coat, the light touch burning itself onto the skin beneath, searing me to my core and branding me as hers forever. I knew then, without any doubt, that I was in love with this girl. I said nothing, however and merely moved aside so she could pass by without moving onto the damp grass.

I watched as she moved lightly through the emerging dawn and bit my lip to stop myself shouting, 'I love you!' at her retreating figure. Even in my drunken state I knew this was a step too far.

I didn't see much of Olivia over the next couple of days as – like everyone else – I was busy registering for my course, meeting my personal tutor and the other members of my degree class and generally settling into life at university. I imagined she was doing the same and yet I did not feel the lack of progress in my quest to attract her attention. We were together at dinner time and in the evenings, albeit as part of a larger group and she always acknowledged my presence with that quiet smile of hers. I had quickly learnt to tell the difference between the one of genuine welcome and the equally polite and only marginally less forthcoming one that appeared when she was merely being civil to someone. I doubt anyone else would have seen the difference, but I watched her so closely, I knew by heart the minute changes in her expression. I like to think she was honestly pleased to see me. I certainly never felt my presence was unwelcome, although other male members of the hall had described her as 'stand-offish'. Her face rarely lost the slightly guarded look I had at first mistaken for shyness and I took 'stand-offish' to mean that she had rebuffed overtures of a romantic nature. I didn't know whether to be pleased or put out by this. I was glad any advances had been unwelcomed, but worried she was being put in a position where she felt the need to discourage them. It upset me that I wasn't able to protect her from them. Not that she ever seemed to need protection. I was discovering that although she was warm and funny and friendly, she never revealed too much of herself in conversation, tending to listen and learn without saying too much about her own life. It's probably true to say that had I cared enough to remember what had been said, I could have told you how many brothers and sisters pretty much everyone else in the hall had, as well as the names of all their pets, their favourite kind of music and a whole host of other information I genuinely couldn't have cared less about. Alone, it was all trivial information but when put together, it built up a solid picture of the person and their home life. With Olivia, however, all I could tell you was that she was an only child. It wasn't like it was a deliberate attempt to be aloof and mysterious, she was just very good at steering the conversation back round to someone else if she didn't want to answer a particular question. She was so good at it, that I don't think anyone else ever noticed that she hadn't actually answered them. I only did because in my desperation to get to know her better, I noticed everything about her. It wasn't just the difference in her smiles, it was the way she folded the ends of her hair around her forefinger and then brushed it against her nose when she was nervous, or the way she examined her shoes and rubbed the toes against the back of her leg, trying not to laugh when to do so would have been unkind; the spark of indignation that flashed through her eyes, darkening them to a wintery storm when something made her angry, before she bit her lip and made her point in a measured tone that only I could detect the silvery bite behind.

Until now, I would never have classed myself as a people watcher, or as someone who was particularly good at decoding body language, but I was so attuned to her every emotion that even after the passage of only a few days, I felt I knew her better than anyone else in my life. The slightest tilt of her head told me everything I needed to know about what she was thinking, except where it mattered most to me. I still had *no* idea how she felt about me. I had cautiously acknowledged that she probably numbered me among her friends, but whether or not her feelings went any further than that, I couldn't say and it was driving me crazy. I knew that if I wanted to find out, I was going to have to be bolder than I had so far been. My ill-advised attempt at Dutch courage had taught me this was not the route to take and spending more time away from her was not an option either – two days had been enough. I had used them wisely and used our evening encounters to establish friendly relations, but it was now time to try for more. I'd got nowhere trying to work out where I stood; in that respect, Zoe would have been the far easier choice. If she liked you, you were never in danger of being left in any doubt about it.

Ever since the night of the Fresher's Party, she seemed to have transferred her affections from me to Eoin, another Thomas Hall resident, much to my relief and his terror. For the last two days I had chuckled to myself every time I'd seen him. He was a mesomorphic North Londoner with Irish roots who had exuded self-confidence until he became the recipient of Zoe's attention. Now, he had taken to peering myopically around the common room door before entering the room. If Zoe wasn't there, the rest of his body would follow his head and he would hide himself amid a group of us, making sure he was protected on both sides. If she had beaten him to it, a preyed upon look would come into his eyes and he would attempt to withdraw without being spotted. If he was too slow (as was often the case) and she caught sight of her quarry, she would pounce across the room and drag him to sit next to her, glaring in an aggrandised manner at any other female who braved her posturing in order to speak to the poor, beleaguered, Eoin. I felt sorry for him, particularly as I was possessed of the knowledge that he was quite taken with Olivia's friend, Sophie, a quiet girl who was on the same course as her, as well as being in our hall of residence. Eoin was reluctant to pursue this interest, for fear of unleashing the vengeful banshee we all sensed was lurking beneath the brittle confidence of Zoe's public persona. It had occurred to me to suggest to Olivia that a joint campaign to get the two of them together might be a good idea, not to mention a way of arranging for us to spend more time together. However, I was fairly certain Olivia would not want to upset or alienate her room-mate and I wasn't totally comfortable with the idea of interfering in someone else's love life, given that I had enough problems trying to kick start my own.

And so it was, that on the next evening, I decided to put my plan into action. I had no great confidence in its chances of success; there were too many external variables that were not under my control, but I was prepared to take the risk and accept the consequences if I failed. As had already become the norm, a group of us had gathered in the larger of the two communal rooms downstairs, drinking everything from tea to a large vodka and orange and in some cases, dragging lazily on a bright tipped roll-up, smoke from which clung covetously to fibres and hung in a dense fug above our heads. Even the non-smokers of the group greedily inhaled the vanilla scented haze that saturated the air.

The room itself was depressingly furnished. On our first evening we'd been treated to a talk from one of the more prosaic third years about how the bare wooden floorboards had once borne the dainty slippers of beautifully ballgowned debutantes. Now, they were scuffed and depressed by years of abuse from black soled trainers and stiletto shod students. She told us – with a nose wrinkled in disgust – that this disgrace was disguised by the formerly rich Persian rugs whose brightly woven patterns were now dulled by dirt and time. Like everything else in the house they were frayed at the edges and threadbare, but she tried to conjure up for us an image of their dazzling beauty, not the moth-eaten tattered rags they'd become.

A pool table graced the centre of the room, the green baize scarred with jagged chalk lines, stirring memories of games fuelled by drink. The legacy of these were the ugly furrows that cut through the dark wood and the ring marks from glasses long-emptied; relics from departed students.

In the corner, a battered grand piano harked back to the house's glory days. She informed us that it longed for someone to play it as it would once have been. One of the boys from the stable had responded to this invitation by sitting down and thumping out a medley of Oasis tunes.

The low bay window with its peeling white paint looked out onto the carriage drive; a long arc that swept up from the road to the front door with just enough room at its apex to swing a carriage – or in more recent times, a car – around.

Much as we took the mickey out of her grand statements, seeing the place through her eyes taught me to appreciate the room we inhabited. My first, disinterested observation of it was as nothing more than another dingy room, with its squeaky-springed sofa and low-lying wooden coffee table. After her lecture I saw a little more of the beauty in it and I quickly fell in love with both the room and the house that contained it.

I wondered if this was what it was like to really *see* things, to *understand* that architecture could talk to you. It was another thing to add to the growing list of new things I was experiencing and appreciating, a new awareness of what life could hold if you knew where to look.

I couldn't help but hear the little voice of hope that suggested perhaps this room would stage the opening scene of the micro-drama of my relationship with Olivia. It was time for my opening line.

'I'm bored,' I announced awkwardly, as we sat that evening. The conversation had been meandering around the room, washing over our semi-reclining figures. My limbs twitched, rebelling against the enticing lure of the faded velvet. 'I want some fresh air. Does anyone fancy a walk?'

For a moment, there was a perplexed pause. No student suggested exercise in those days. We were creatures of the video game, the book and the library, not the gym. Olivia's quiet voice soothed the silence.

'I'll come if you like,' she offered. 'I'll just grab my coat.'

She disappeared through the door, leaving a lingering trace of her delicate scent behind and I arched myself over the sagging back of the sofa to retrieve my coat from where I had stowed it on my way into dinner.

'I could...'

I cut Eoin off with a glare that would have turned tungsten to liquid and he subsided back into his seat with a smirk.

'Maybe not.'

I squirmed uncomfortably, not enjoying the fact that my motives had been discerned so easily, but it seemed that nobody else cared. The conversation had resumed, shaping itself around the gap I'd created and the tension left my shoulders until Olivia returned, wrapped in a patchwork coat that enveloped her small frame. Springing to my feet and throwing a hasty 'See you in a bit' over my shoulder, I hustled her out through the TV room and into the night, before anyone else could attempt to join us.

There was a biting chill in the air that night and Olivia's hands were thrust deep into her pockets, her shoulders hunched to ward off the cold, giving me no opportunity to 'accidentally' brush my hand against hers. We walked slowly, with no sense of purpose or directions, just content to be together. I couldn't believe I had finally got her alone and found myself frustratingly tongue-tied on the one topic I wanted to discuss. Every other part of the conversation flowed freely though; it was like talking to an old friend and I loved the way her hands waved in the air, growing increasingly animated the more passionate she was about the subject.

I tried to induce her to talk about home, to find out if there was a boyfriend waiting in the wings for her. Was there someone ready to snatch her away from me before I'd even had my moment in the spotlight? As usual though, she steered the conversation away from her and I found myself telling her all about my parents instead. In the end, I adopted a more direct approach.

'And what about you? Any jealous boyfriend waiting anxiously for the holidays?'

I kept my tone as light-hearted as possible; a casual enquiry from someone with a passing interest. I could hardly breathe though as I waited for her to answer.

We had ended up on a walkway on the far side of campus in a small, wooded area and the darkness created by the canopy of trees was reflected in her face. Although she kept moving, her whole frame vibrated with stillness like a cornered animal choosing between flight and fight. The tension coming from her stretched out over the surging black silence, then suddenly, unexpectedly, she laughed. The sound of it didn't reassure me. It was brittle, a harsh expulsion of air that cracked like a frozen windscreen under hot water, cutting through the cold night air and vanishing into corners, unstoppable and dangerous. I couldn't speak for fear of splintering the fragile stillness that followed in its wake.

'Sorry,' Olivia said at last, patting my arm, as she might to reassure a small child, 'But if you knew anything at all about my life, you'd know why that was such a joke.'

'Why don't you tell me then?' I suggested, capturing her hand and drawing it through my arm, so that it rested in the crook of my elbow.

She looked at me doubtfully as though wondering what to say. I tried to smile encouragingly; no-one had managed to glean any information from her and if I could get her to open up to me, then surely that was a sign she felt *something* for me. I guessed that a person as private as she clearly was, needed to feel a connection with someone to let them see her inner self. I tried to pour all of that understanding into my eyes as I gave her hand a gentle, but guiding squeeze, inviting her to talk. For a moment, she held my gaze through the inky blackness, her eyes searching my face for something. Whatever she was looking for, she evidently found it, as she took a deep breath and spoke, her words quiet but authoritative, as if she was detaching herself from the experiences she was relating, giving herself the distance she needed to tell her story.

'I guess I had a fairly conventional upbringing until I was about thirteen,' she told me. 'I had dance lessons from being quite young, tap, ballet, the usual stuff. I got a scholarship to a private school when I was eleven and had to work my butt off to keep up with everyone else. The broad Lancashire accent had to go as well, hence this...Middle England nonsense.' She waved a hand in the direction of her throat and smiled self-deprecatingly, almost mocking the transition she had made. 'That's why the idea of me having a boyfriend is so laughable. I had some good friends at school but the boys at that school weren't interested in someone like me.'

'Then they were either blind, or stupid, or both' was the retort on my tongue, but I kept my silence and allowed her to continue with her story uninterrupted.

'Then when I was thirteen, everything sort of fell apart a bit. My parents divorced and I couldn't handle it. There was other stuff going on as well and life was out of control. Nothing seemed to make sense anymore and I didn't know how to deal with it. The only thing that was in my power to change was what I ate and you know what teenage girls are like; always think they can stand to lose a few pounds and that's how it started.' She shrugged and pulled a face, her mouth turned downwards.

'You had an eating disorder?' I couldn't quite bring myself to believe what she was telling me, even while I knew this was not something she would lie about. It simply didn't fit with the image I had created of her.

'Still do,' she said matter of factly. 'Anorexia isn't something that just goes away. It's a nasty little sod that sits at the back of your brain, ready to attack if you let your guard down. It took trips to the doctor and threats of hospitalisation to make me start eating again and twelve months to get back to a healthy weight. Even now, if I get stressed, I stop eating and I have to remind myself that I actually need to have food if I don't want to die.' She quirked a grin at me with the last part of her speech.

I couldn't comprehend what she was saying. I was a food lover through and through and I couldn't conceive of a time where I would ever have to be reminded to eat. I chose to say nothing, for fear of saying the wrong thing and waited for her to continue.

'My dad left and I lived with Mum for a while and then the year I did my A-levels things got really bad and I ended up moving into a place of my own. Dad was too far away and I couldn't live with Mum anymore, so the school were brilliant; they talked to the council and eventually, I got my own flat. I gave it up though when I came here; there's no point in it sitting empty for three quarters of the year while I'm here. Someone else will have a much greater need for it.'

I was overflowing with questions I couldn't ask, all

jostling for position inside my head and fighting to be let loose.

'What will you do in the holidays?' seemed the only safe one.

'I'm going to Dad's for Christmas. After that, I don't know. If I can get a job somewhere that comes with accommodation I'll do that. If not, I'll probably go travelling and find work as I go. I've got a little while to organise it, so something will come up.'

She gave me a confident smile; a mega-watt of brightness, as the light from a passing headlight on the road beyond illuminated her face. We walked back to the hall in near silence, although her hand remained locked in mine, resting on my arm. I needed time to process what she'd said, to rein in my anger at her parents. All my illusions about her had been shattered, but she was more real than ever. However, it was a reality I needed to tread carefully on it in case the frozen surface cracked beneath my feet. The only question in my head was 'am I ready to risk plunging into the freezing water?' It was fanciful, but that was how I felt. That was how *she* made me feel and it was terrifying and exhilarating all at once, like diving over a waterfall, hoping that the rope attached to your leg was going to snap you back in time. Whatever my expectations had been for that evening, they had been crushed and reconstructed with such dizzying speed that I no longer recognised them and had to search for the foundations of them in my fuddled brain.

When we parted at the door to the house, she reached up and brushed the briefest of kisses against the stubble of that morning's shave, her lips burning an icy scorch into my already numbed flesh.

'Thanks for listening,' she murmured, her breath hot on my ear, then her hand was pulled from mine and she was gone.

My arm felt bereft and weightless without the touch of

hers and I stared at it for a moment, wondering how it was possible to feel so detached from one's own limb. Sleep eluded me for much of that night and when it finally paid me a visit, I was restless throughout, visions of Olivia parading through my dreams. Dreams, not nightmares, but just as unsettling in their own way.

I mostly kept to myself the following day, heading up to the campus quite early and hiding myself away in the library until lunchtime. I told myself I needed to find my way around the sections I needed for my joint honours degree, but much as I loved my subjects, there was only so long I could spend reading books on German literature and the history of Czarist Russia before my eyes started to glaze over. In reality I needed time to think about Olivia. Her revelations of the previous evening had really shaken me and I wasn't sure how I felt about them or her. Discovering that she had suffered from anorexia had shocked me and destroyed the illusory Olivia I'd built up in my mind. She was now a real person with everyday problems and I had a decision to make. Did I want that reality, or was it only the Olivia of my imagination I desired?

My sole alternative to the library was to smoke and I could feel the lure of the nicotine beckoning me, the siren call of its soothing sensation whispering in my willing ear. A deep sigh escaped at the thought of it. *You're giving up, remember?* I'd hidden this vice from my parents, but away from the fear of their disapproval it had been too easy to become part of the smoking crowd. *Will I lose my friends if I quit?* I looked again at the open book in my hand seeing nothing but a blurred block of black. *Olivia. What are you going to do? Are you really ready for a relationship? Do you even want one with the real Olivia?* Leaving the library, I sought solace in a cigarette.

After lunch, I walked into town and spent a few hours familiarising myself with the High Street and its extended row of shops, most sporting huge posters in the windows that shouted about the student discounts that were currently being offered. There wasn't a huge amount that appealed and there was certainly nothing I needed as my parents had seen me well stocked in clothes and other necessities prior to my leaving home. Nevertheless, by the time I boarded the N bus to go home, there was a hole in my grant money and I was weighted down by carrier bags from Waterstones and MVC. Secreted between the Tom Clancy and the biography of Catherine the Great, was a copy of Jane Eyre. I'd never read it; it had never appealed before, but I'd overheard Olivia mentioning that it was one of the books she was going to be studying this term.

The journey home wasn't long, but it gave me enough time to go over an odd encounter I'd had in the book shop. As I'd made my way to the tills I'd caught sight of a dark head secreted away in one corner of the shop.

'Hi Zoe.'

She dropped the book she'd just taken off the shelf and shooed me away when I tried to help her retrieve it.

'I've got it!' she snapped, snatching it up and stuffing it back in its place.

Apologising, I left her to it, musing that the self-help section was probably the right place for her. Despite complaining about Peter's lack of personality, I'd never envied Olivia the joys of sharing a room with someone so mercurial, but even by Zoe's standards, her behaviour today had been peculiar. She was an odd girl. Olivia liked her and that should have been enough, but her intensity terrified me at times. 'Desperation' clung to her and it was a perfume I tried hard to avoid. I smiled at my own wit.

I arrived back in time for dinner to find Olivia had contrived to keep a space for me. She seemed pleased to see me as I took my place but I noticed she was pushing her food into little piles. Beneath the cover of the conversations around us and the clatter of cutlery against the thick white dinner plates, she touched my hand lightly.

'Do you fancy going for a walk again tonight? I've been stuck inside most of the day and I could do with getting out for a bit. I wondered if maybe you might like to come with me? I mean, it's fine if you don't, but I just thought I'd ask.'

'No! I'd love to.'

The look of uncertainty disappeared from her face and she smiled again then returned her attention to her meal, the neglected food now being consumed at great speed.

I decided it would be much easier if we did away with the pretence of asking anyone else to come with us, so as we left the dining room I pulled Olivia to one side and whispered that I'd wait for her outside the front door. She nodded and raced off, taking the big formal staircase two steps at a time. Less than two minutes later, she had joined me on the gravel drive and we were crunching our way down to the road below.

Already, Olivia had changed the way I viewed the countryside around Thomas Hall and I breathed in deeply as we walked. It truly was a beautiful evening. The air had that kind of crisp autumn loveliness about it: cold enough to need a coat, but not so cold you could see your breath. The moon hung low in the sky, its silvery light casting dancing shadows that welcomed you in, inviting you to come and play with them. A calm hush had fallen over the whole countryside, broken only by the occasional purr of a car engine as its headlights loomed out of the darkness then disappeared into the noiseless distance, leaving only a faint white trace that vanished as soon as you blinked.

Once again, my power to speak coherently had deserted me in Olivia's presence and I was unable to think of a single thing to say. The silence wasn't strained, but nor was it companionable and there was a sense of something hanging in the air between us, a barrier I couldn't navigate my way past.

'Where have you been all day?' Olivia asked eventually, her hands twisting together as she spoke. 'No one seems to have seen you since this morning.'

'Yeah, I've been out. I spent most of the day in the library. Not the most interesting thing to do I know, but you know what it's like - I needed some books for my course and then after that, I just popped into town for a bit; did some shopping - books I needed – you know the kind of thing, boring but necessary.'

She seemed to accept my explanation, as a low chuckle bubbled over her lips and she patted my cheek with her hand.

'Poor baby,' she teased, a small smile tugging at one side of her mouth.

I flinched as though she'd struck me. Although the slight caress was welcome, my face stung as much as if she'd slapped me.

'Your hands are freezing!' I gasped. Then the indrawn breath expanded like a cartoon balloon and got stuck in my throat, as that ironic, teasing quirk lengthened and morphed into a cheeky grin.

'You could always do something about it!'

Her eyes and her hand dropped a mere half second later, so I could almost have believed I'd imagined the hint of flirtation. Fortunately for me, that split second of uncertainty freed my body from the controlling influence of my brain and provided just enough time for my hand to take matters, quite literally, into its own hand and jerk out to grab hers. She looked quizzically at our joined hands, seemingly as puzzled as I by the contact and I wondered if she was experiencing the same strange liquefication of her limb as I was.

I was a jumble of sensations all starting at the point of connection between our fingers; aware of everything and nothing, floating away but anchored to the ground through that link to her. Glorious warmth spread through me; not the heated flames of adolescent passion, but a gentle course of melted gold, a rippling stream that softened everything on its journey through my body. I could see every crease and indentation in the back of her hand without looking at it, hear the blood washing through the veins in her palm and feel every contour of her knuckles as I brushed my thumb gently over them, a feathery touch that bound me to her as tightly as any rope could have done.

We continued to walk along, not speaking, just enjoying the experience of this new closeness. A shift had undoubtedly happened, but I was still teetering nervously on the edge of this moment, torn between the safety of the ground and the joyously anticipated release of flight; still not sure enough of myself to take that final step into the unknown.

On the bridge at the bend in the road, Olivia stopped and released my hand to lean over the cobbled stone parapet and gaze down at the stream below. I could hear the gentle rush as it passed beneath us, slipping silkily smooth over the jagged stones that littered the stream bed, blithely ignoring them as they tried to divert it from the course of its downward journey to meet a second stream; old friends that whirled around each other in the joy of their reunion, laughing and giggling as they continued their journey together and I envied them their carefree familiarity. The moon dimpled and rippled on the surface of the water, its movements mesmerising. Olivia shivered and I put my arm around her shoulder, drawing her closer and inhaling the scent that left me befuddled every time I encountered it. I felt the hitch in her breathing and pulled her upright, my hands on her arms, rubbing heat back into her.

'It's so beautiful isn't it?' she whispered, her warm breath tickling my cheek as I leant down towards her.

'Come on, let's go,' I said. 'It's too cold to stand here all night.'

She said nothing further but allowed me to reclaim her hand as we began to retrace our steps. As we walked away from the bridge and its friendly little stream, I cursed myself for missing the opportunity to kiss her. The setting had been perfect and it wasn't as if I hadn't been imagining that moment for almost a week now. *What's wrong with you? All you had to do was lean in a bit more.* I could feel the unyielding presence of Olivia's arm next to my own, but it was less moulded to mine than it had been and her shoulder no longer leant into me. Her gaze was fixed on something I couldn't see and it was impossible to catch her eye.

The road had become busier as the evening grew later and more people were returning home from work, their headlights mocking my desire for a quiet corner of privacy. We were not far from the barred wooden gate that separated our hall of residence from the pavement and I was reluctant to return with things still unresolved between us, so in a minor state of panic I blindly guided Olivia down a narrow alleyway that led onto a small housing estate and we wandered wordlessly with no real idea where we were going, my brain still struggling to formulate what I wanted to say to her. In the end, it was Olivia herself who broke the silence.

'Shall we head back to the Hall? It's getting cold and I don't want to get lost.'

Her voice was flat and lifeless, dulled by what sounded like disappointment. I hoped that's what it was anyway. Things had been going well until we left the bridge and then she'd stopped talking to me. I had sunk into a fug of despondency, too caught up in berating myself for not acting to consider how *she* might be feeling. Was that why she wasn't talking? It had to be. There was only one way I could repair the situation and make amends for my selfish stupidity.

Not by a long shot was it the location I would have chosen, but I was a desperate man and I was past caring about having the perfect setting. The conversation of the previous night had shown me that Olivia herself was not the perfect being I had imagined her to be, she was flesh and blood, a living breathing human, as fallible and flawed as the rest of us. Much as I wanted everything to be just right, I realised that it didn't need to be perfect, it only needed to be perfect for us and there it was, standing triumphantly before us. A rickety looking bus shelter.

It was one of those small wooden structures you find out in the country with interlocking wooden slats that supported a sloping roof. Inside, a dilapidated bench that lurched drunkenly to one side, so that you could never quite 'sit' on it, unless you were no more than three years old, or had the bottom of a Mexican wrestler and on the colder days, the wind would whistle through the punctured knot holes and splintered slats, rendering its protection from the elements all but non-existent.

'Do you want to sit down for a bit?'

Pre-empting her answer, I determinedly steered her towards it and she frowned, looking from the bus shelter to the point at the top of the hill ahead of us where we could just see the lights from the top floor of the hall. We perched on the seats, our hands still locked together and I stared at the scuff marks on my DMs, polishing the worn toes on the back of my jeans. Silence fell over us again, shielding us from the prying eyes of the traffic, muting the sounds of homeward travel and cloaking us in a veil of privacy. I cleared my throat.

'Would you mind if I kissed you?' I asked, the words falling over themselves in their adrenaline fuelled attempt to escape before I could bite them back. 'It's just that I've been dying to do it for ages.'

A shy smile spread slowly across her face and she shook her head.

'I don't mind at all.'

So, I did. It was like seeing the warm glow from your living room lights at the end of a lengthy journey. A feeling of safety. Her lips were soft and yielding beneath mine; my fingers tangled in her hair, her arms wound themselves around my neck and when our mouths finally parted, needing to catch our breath, for a long time, neither of us moved, our foreheads resting together, connected still. I traced her cheekbone with my thumb, grazing the soft skin, needing to reassure myself that this was real and there we sat as the minutes ticked past, content just to be.

GRACE

It had been one of those weeks, the ones when absolutely nothing goes your way. Ever since our eldest had been born and Olivia had gone back to her job at the university library, I had worked from home, juggling my translation work with looking after our son, Theo. Two years later, his younger brother, Xander, had come along and joined our makeshift little nursery, followed two years after that, by our daughter, Elodie. Most of the time, it worked well and with Mum's help I was able to keep on top of everything, but sometimes keeping the work-home balance right could be tricky. The boys were at school now, with Elodie at the pre-school that was attached, so I was able to work during the day when the house was quiet. This week however, a client had been late sending me the information I needed and just when I had decided to abandon my desperate attempts to encourage her, Elodie had finally decided to begin potty training. In my opinion, at the age of almost three, this milestone was overdue; at the same age, her brothers had been dry for months and had almost cracked the overnight dryness as well.

In the days when she still spoke to me, Olivia used to tease that it was my fault. I was too lenient with her. Definitely more so than I had been with either of the boys. To her of course, I gave an outraged denial, but as was often the case, she was absolutely right. Not only was Elodie our baby and the only female of the group, she was also the spitting image of her mother. It felt as though I was being given the privilege of watching Olivia herself grow up. The boys, who both took after my side of the family in physical appearance, doted on Elodie and I was often forced to remind them that she was not a doll. She was a living, breathing human with a mind of her own, who did not always *want* to be cuddled and petted. When the boys had had enough of a situation, they could leave and escape to their bedrooms, but the various baby gates that still barricaded parts of the house, meant that Elodie didn't have that option and the tantrums that inevitably followed the boys' over-enthusiastic love for her, were not only a sight to behold, but an experience to be avoided if at all possible. My darling girl was like a summer storm in those moments. A squall whooshing up out of nowhere, then just as quickly blowing itself out, fading away to nothingness. Then the sun returned in all its golden glory to shine on everyone again.

It was impossible to stay cross with her when she bestowed the full force of that beaming smile on you and even at her tender age she was well aware of the effect it had on her father and brothers and used it knowingly to twist us to her every whim. Not that she was a spoilt child; she was loved and indulged, yes, but never to the extent it risked becoming a character defect. Olivia would never have allowed that, even had I been so inclined. She was determined our children would have the kind of childhood she had wanted. They would grow up free from care and worry; confident in their parents' love, safe in the solidity of our little family unit.

Nevertheless, she had pointed out – rather more forcibly that I felt necessary – they would grow up with a social conscience. Their own sense of self-worth was important, but not at the expense of the well-being of others.

'They need to know their place in the world,' she argued, when I questioned the suitability of exposing Theo, at the age of five, to the issue of homelessness.

'It won't kill him, Tom!' she said, throwing her hands in the air. 'I just want him to realise that not everyone is as lucky as he is! He had a tantrum because we told him he couldn't have a game. It's ridiculous that something so small makes him think he's so hard done-by.'

I felt her solution was extreme, but that was Olivia; always thinking of others and desperate to ensure our children grew up with what she considered to be the right values. I knew from experience there was no point arguing with her when she felt this strongly about something.

That morning had been particularly challenging and after dropping Elodie off at the pre-school and walking the boys round to their respective classrooms, I trudged home, head down, hands thrust deep into my pockets, ignoring the beautiful spring day around me. In my world everything was bleak and blanched of colour. When I reached the front gates, I paused, one hand on the cold metal of the door handle, immobile, unable to make the final movements that would take me up the drive and into the empty house that was silent and leeched of life.

Thoughts of the empty cereal bowls and breakfast detritus that lay piled in the sink like mountains of misery, islands in a dirty grey sea, waiting to be loaded into the already groaning dishwasher, filled my head. I could feel the panic rising and I quickly tamped it down, coercing the bile back. I took a few deep breaths, forcing the nausea to retreat from its determined assault. Waves crashed over my head and

I was back in the swimming pool nightmare of my childhood. The water was heavy, keeping me trapped below the surface, until finally, gasping for breath, I broke free. An insistent buzzing noise filled my ears, bringing me back to myself. My leg was vibrating; no, not my leg, my pocket. My phone. I scrabbled around for it, fumbling fingers through layers of clothing and finally located it, just as it stopped ringing. Eoin.

I'll call him back later, I promised wearily.

'Are you OK, Tom?'

I turned to see Mrs Barlow from next door, a slight frown creasing her already well-lined face. I had no idea how old she was, but she looked like Miss Marple; lined face and fluffy hair and the same air of vague amiability that concealed a core of solid steel. I'd once had the pleasure of witnessing her berating a group of youths who'd dropped their crumpled crisp packets and half-eaten sandwich carcasses by the war memorial. She was magnificent: walking stick waving wildly above her head, she was a vengeful nemesis of wrath and retribution as they ducked and dived out of its path. Unsteady on her feet she may have been, but her aim was true as she swung the stick around her, scattering them like skittles as they scrambled to collect the remains of their makeshift picnic.

I forced my face into the semblance of a pleasant expression, my stooped shoulders rearranging themselves.

'Yes thanks, Mrs B. Just one of those weeks, you know?'

She nodded sympathetically and patted my shoulder.

'I had weeks like that when I lost my George,' she said. 'But it will pass. The bad days always do.'

I nodded, a weak parody of a smile smuggling its way onto my mouth, then slithering away again the moment her front gate closed. She didn't understand of course. How could she? I decided the washing up could wait. It would still be there this afternoon and by then I might feel more able to face it.

Unlocking the front door, I went inside only long enough to retrieve my car keys and wallet, then slid into the driver's seat and set off with no real consideration of where I was going, only knowing I needed to get away from the house and its suffocating aura of misery. I couldn't remember the last time I'd stepped through its door and actually felt happy.

I depressed the accelerator, shifting through the gears and the fleeting idea, *What if I just kept pushing?* flashed through my mind. For a long half second, I fantasised about the crunch of crumpled metal, jagged blue shards sticking out like the wreckage of a ship at low tide, of my head slamming into the windscreen, scoring its pristine surface with thin trickles of life, like cracked riverbeds in a summer drought. And then I thought of the children. My foot shifted infinitesimally on the pedal and the moment had passed; I was ashamed it had ever existed.

A brown tourist sign caught my eye and a few metres up the road, I turned into a narrow, fence lined road. The car bumped its way down the track, throwing me from side to side as the wheels ground deep furrows into the surface. One rotation crushed the gravel, the next sent it spinning out of control, until it lay exhausted, waiting for the next set of tyres to come along and fling it to a new resting place. I knew how it felt and I sympathised.

For some time after I switched the engine off, I sat in silence, listening to the sounds within it; the faint 'tick tick tick' of my watch, measuring the seconds as they passed relentlessly by and the distant buzzing of an omniscient helicopter flying overhead, observing the patchworked landscape below where people and vehicles scurried from one place to the next. Caught up in their own concerns, they spared little attention for the insignificant people they passed, seeing only the superficial, heedless of the pain beneath the smiling masks presented to the world. The occupants of the helicopter would be able to see my car, ant-like, below them, unaware of the miserable creature it contained. I watched as the remnants of the previous night's rain trickled down the windscreen, dividing it unevenly down the middle and I reflected idly that it rather neatly echoed my life; one half before 'this', the other half after. I hated feeling like that, so dissociated from everything around me, as though I was observing my own life, rather than living and experiencing it as a fully functioning human should do.

Wherever I'd ended up, it wasn't a place I'd ever visited with Olivia and eventually, curiosity got the better of me. I dragged my protesting body from the car, attempting to leave behind the blue mood that had followed me from the house. It clung to me like smoke from a burnt out bonfire and I was never quite able to shake it off. I would think it had left me for a while and then, sometimes mere minutes later, I'd catch a whiff of it and there it was again. It wound itself around me, weaving its way through my clothes to my skin, where it lay solidifying and congealing until I feared it would never leave, would be my eternal companion, oppressive and cloying, taunting me with its very existence.

The shop and visitor entrance were only a short walk across the loosely pebbled car park, but it was not the glossy, chrome covered reception often found in such places. In fact, it rather reminded me of a large garden shed, crammed full of blue and green glazed plant pots, beautifully coloured gardening books and other present-worthy paraphernalia, all waiting for the discerning visitor to purchase them and take them home, allowing them to fulfil their purpose. It had a homely atmosphere, comforting in its promise of the joys of nature to come. Its brightly coloured displays reassured me that – contrary to how it felt – there were still a variety of colours in the world.

'Good morning, Sir.'

The cheery, customer friendly greeting seemed almost

alien in tone and yet I found myself automatically smiling and returning the greeting. I did not recognise the voice as my own, so different was its hue to the flat greyness I had come to recognise and loathe in equal measure. This muted neutrality was an anathema to the person I knew myself to be. The person I had once been. Before this. This stultifying oppression I felt. Every. Single. Day.

'One adult, please,' I said, passing the crisp five pound note over the counter to her.

'Have you visited us before?'

I shook my head and she slid a brightly coloured map across the smooth surface.

'I'll give you this then,' she said. 'You won't get lost, but it shows you where all the different styles of garden are. Enjoy your visit!'

Again, she flashed the gleaming, white-toothed smile and I was summarily dismissed to make my way through the gravel garden towards the main entrance and the larger garden environment. The gravel garden itself was surprisingly interesting. Designed to mimic drought-like conditions, it hosted plants that could survive in dry weather and I spent a few minutes wandering along the paths that criss-crossed the islands of flowers, admiring the hardiness of nature. The ability of the delicate stems to survive adversity and come back stronger each season was something I admired and I paused for a moment in front of a particularly pretty verbena. I recognised it as Olivia had bought one to plant in our garden, after seeing it in one of the National Trust gardens we had got into the habit of visiting.

'Isn't it beautiful?' she enthused. 'It says it's perfect for attracting bees and butterflies as well, so that's good. A couple of those would look lovely in that bit at the back by the fence, wouldn't they?'

I didn't have any strong feelings on the matter, but it was hard not to get dragged in by her eagerness and so I dutifully loaded the two plant pots into the boot of the car. Having planted them in the spot she requested, I then spent every year following that summer, digging rogue verbenas out of the rest of the garden and eventually we got into the habit of potting them up and leaving them outside the front of the house for our neighbours to help themselves to. I lost count of the number that had sprouted over the years, but it seemed as though every house on the street had our verbena growing in its front garden.

The one in the gravel garden had obviously been well tended to keep it under control and it had flowered early; the ones in our garden were still just green stalks, but this one was in full bloom. Its long, thin, delicate stems danced prettily, bending with the breeze, the clusters of purple flowers, delicate and dainty, weaving unsteadily through the air, free-forming to music only they could hear. A bumble bee landed on one head, bending it under the weight of its body, greedily draining it of nectar, before hovering gracefully to the next section of the plant. The dark stripes created a pleasing contrast with the bright blooms and I whisked my phone out of my pocket, managing, for once, to capture the perfect shot; the bee in glorious technicoloured close up, balancing on the verbena, its proboscis extended right into the heart of the flower. I could see the individual hairs on its body outlined against a backdrop of lavender petals and I marvelled at the complexity contained in this tiny creature. Bees were beings to be admired, I thought, working together to create something much bigger than each individual, each having their own place in society and sticking to their task, regardless of its difficulty or monotony, because it was the right thing to do for the community.

My study of the bee had lifted my spirits briefly and it was with a marginally lighter step that I followed the map's suggested route and made my way towards the ramp to enter the water gardens.

My first impression of it was that it looked like the external set of one of the Hollywood musicals that Olivia loved so much and the thought momentarily lifted my spirits. As I walked along, I found myself singing, *Stereophonic Sound* from *Silk Stockings* under my breath, but the song brought tears to my eyes, so I stopped.

A huge weeping willow hung low over one of the ponds at the centre of the grounds, the feathery fronds of its yellow-green leaves tickling the placid surface of the water, sending gentle concentric circles rippling outwards every time it dipped and bobbed in the breeze. Through the gaps between the fringed branches, patches of brilliant blue sky peeped cheerily, defying an observer to be miserable in the face of its unrelenting positivity. I was surrounded by hundreds of shades of green, punctuated by splashes of pinks, purples, oranges, yellows and reds, all competing for my attention, the colours clashing violently, cymbals vibrating after a short, sharp rim shot. Ducks disturbed the smooth surface of the water, diving down from the sky like nature's Stukas, honking angrily at each other, squabbling over their food, the will to survive present, even in a setting where they were well cared for. If they were to lose the fight, it would not be through lack of effort on their part at least.

It was like walking into a colourised photograph; the colours were too bright, too intense to be real and a gnawing headache began making its presence felt. It pricked at my temples, an internal itch I couldn't scratch, sending pointed pin pricks of pain darting through every nerve in my head. White jagged streaks of light seared across my field of vision. I had half decided to just return home to the grey, uninspiring tepidity that awaited me, where I would be safe from this dangerous onslaught of life, when I rounded a corner and saw *her*.

In an instant, I was surrounded by a comforting cocoon of warmth. The headache, which only a moment earlier, had been threatening to invade, now retreated, grumbling, to lurk in the shadows; I was protected from its attack and it didn't like it, but it was powerless in the face of the feelings that flooded through me. They swept away everything in their path.

I was acutely aware of everything around me. The delicate beat of the butterfly's wings, a throbbing pulse of delight revelling in the freedom of flight. Bees buzzing past, accompanied by the lower pitched drone of another insect I couldn't identify. Muffled sounds were clarion calls; the soft scuffle of feet through grass, the truncated click of a camera shutter and the murmuring voices of other visitors discussing the different species of hydrangea.

Above her head, a single strand of gossamer thread from a spider's web stretched like a flea circus tightrope between a Larch and a Swamp Cypress; fragile but strong. A rope drawing me inexorably towards her, even as I stood paralysed, rooted as firmly to the spot as the trunks of the trees around me.

The rays from the sun bounced off the red curls that crowned her head, reflecting off the lenses of the purple-rimmed glasses that were perched precariously on the end of her nose. A long, slim finger reached up unselfconsciously and pushed them back up to their rightful place, purple glittery nail polish winking and blinking, playing hide and seek with the sun.

She had a book propped up on her crossed legs, a thick, weighty looking thing that seemed too heavy for her slender frame. I studied the cover, trying to make out what she was reading, but all I could see were the big blocks of colour that decorated the cover. It was clearly an academic book of some kind; *No novel would have such a bland cover,* I thought, *Not if it ever wanted to be picked up and read.*

She shifted her position on the bench, transferring the weight of the book from one leg to the other, smoothing the knee length skirt back down, before resuming her study of the page. Soft tendrils clustered around her temples and she twisted a longer curl around her index finger, a slight frown creasing the gap between the well-defined brows.

I ran a hand through my hair, scared to acknowledge the familiar feeling, unsure of what my next action should be and the movement must have caught her attention, because she lifted her head and removed her glasses, peering across the pond to see what had distracted her. I knew the moment she saw me because a slight smile of acknowledgment flickered across her face. I returned the gesture with interest, not deterred in the least by the instant return of her attention to the book and suddenly, I knew exactly what I needed to do. I crossed the narrow wooden plank that divided the two main bodies of water and made my way towards her bench.

'Hi,' I came to an abrupt halt to one side of where she sat.

She looked up, shielding her eyes from the sun. A puzzled frown half-formed then fell away.

'Hello.'

For a moment, we occupied the awkward silence. I felt it forming around me, tying my tongue into tangled knots, then I shook it off, reminding myself there had been a purpose for the interruption of my walk.

'It's so beautiful here, isn't it?'

She nodded, the irritated frown warring with the polite smile; the battle for supremacy playing out across the pale face.

'Yes.' A long pause, during which I did not move. 'That's why I come here. It's somewhere quiet to read my book.'

As she gestured to the thick volume on her knee, I caught sight of another, slimmer book just poking out from the top of her bag.

'The Joy Of Creative Writing,' I read aloud. 'Doesn't reading that rather take away from the joy of creative writing?'

It was a pitifully weak attempt at humour, but she laughed, nonetheless; a light, tinkling sound like raindrops on a windchime and it broke through the barriers of social constriction that had thus far kept our conversation muted.

'It does a bit,' she admitted, 'But,' she dropped her voice to a conspiratorial whisper, 'I've got an old favourite to keep me company if I get bored.' She inclined her head towards the copy of Jane Eyre I'd spotted.

'I've read it,' I smiled. 'It was quite a while ago, but I can just about remember the story. I never understood why she went back to Rochester though. He treated her so badly and yet she still went to him when he needed her.'

'You don't stop loving someone because they're unsuitable,' she said quietly and I pretended not to notice the tear that escaped from the corner of her eye, suddenly finding my feet awfully fascinating.

'So, if you'd rather be reading Jane, what's with the Joy?' I asked, a little too loudly.

'Oh, that I *have* to read,' she said, dismissively. 'It's course recommended reading.'

'What course is that then?'

'I'm doing a Master's in Creative Writing.'

'Wow.' I was genuinely impressed. 'That sounds amazing.'

Her smile was broader and more genuine this time.

'It is,' she said, 'That's why I'm here really. I have an assignment due in a few weeks and I'm here to get some inspiration.'

'I can see why,' I admitted, looking around with newly appreciative eyes. 'It's a beautiful place to sit and think. Do you get many ideas sitting here?'

She shook her head. 'No, it's not that. I've got the basic plot in my head; I just need some descriptive detail.'

She patted the bench and moved to one end of it.

'Sit down. I'll show you what I mean.'

I did as I was told.

'OK. Look around you and tell me what you see.'

'Flowers, trees, the ponds,' I started listing things and she laughed.

'What can you hear?'

'You, the ducks.'

'Right. Now close your eyes. OK, tell me what you can hear.'

I told her about the drone of the helicopter I had noticed earlier, that was still marking lazy circles in the sky above, the muffled sounds of the cars as they passed along the lane outside. Encased within that were smaller sounds, the rapid fire rattle of a duck's wings in flight and a myriad of other sounds. I described them all until I felt her light touch on my shoulder.'

'Now open your eyes and tell me again what you see.'

When I opened my eyes, I did not see the clashing colours of nerve-jangling iridescence that had greeted me on my arrival. Instead, it was the paint palette of an artist in his or her green period – from the almost silver green of the Jack Frost to the purplish-green tinge of the ornamental sweet potato. The splashes of colour I had observed on my arrival transformed themselves into silky soft shades of butter, honey, marmalade, cyclamen, watermelon, lilac and periwinkle; each one angrily shaking its heads at my former simplistic descriptions. She nodded her head as I spoke, a knowing smile illuminating her face with a healthy glow.

'That's it,' she said. 'That's why I come here; I can't *imagine* those descriptions, I have to *experience* them, or the words just don't come.'

I was acutely aware that her hand was still resting on my shoulder and I was afraid to move, almost afraid to breathe, in case she realised and moved it. The pleasure she took from her surroundings was writ large across her face and I shared her appreciation; this was indeed a beautiful place and I closed my eyes, the skin at last stretching anew over the raw, unhealed wounds. It would take a long time and scars there would certainly be, but it was a beginning. Just the simple contact between her hand and my shoulder had begun the healing process. Knitting everything back together was bound to be a painful process, but for the first time in months, black was not the overpowering emotion running through me.

Slowly, I became aware that she was looking at me quizzically.

'What is it?'

'You were miles away; I was wondering where you'd wandered off to.'

'Nowhere important,' I told her, 'But we should probably introduce ourselves. I'm Tom Blythe.'

'Grace Walker.'

She removed her hand from my shoulder and offered it to me to shake. Her grip was tentative and she shoved her hand deep into her pocket the moment I released it, but when I suggested having a coffee together, she surprised me by agreeing.

'The café here is lovely,' she told me. 'Their soup is to die for.'

I laughed at the dreamy expression on her face and a light blush coloured her cheeks.

'I'm a bit of a foodie,' she confessed, lowering her eyes.

'Nothing wrong with that,' I hastened to reassure her. 'I've yet to meet a food I don't like.'

We sat down with our coffees and I observed her over the rim of my mug. Her bright ginger hair was bobbed in what I thought might be a 1920s style and stood out vividly against the high-necked black jumper she wore. Her lips were full and pink as she blew across her cup, sending miniature ripples across the frothy surface. She wore a tear-drop pendant around her neck and the only other jewellery she wore was, what looked to my untrained eye like a pair of diamond studded earrings. She caught my gaze and smiled, setting her cup down.

'Well, this wasn't how I'd planned to spend my morning,' she said. 'I'm totally skiving now.'

'I hope I provide more stimulating company than that thing,' I said, gesturing to 'The Joy of Creative Writing' where it poked out from the top of her bag.

'Don't worry, you do!'

'Mind you,' I joked, 'I don't suppose that's saying a lot!'

She laughed and then immediately, her face fell and she looked worried.

'Oh no,' she shook her head. 'I didn't mean to...'

I held my hand up to stop her apology and she flinched.

'I was only joking,' I told her gently.

She turned her head away for a moment and brushed the back of her hand across her eyes, then turned back to face me again, a smile once more on her lips.

'I'm sorry,' she said.

Once again, I pretended not to notice the single silvery trace at the corner of her eye and changed the subject.

'So, tell me about yourself,' I said. 'How did you end up doing this MA?'

'I always wanted to be a journalist,' she said, 'But in my final year at uni, my...things changed and I decided to become a librarian instead. I've always loved books and it kept me closer to home than journalism would have done. Then, about a year ago, I got the opportunity to do this course, so I decided to take the plunge and become a student again. I'm only twenty-eight and I don't want to be a librarian all my life. Not that there's anything wrong with that!' she added hastily. 'It's just not for me. I've dabbled with writing on and off for years, but I never thought any of it was any good until recently. This course will help me to improve it and hopefully give me an idea if what I write is good enough to get something published eventually.'

She looked down at where her hands where clasped tightly around her mug and took a sip from it, the mug shaking slightly as she set it down again, the china making a loud clatter as it made contact with the table.

'I think it's brilliant that you're doing it,' I said. 'I love my job and I can't imagine doing something I wasn't passionate about.'

'What do you do?' Her eyes were curious now that I hadn't laughed at her ambitions.

'I'm a freelance translator. At the moment I'm working on a novel. Not writing it,' I amended hastily, 'I'm translating it from German to English for a small publishing company.'

'That's incredible,' she said. 'I'm a complete dunce at languages; always have been. English Lit was my subject at uni. It was hard enough analysing books in my own language; I can't imagine doing it in a foreign one. The only other thing I've ever been any good at is dancing.'

'Oh yes? What kind?' I asked.

'Ballroom and Latin. My whole family are dancers, so I've been doing it since I was tiny.'

'How tiny is 'tiny'?' I was suddenly struck with a wonderful picture of a pretty red-headed little girl waltzing around the floor with an equally tiny partner.

'Apparently I was dancing almost as soon as I could walk, so certainly by eighteen months old. My brother is a couple of years older than me, so we did competitions together as soon as I was old enough, but we had to stop them a few years ago when Ash broke his leg. It still aches if he does too much on it so we couldn't do the hours of practice anymore. We still go most weekends to the Tower though.'

'I might see you in there then,' I blurted out, before my brain caught up.

I hadn't danced in years and even when I'd been doing it regularly, I'd only visited the Tower sporadically. Olivia had always enjoyed dancing and had persuaded me a few years earlier that ballroom dancing would be something we could do as a couple, to give us a hobby together, away from the children. I was initially reluctant, believing that with two left feet, putting them on a ballroom floor and expecting them to be co-ordinated *and* move in time to music would be nothing short of disastrous!

I reminded her of how she'd described my dancing at the Fresher's Ball. Did she really want to risk recreating that? But she begged and pleaded and cajoled and eventually wore me down enough for me to agree to give it a try.

To my surprise, I was nowhere near as bad as I'd feared I would be and after a few lessons I learnt enough to be able to get round the floor without making a complete fool of myself. As a partnership, we made steady progress and I even grew to enjoy it, but then when Olivia fell ill for a while we were forced to stop the lessons and it was something we never went back to. Somewhere in the course of those lessons, our teacher had managed to instil in me a sense of both rhythm and timing and I was fairly confident I could remember enough not to embarrass myself. The ethics of using something I had learnt to do for my wife, to impress another woman, pricked at my conscience, but I subdued it with the reassurance that I had everything under control and wasn't *really* doing anything wrong. It wasn't as if anything had happened between us except a conversation, a coffee and a vague notion of perhaps seeing each other again someday.

'Are you OK?'

Grace's hand on my arm and concerned face made me realise I'd once again been wool-gathering.

'Yes. Sorry.' I smiled self-consciously. 'What were you saying?'

'I was just asking if maybe you were planning to go to the Tower at all this weekend?'

My conscience was now red-faced and angrily shouting at me, but I turned my back on it.

'I might go in on Sunday,' I ventured hesitantly, the words sticking in my throat.

'Oh lovely!' she said, her face splitting into a smile. 'I'll speak to Ash and see if he's free and we could meet you there, maybe?'

'That would be nice,' my voice said, as my brain back-pedalled furiously. What was I doing?

We sat in companionable silence for a few moments, listening to the quiet chatter from the other customers. One lady a few tables over from us was clearly in the latter stages of pregnancy and was holding forth to her bleached blonde friend on the subject of baby names.

'I'm just struggling, you know? It's so difficult to think of names beginning with 'M'. It's doing my head in!'

'Does it have to be an 'M'?'

'Yeah. Mark's determined. It's some family tradition of theirs. I wouldn't mind, but it's muggins here that's got to come up with the names and all I can think of is Megan for a girl and Miles for a boy. Whatever I choose has to go with Mitchell and I'm running out of 'M' names.'

'How many kids have they got if they're running out of Ms?' I whispered behind the cover of my coffee cup.

Grace smothered a chuckle.

'If they get really stuck, they could always take a leaf out of the Nevilles' book and double up the surname and call it Mitchell Mitchell.'

It was my turn to suppress a grin this time.

'If it's twins, maybe they could call them Mork and Mindy.'

Grace choked on her coffee, unable to stop the giggle, causing us to become the focus of attention for one or two of the other patrons, until she managed to catch her breath and smilingly said she was fine, as other conversations bobbed and wove their way around us.

'You've changed your number now, so don't give it to him again,'

'One day, everything will come right and I'll get my own place.'

'We went to The Counting House on Saturday. You should've come, it was a great night.'

'I don't understand why these places get just one person to sing. You might as well have karaoke. Except they can sing, obviously. It's different if they have an instrument.'

It was odd, listening to these snapshots of people's lives and wondering how much of the speaker was revealed through them. I didn't want to consider what kind of picture Grace and I presented to the other people watchers. I didn't want to know what kind of story they would create for us.

Eventually, Grace drained her cup and stood up, her hand outstretched.

'I'm afraid I really must get on now,' she said ruefully. 'I have to get this piece started today.'

'Of course,' I agreed, shaking her hand. 'And my novel isn't going to translate itself, so I should probably get back to it. Until Sunday then, hopefully?'

She smiled and nodded, then gathered up her bag and headed to the door, before returning abruptly.

'I just had a thought,' she said apologetically. 'Shall I take your number in case we can't make it? I'd hate to think of you sitting on your own waiting for us not to turn up.'

I handed her one of the business cards I always kept in my wallet, resolving not to ask for her number in return. The fates would decide if I saw her again, not me. I was still telling myself I was doing nothing wrong; it wasn't a date if her brother was coming as well. We were just two people with a common interest who wanted to further our acquaintance.

On my way home, I returned Eoin's call. He answered after only one ring and knew immediately that something had changed from the last time he'd spoken to me.

'What do you mean, what's happened?'

'Your voice is different,' he told me. 'Lighter. More like yourself.'

'Nothing's happened,' I lied. 'I'm having a better day today, that's all.'

He was one of my oldest and dearest friends, but I wasn't ready to tell him yet. It was too soon and I wasn't sure how he would react; he and Sophie were Olivia's friends too. I moved the conversation onto more neutral ground by asking how Sophie and the kids were.

'They're good thanks. We saw Zoe last weekend and we were only saying then that it's been too long since we saw you. Why don't you come down in a couple of weeks and bring the kids for the weekend?'

A little reluctantly, I found myself agreeing to a visit in the not too distant future. Eoin and Sophie were like family after so many years of friendship; they'd been with us through all the ups and downs of the last few years, but I knew I could expect the third degree about the state of my mental health when we met. Although it was done out of love and with the best of intentions, it was draining and I was already exhausted by it all. Some weeks were more of a struggle than others, but it had always been like that; it was all part of the job description of a working from home parent. You got the joy and exultant high of being there to witness the first word and the first step, but there was no 'boss' to ask for help when you were on your third set of clothes of the day before it was even nine o'clock because various breakfast foods and bodily fluids had been deposited on the previous two sets. Or when you felt that if you had to spend the rest of the day wrinkling your nose and wondering where the godawful smell was coming from – only to belatedly realised that it was you – you were going to scream!

After a few tense months of this, we'd worked out a more manageable routine. Saturdays were our family days where we would go out and do something fun together; the cinema, bowling, bike rides, hikes, anything in fact, as long as we could all join in. Sundays, however, were *my* days; my day away from work, away from our relationship and away from the kids, a time to recharge my batteries. It was thoughts of Sunday that kept me going on those days where Elodie spent the whole day screaming, or in earlier years, the boys argued over toys, hitting each other over the head with plastic trains and wooden bricks.

However, I approached the next Sunday with a mixture of dread and anticipation. Grace had texted me on the Friday morning to confirm that she and her brother would be in the Ballroom that weekend and I spent the two days following her message feeling nauseous. So many times, I got my phone out to text and tell her something had come up and I wouldn't be able to come after all. Every time, I stared at the blank screen, willing a message to come up, praying it would be from her saying they'd changed their plans yet at the same time, hoping fervently that no message would appear. As for breaking the engagement myself, that was impossible. I couldn't do it. My phone stayed infuriatingly silent. The only time it rang was a call from my client checking in to see how the translation was progressing. I was actually able to tell him that it was coming along very well. In a futile bid to distract myself I'd put in extra hours at work in the evening, leaving myself as little time as possible in which to ponder my situation.

Sunday morning arrived and I pulled my black suit out of the back of my wardrobe, trying not to think about the last time I'd worn it. I didn't have much call to wear a suit working from home and so it had been some months since its last outing and it was not an occasion I wanted to remember, especially not today when I was anxious enough already. Pushing these thoughts to the back of my mind, I drove the few miles into Blackpool and parked up in the centre of town.

The car park backed onto the rear of the promenade and was the most convenient for the Tower, but it was a singularly miserable place, even by car park standards. The gaudiness of the brightly lit arcades on either side of it contrasted sharply with the dishearteningly grey and austere sprawl of tarmac. Nearby, tattered and faded awnings fluttered above some of the shops undermining their attempt to appear prosperous and popular. It was important to fake the seaside good cheer for the tourists who always seemed to occupy Blackpool's streets. The reality of living in the town outside of the summer season could be very different from its public persona.

For the outside observer, it was a depressing place, the faded grandeur of the Victorian era and beyond, a mere memory now. Like most British seaside towns, drugs and homelessness were more its watchwords than the family entertainment and holidays of earlier decades. Yet for the locals, Blackpool still somehow managed to hold on to much of its charm, due in no small part to the increased attraction of the Tower Ballroom, after multiple appearances on Strictly Come Dancing. The town engendered a deep-seated loyalty in people like me who had spent many happy hours enjoying the entertainment it had to offer. Yes, I could see that North Pier was being allowed to fall into ruin, but in my mind's eye it was still as beautiful as it had been when I'd first visited with Olivia in the early days of our relationship. Little was the same in Blackpool, yet in some respects, nothing had changed. The town had stagnated, but people still felt drawn to it; popular as it was with hen and stag weekends, in the summer you still found families playing on its wide expansive beach and although my days of riding the donkeys were in the past, the children loved it. In South Shore, the rollercoasters of the Pleasure Beach still carried screaming thrill-seekers around their rickety tracks, the old rides as popular as ever, even in the facc of the gleamingly new metal structures of their more modern counterparts.

Once inside, I made my way up to the third floor, taking the stairs to allow myself just a few seconds more to prepare for this meeting. It was a tiring trek up the red carpet and I had to pause at the top to get my breath back, calming my pounding heart by looking out over the sea, watching the people on the promenade and the trams carrying people backwards and forwards along the length of the promenade, from Starr Gate in the south, almost to Cleveleys, where the tracks went inland to their end point in Fleetwood. The normality of it all soothed my nerves and eventually, I plucked up the courage to step through the weighted wooden doors and cross into the Ballroom.

I had been an occasional visitor to the Tower Ballroom before, but the beauty and sheer unadulterated opulence of it never failed to impress me. On this occasion, after so long away from its grandeur, it took my breath away. Three sides of the magnificent block parquet floor were surrounded by a two-tier balcony supported by rectangular Corinthian-style marble columns with triple bowled chandeliers spaced at regular intervals along the sleek undulations of both tiers. Beneath this were walls of brown and burgundy tiles, smooth and sleek in the main, but some were decorated with stippled flowers and the whole was topped by Victoriana wallpaper that harked back to the era in which it had been built.

At the end of each balcony, gold scroll work concealed the speakers that were filling the cavernous space between them with the sounds of the organ; chipped gold leaf cherubs holding lyres and bunches of grapes channelled the spirit of Dionysus while the names of composers such as Haydn, Chopin and Liszt looked down at the dancers below, moving mellifluously to the strains of an unfamiliar tune.

My eyes were drawn again to the far end of the room, where the faux elegance of the white and gilt staircase with its mockery of a red carpet led guiltily up to the true centrepiece of the room; the magnificent Wurlitzer organ being played by Mr Blackpool himself, Phil Kelsall.

Grace appeared at my side and tucked her arm through mine to lead me to where she and her brother were sitting.

'It's stunning, isn't it?'

I nodded, still too enthralled to give her a proper answer.

'You'd never believe it wasn't original, would you?'

I stopped walking, pulling her off balance and making her stumble in her heels.

'What do you mean?'

'It all had to be redecorated after the fire in '56,' she explained. 'None of the decor in here is more than sixty years old. The structure and the Wurlitzer survived, but the floor was completely destroyed and obviously everything else was either fire or smoke damaged. They did an incredible job restoring it though. It's pretty much exactly as it was before then.'

I looked up at the classical style frescoes and then at the backdrop of the Bay of Naples on the stage and shook my head.

'I know,' Grace said, as she tugged me along. 'It's got to you too.'

She made it sound as though the Ballroom was a living breathing personality, but she was absolutely right. I'd had a visceral reaction to the thought of all this beauty being destroyed; the charred ruins smoking, choking the air.

Bid me discourse and I will enchant thine ear.

It was in big letters above the stage, but it was as if the Ballroom itself had spoken to me. She knew her purpose and she wanted to fulfil it, wanted to welcome you into her warm embrace and surround you with beauty of every kind. I could almost see and feel the notes dancing through the air around me as the music played and the dancers twirled. I was becoming fanciful again; a sure sign that I was nervous and I gave myself a strict talking to as Grace guided me between the maze of tables and up to the other end of the room where a man sat alone at the table nearest the organ.

'Ash, this is Tom. Tom, this is my brother Ashley.'

His grip when he shook my hand – like the gaze which fixed on me – was polite, inquisitive and stern. He wasn't sure about me and I didn't blame him. I wasn't sure about myself.

'How d'you do,' he said, his face impassive.

'Good thanks. It's nice to meet you.'

He nodded in reply. It seemed that polite but guarded was the approach he was going to take and that was fine by me. I didn't know what I was letting myself in for any more than he did; wasn't sure how to proceed, or what the etiquette of the situation demanded. I decided to change my shoes; it would give me something to do, an excuse to not talk for a few moments.

'Would you like to dance?' Grace came to my rescue. It was a Quickstep; one of my favourite dances and one of the few I could remember well.

It felt so natural to hold her in my arms as we flew around the floor, which bounced beneath our feet and I recalled my old dance teacher telling me that it was one of the only sprung dancefloors in the country, which meant it could be loosened or tightened, depending on how many people were dancing that day. The speed of the dance left little breath for conversation which meant I could concentrate on getting the steps right and I came off the floor at the end quite satisfied that I had not made a poor showing of myself during my first foray onto the floor for a few years.

It seemed that everyone in the room knew Grace and her brother and in between dances I would be introduced as 'Grace's friend Tom' to the myriad of people who came to speak to them, clearly angling for an introduction to the interloper into the group.

'I've been coming in here all my life,' Grace said by way of explanation. 'I grew up in front of these people, so naturally they want to know who you are. Phil knows my parents,' she added, as the organist smiled and nodded at her between songs. 'I've got so many photos of him holding me as a child and somewhere I still have a wind up clock toy he gave me when I was about three.'

I excused myself to go to the bathroom, feeling a tiny bit overwhelmed. It was as though I'd fallen through the Looking Glass into a bizarre and unfamiliar world where it was normal to know everyone else's business and it felt like I was frantically trying to catch up with a runaway train that never seemed to slow down. It was intrusive, yet everyone else thought it was perfectly reasonable.

On my return, Grace and her brother were sitting with their heads close together. I was too far away to hear that they were saying, but she looked angry and hurt.

'Ashley was just going to get us some drinks,' she said through gritted teeth and a forced smile. 'Would you like one?'

'I'll have a coffee please,' I said, sitting down.

I would usually have offered to get them myself, but I sensed that brother and sister needed a few minutes apart.

'Shall we dance?' I offered Grace my arm and she took it straight away, casting a defiant glare at her brother before her expression relaxed into a more natural one.

The Foxtrot was not the easiest dance to do and my feet kept getting into a terrible muddle, but luckily Grace had the skill to keep manoeuvring me around the floor without crashing into any other dancers.

I was starting to relax a little and enjoy myself when the organist changed tunes and my breath caught in my throat. That song. Red hot rivers of guilt flowed, lava-like across my skin, smothering me with its suffocating self-reproach. What was I doing? How could I be dancing with another woman to that song? Our song. I stumbled off the floor, cold and sweating, a sheen of perspiration glistening on my face, allowing Grace to guide me back to my chair, listening to the roar of blood that pounded in my ears, the dull thud of my heart an accusatory beat. Cheat. Cheat. Cheat. Cheat. Everything else was reduced to a faded buzz behind that one word, repeating loud and clear. Over and over again. Getting louder and louder until it occupied the whole world and nothing else existed. And then, suddenly, the space in my head was filled with silence, my ears ringing with the deafening lack of noise. Grace was stroking my face, talking to me. I could see her lips moving, but at first the silence was too loud for me to hear her and then gradually, her voice penetrated the thick sludge of noiselessness, calm and quiet, wavering just slightly.

'Tom, it's alright, I'm here. Everything will be OK, but I'm going to need you to breathe for me.'

A sudden expulsion of air released itself from my lungs and everything righted itself. Things resumed their normal shape and form around me, comforting in their normality. My head twisted from side to side, doing its own frantic dance, until Grace squeezed my hand.

'Don't worry,' she murmured. 'No-one's looking.'

I nodded, still not trusting my ability to form words and allowed the music to wash over me. The song had changed. Its power had been lost and I relaxed a little. Grace resumed her seat and sat quietly at my side, her hand resting, coolly reassuring, on mine, waiting.

'You had a panic attack,' she said eventually. ' Have you had them before?'

I shook my head, then paused mid-denial and nodded. I had. Several in fact, over the last few months.

'I used to have them as well,' Grace continued. 'I recognised that look of helplessness. It's OK though,' she repeated, the pressure of her fingers on mine increasing ever so slightly. They can be managed if you know the right techniques. I can show you some another time if you like?'

I smiled weakly at her, grateful for, but embarrassed by her concern. I was an awful person and I didn't deserve her sympathy.

Ashley returned with the drinks and set them down carelessly, sloshing coffee all over the table.

'Sorry,' he muttered, thrusting a bundle of wadded up napkins at us.

Mopping it up gave me something else to focus on, watching the murky brown liquid soak into the thin paper turning it limp and useless to render any further assistance. Futile attempts to stop the liquid spreading across the table seemed to just send it skating further across the surface, creating a soup like substance that vibrated and jumped every time a couple danced past us, the sprung floor conspiring to hinder my cleaning attempts. Then Grace stepped in with another handful of tissues she'd found and swept it back towards me, our joint efforts catching the runaway drink like a dog herding sheep and we managed between us to mop it all up. We were left with a table that was sticky with milk residue, but at least it was dry. Leaning on it was reminiscent of the university bar at the end of a night serving Snakebite, when you were never quite sure what you were putting your elbow in and it always left you feeling rather unclean and desirous of washing rather hastily.

'What are your intentions towards my sister?'

Ashley's question came out of the blue and was fired at me; it had obviously been simmering in his brain for quite some time and as soon as Grace had left the table to go to the Ladies, it burst forth. At first, I didn't respond, just blinked in surprise. Where I came from, people weren't generally so blunt and even having lived with a northerner for fifteen years, six of those years spent living in the north, had not rendered me immune to this kind of full-frontal attack. It seemed to be something built into northern DNA, an instinctive ability to get straight to the heart of the matter without the need for the meandering politeness of most southerners. *Or perhaps*, I thought, *On reflection, maybe it's a certain class or type of person who has this 'honest to a fault' gene. After all, some of Mum's relatives had this same knack of catching you off guard with their straight-forward way of talking and they're all Londoners born and bred.*

'I have no intentions of any kind,' I lied. 'We met by chance and got talking and she invited me to come with you today.' I paused for a moment, then continued, my guilty conscience cloaking itself in righteous indignation. 'And I don't mean to sound rude, but even if I did, what possible concern is it of yours? Grace is a grown woman who can make decisions for herself and I'm not sure she'd appreciate you poking your nose into her business.'

'I'm damn sure she wouldn't!' His grim face softened momentarily and a small grin appeared. 'Actually, she'd be furious with me.'

'Then why do it?'

His mien hardened again.

'Because someone has to. Ordinarily, I wouldn't dream of interfering, as you put it, but the fact is she's had a pretty tough time lately. I've only just got my sister back, the sister I knew growing up and I don't want her disappearing again. I love Grace dearly and if I have to piss her off to protect her, then I'll do it and willingly face the consequences.'

I nodded, understanding. Naturally, I was dying of curiosity, but now was not the time to be nosey. No, I corrected myself, it wasn't nosiness. I only wanted to know because it was about Grace.

'I won't tell her if you don't,' I said placatingly. 'And I wouldn't ever want to hurt her.'

He didn't reply but nodded briefly as Grace returned. His demeanour thereafter, while it could not be classed as friendly, was definitely less uptight than it had been. It seemed I had passed some kind of test, but this only left me more conflicted than ever. I'd said I wouldn't want to hurt Grace, but there was still the one big secret I'd not shared with her and if anything might hurt her, that would. Actually, given that this was only the second time we'd ever met, there was a lot she didn't know about me and vice versa. There would be plenty of time in the future to find out most of them and it seemed that we each had parts of our lives that were going to be painful to reveal. The difference was that while I was fairly confident that there was nothing she could tell me about herself that would stop me wanting to see her again, I couldn't guarantee she would feel the same about me and my secret.

There were also the children to consider. We were very much a package deal and unsurprisingly, the question of whether or not she wanted children had not been one of the areas our conversation had covered. The fact that they would not be her own was an added complication and I had no idea how they would react to her either.

After a few hours my legs were beginning to protest about the unaccustomed exercise, so I made my excuses and prepared to leave. At a sharp glance from Grace, Ashley bid me goodbye and left the table, not even bothering to make an excuse for his less than subtle departure.

'Will I see you again?' she asked me, her voice quiet and unsure.

I didn't know what to answer her. My whole body was engaged in a raging war with itself, all the different limbs and organs shouting conflicting responses at me.

'Would you like to?'

'Very much so,' she said, 'But only if you would as well.'

I looked her straight in the eye.

'Why?'

This seemed to confuse her for a moment.

'What do you mean?'

'I mean, why me? Why do *you* want to see *me* again?'

She frowned. Her reply when it came was barely above a whisper and I had to lean towards her and strain to hear it.

'You're attractive, you make me laugh and you didn't make fun of me when I said I wanted to be a writer.'

I wanted to tell her, but to my shame, I couldn't. The words just wouldn't come. Instead, I merely nodded.

'Give me a call.'

II

OLIVIA 1997-1998

The morning after our kiss I awoke with a grin on my face. It had finally happened and she was mine. There was no more worrying about whether or not she liked me: she did and we were dating. Everyone in the Hall was going out that night to the Lemmy, but we'd agreed to go for a few drinks on our own beforehand. It would be our first proper date.

I met Olivia at the foot of the main staircase, having watched her descend like a dandelion clock, seeming to float from step to step until she reached my side. I could almost picture her in an old-fashioned ball dress, her hair curled high on her head, an anxious debutante, eager to meet the man who would sweep her off her feet and marry her.

'Are you ready?' Olivia's amused voice broke into my thoughts and the debutante promptly vanished.

She was wearing a short skirt with a navy blouse that sparkled under the chandelier and chunky heels that raised her level with my nose.

'At least when you're wearing those I won't get neck ache if I kiss you,' I smiled.

'If?' her eyebrows quirked expressively.

'*When*,' I corrected firmly.

The Ram – the main campus pub – was right at the centre of the campus and as we stopped every few hundred metres for one of us to steal a lingering kiss from the other, it took us quite some time to get there, but we were lucky; it was still early and it wasn't quite as crammed as I'd feared it would be. Drinks bought, we found ourselves a corner table that while not exactly cosy, offered us a little seclusion from the rest of the pub, which only got busier as the hour grew later.

I was content for a while, to merely sit and revel in my good fortune. Less than a week into my new, independent life and there I was, sitting in a pub with my beautiful girlfriend. My introductory lectures had not been too challenging, particularly in German, where the first year was designed to bring us all up to a similar standard of fluency. Life was good.

'You look pretty pleased with yourself,' Olivia observed drily.

'Is it that obvious?' I blushed.

'Any more obvious and you'd have been presenting yourself with a trophy!' she laughed.

I had to smile.

'Sorry,' I said. 'I was just thinking how nice this was.'

'Being at uni or being here?'

'Both, I guess. I'm looking forward to lectures starting properly, but it's also nice not to have to tell someone where I'm going the whole time. What about you?'

She looked thoughtful for a moment.

'I suppose I'm more used to being independent,' she said, 'so it's not so much of a novelty for me. Actually, it's quite nice having other people around all the time.'

A wave of guilt washed over me as I remembered what she'd told me of her recent home life. All the evenings I'd spent at home watching TV with Mum while Dad cooked dinner, or vice versa, Olivia had spent in a lonely flat, cooking her own meals and doing her own washing, the only conversation coming from the TV. It must have been a solitary existence and I was in awe of how she'd managed to cope with that and still come away with good A-level results. I wasn't a complete incompetent around the house – Mum and Dad had seen to that – but I was by no means sure I'd have been able to do everything for myself in the way that she had.

'Don't look so grief-stricken,' she said, patting my hand. 'It wasn't so bad. I don't need your pity!' she added in a sharper tone, guessing the direction my thoughts had gone in.

'I know you don't,' I said defensively, a little taken aback by the anger in her voice and the sudden withdrawal of her hand. 'And I wasn't pitying you. Not exactly.'

I reached over the table and pulled her reluctant hand back into mine. 'If you must know, I was actually thinking how amazing you are. I was wondering whether I'd have coped as well and I don't think I would've done.'

'I won't be pitied,' she said again, but the fierceness has left her voice and she sounded unexpectedly vulnerable.

'What happened with your mum?' I asked tentatively, 'And why couldn't you go to your dad's if it was so unbearable?'

I was angry at the man who seemed to have callously abandoned his daughter at the same time as his wife and I squeezed Olivia's hand a little too tightly.

'In his defence, Dad would have had me,' she said. 'I didn't want to go. As for Mum,' she broke off and a strange look came into her eyes, a combination of despair and anger. 'Look, do you mind if we don't talk about this now?'

'Of course not,' I said immediately, feeling bad that I'd pushed her on a topic which clearly still upset her.

'I will tell you one day,' she said. 'Probably. Just not now. It's not a first date conversation and I'd rather enjoy tonight.'

'What shall we talk about instead?' I asked, knowing even as I did so that it was a question guaranteed to kill any hope of natural conversation.

'Oh, I don't know!' she said, throwing her arms in the air and laughing. 'Something else. Anything! What about your parents? What do they do?'

So, I told her how my father ran a wine bar and my mother worked at the Job Centre. I regaled her with the tale of how they'd met at the age of seventeen at the local Sixth Form College. Mum had thought Dad was a bit of an idiot at first, always showing off in front of his mates, but as she'd got to know him, he'd gradually shown her another side to him and it was this part she'd eventually fallen in love with. She finally agreed to a date after months of him asking and her turning him down. She said she'd always liked him, but he was too much of a jack-the-lad and so she kept saying no. Eventually he realised that it was the front he was putting on for his mates that was putting her off and he changed his behaviour.

'Basically, he grew up,' I said.

They'd got engaged at nineteen and were married at twenty but had been forced to wait ten long years until I was born. Dad told me they'd just about given up hope and accepted that maybe they weren't going to have kids and then one night when he was at work, Mum rang to say she was pregnant with me. Apparently, he was so shocked he dropped a bottle of wine on the floor.

'He always says it's lucky I wasn't a girl. He reckons Mum wanted to call me Chardonnay if I was, but she says it's just him talking nonsense as usual.' I laughed at the memory of Mum's indignant face as she swatted Dad affectionately with a tea-towel.

My home life had clearly been very different to Olivia's, but she laughed nonetheless when I told her about all the ridiculous things my parents had done over the years; memories I thought I'd forgotten, that left me if not exactly homesick, then certainly a little nostalgic and with a lot more appreciation for what I'd had growing up.

She changed the subject and we moved on to talk about

our hallmates. She agreed with me that Sophie and Eoin had a bit of a thing for each other, but we had to agree to disagree on the subject of Zoe. To me, she was a nuisance; a loud, overbearing vamp who preyed on an unsuspecting male populace. Olivia, however, held a somewhat kinder view of her roommate.

'Come on, Tom,' she chided. 'There's more to her than that. She can be lovely sometimes, when she's not being loud. You saw her at the Lemmy the other night, she was in a right old state, thinking everybody hated her. If she really was like you say she is, she wouldn't have reacted like that. She wouldn't have noticed or cared what anyone else thought. You're being too hard on her.'

I smiled and said nothing. I couldn't help feeling Olivia was too keen to see the best in her friend, but I didn't want to argue about her and so the rest of the evening passed by in a warm, alcohol-induced feeling of fuzziness, setting the tone for the next few weeks of university life. Days were spent in small lecture rooms, making notes at dizzying speed, then grabbing cheap priced and fat laden breakfast rolls from the campus café, hoping, as you crammed the food into your mouth, that the ache in your wrist would subside before your next lecture began.

Dinner in the Hall – at its best bland, at its worst, varying shades of brown mush – was followed by a frenetic period of activity in which everyone rushed to get ready for the evening and then we'd convene, sometimes in the Common Room, often in someone's room, clutching varying bottles of wine and spirits to 'pre-drink' before we jumped on the bus into the city to hit whichever nightclub had its student night. Of course, there were occasional hiccups to this routine, like the night I thought it would be a good idea to drink the best part of a litre bottle of vodka to myself, only to have it re-emerge the moment I stepped foot off the bus, or the night Oliva didn't realise that doubles were on offer and couldn't understand how she'd got so drunk so quickly when in her own words, 'I can normally hold it much better than this,'. Whether she was referring to her ability to drink, which was moderate at best, or her ability to hold the handbag she kept dropping, which she usually did well at, I wasn't quite certain. Nevertheless, a pattern emerged for each week. On Mondays, it was off to Club Rococo for their 70s night, Tuesdays were spent in Volts, dancing the night away to old-school Madonna, A-Ha, Culture Club and the like, Timepiece was our venue of choice on a Wednesday and on Thursdays we were spoilt for choice; Warehouse, Boogies and Boxes were clubs within a club. Three floors in the same former quayside warehouse, all pumping out different styles of music but serving the same cut-price drinks; £1 for a bottle of Reef – not great under normal circumstances, but if we were particularly short of cash we soon worked out that you got drunk far quicker (and consequently, far more cheaply) if you bent the straw over the side of the bottle neck and downed the contents in one. The thing I remember most clearly about those nights is Olivia, along with the other girls, going to the toilets as soon as we arrived and stuffing their handbags full of toilet paper, so that when it inevitably ran out later in the evening, they were well prepared. Of all the things I recall about those early days, this is the memory that puzzles and impresses me in equal measure. I think it was their forward-thinking that appealed to me; this level of planning would never have occurred to me, nor I suspect, to any other male. It wasn't something we ever truly understood the logic of, for surely, if all girls did this, that was why the roll ran out?

Fridays and Saturdays were usually spent in The Lemmy, unless Olivia and I had arranged to have a date on our own. Whenever we did, we tended to go into Exeter city centre, as we were less likely to bump into any of our Hallmates there. At times it felt as though we were a small part of one big relationship with the whole Hall, so much time did we spend in company with each other. It wasn't just us – Eoin and Sophie, who had finally got together about a month into term, had to deal with all the same issues, it was simply a natural result of living in Halls and sharing rooms with other people. When you argued, everyone knew and gossiped about whether or not you'd broken up. When you made up, everyone talked about it and speculated how long it would be until the next fight. When you tried to find some privacy to do the things that couples do, inevitably someone would walk in on you and then it would be all around the Hall that you had been caught 'mid-snog' *again*. There was very little privacy to be had anywhere until after everyone else had gone to bed and it wasn't always practical to stay up until two o'clock when you had a nine o'clock lecture the next morning. Occasionally on our date nights, we'd have to co-ordinate with Eoin and Sophie about where we were going to ensure we didn't inadvertently end up on a double date, but generally speaking, we would be the only students in a restaurant full of locals. Particular favourites were The Ship, where Olivia had a strange (at least to my eyes) partiality for their sandwich and chips menu and Chaucer's Inn, an underground restaurant on the high street, where the waiters were all dressed as monks. There was nothing particularly exciting about any of these date nights individually, but taken as a whole, they made us feel more grown up, as though we were doing something outside of the student norm, something more adult and 'real world'.

Exeter was a city very much orientated towards its vast student population. Most of the shops and restaurants offered a student discount of some kind and although there was a degree of inevitable tension between the students who benefitted from these and the local residents who didn't, but kept those same businesses open outside of term-time, by and large the disparate groups muddled along together in relative harmony. However, there were certain pubs we were warned about by those in the years above; establishments such as The Turk's Head which were known to be 'squaddie pubs'. The Royal Marines had a base not too far away and the cocktail of squaddies, students and alcohol was not a pleasant one, or so we were informed via a multitude of horror stories about what happened to unsuspecting students who wandered in there. The level of punishment meted out seemed to increase with every telling of the tale, but it succeeded in making most of us at least a little bit wary of venturing into these places. Not so Olivia. She dragged me in there for a drink on a number of occasions, just to prove we could do it without starting a riot. I thought these jaunts were foolhardy to say the least, but that was Olivia all over; she hated being told what to do and would always rebel against anything she viewed as limiting her freedom. I, by contrast, would have been quite happy to stick to 'our' parts of the city where it was safe and generally welcoming of us.

Even more worrying were the days when Exeter played local rivals Torquay and the streets were suddenly occupied by an alarming number of police officers. It wasn't my own safety I was concerned about on any of these occasions, but rather Olivia's; I was streetwise enough to spot trouble before it started and remove myself from the area, but Olivia was always blissfully unaware of it until it had engulfed her. I'd lost count of the number of fights in clubs that I'd had to extract her from the middle of; she was usually unscathed and unruffled, unlike my nerves which were completely in tatters. Her habit of attempting, when drunk, to placate the warring parties were particularly trying and would undoubtedly have resulted in her getting injured on more than one occasion had I not been there to pull her out of harm's way.

'Why do you always have to get involved?'

'I didn't want them to fight,' she slurred, gesticulating vaguely towards where the bouncers were separating the two combatants. 'It always spoils people's night.'

'Olivia, look around you! No-one else cares!'

'I thought it I could get them to talk to each other, they might not resort to using their fists.'

She swayed ever so slightly and peered at me sadly.

'You can't save the whole world, mate.'

'I'm sorry Tom.' She stroked my face. 'I didn't mean to scare you.'

I gathered her close and tucked her head under my chin.

'I don't want you to get hurt,' I said into her hair. 'You're only little and one punch from them would have had you in hospital. I won't always be here to protect you; you've *got* to be more careful.'

The culmination of this conversation eventually happened in the early hours after the Fresher's Ball and it was the first really serious argument we'd had. The evening had started so well; I'd rented a tuxedo for the occasion and Olivia looked stunning in a floor length burgundy dress with a matching jacket. Along with Eoin and Sophie, we'd shared the cost of a taxi to the centre of campus after the girls had complained that they couldn't walk up all those hills in their heels, but it had been with a not inconsiderable degree of pride that we had helped them out of the taxi and escorted them inside; they looked stunning and we knew it.

Inside, the exam hall had been transformed with disco lights and silver streamers that stretched across the length of the high ceiling. We met up with everyone else from our Hall and spent the night dancing and drinking, as was expected on these occasions. Then, just after midnight, Olivia said she was tired and wanted to go home. I was having too much fun and wanted to stay, so she said she'd get a taxi back on her own. Under normal circumstances I would have tried to persuade her to stay or gone out to wait with her, but we'd already had a minor disagreement about me dancing with some of the other girls, particularly Zoe, who, as usual, was all over every male within reach and I couldn't be bothered to have another one about me being overprotective, so I simply asked her to wait up for me in the Common Room.

She left to go and wait outside for her taxi, but when the rest of us got home just after two there was no sign of her, although there were a handful of the older students still up and watching TV.

'Has Olivia gone to bed?'

'Haven't seen her, sorry. Is she not with you?'

It was a fair question, we were rarely not together, but it irritated me; if she'd been with me I wouldn't have been asking about her.

'Would you mind checking to see if she's in her room?' I asked Sophie, who was supporting Zoe on her way upstairs.

She nodded, but her face was grave when she reappeared a few minutes later.

'She's not there Tom. There's no sign she's been back at all.'

My first instinct after berating myself for not ensuring that she made it safely into the taxi, was to telephone the police.

'I'm sure she's OK,' Sophie said quietly. 'She wasn't particularly drunk and Liv knows how to look after herself.'

I knew she was right, but it didn't change the fact that Olivia had left over two hours ago to do a journey that was no more than five minutes by car. Even allowing for a short wait for the taxi, or a diversion to get cash out, she should have been home long ago; I didn't even know which taxi firm she had used.

'Oh, you're back! Did you enjoy the rest of the night?'

I spun round to see that Olivia had come in through the big front door, looking tired, but otherwise free from harm.

'I'm knackered,' she said, kicking her heels off. 'I'm going to go straight up I think. Sorry Tom, I'll see you in the morning.'

She reached up to kiss my cheek and something inside me

snapped. I grabbed her arm and pulled her away from the others, into the laundry room.

'Tom let go! You're hurting me.'

I released her arm with barely an apology and watched as she rubbed it with a frown on her face. My whole body was vibrating with anger and fear and relief and I couldn't work out if the buzzing that filled my head was a result of the tempest of emotions, the amount of alcohol I'd consumed or the tumbling of the ancient washing machine.

'Where the hell have you been?' I roared over the buzzing, the volume of my voice taking me by surprise as it filled the room. I slammed my hand down on the top of the washing machine, making it jump on its rubber feet, the resulting 'clunk' echoing around the room. 'I've been worried sick!'

'Don't be ridiculous!' she blazed back, 'You've clearly only just got home yourself!'

'Yes, expecting to find you already here! Can you imagine how I felt when they said you'd never got home? I didn't know *what* had happened to you!'

'Well maybe you should have *asked* instead of yelling at me!' she spat out, pushing past me towards the door.

I grabbed her arm. I couldn't believe she was leaving.

'Olivia, please! Will you just tell me where you've been!'

'Why?' She pulled her arm from my grasp. 'Because I wasn't sitting meekly waiting for you to come home, like a good little girlfriend? You think I've been with someone else? *I* wasn't the one flirting with everything in a dress tonight.'

That stung. I really hadn't been flirting. I was friendly to everyone and I couldn't understand why she'd suddenly got so sensitive about me dancing with the other girls; we were all friends and it wasn't as though there'd even been any physical contact. We were just dancing.

'That's not fair,' I said, more quietly. 'I wasn't flirting tonight and it never crossed my mind that you'd been with anyone else. Can't you understand? How would you have felt if it had been me who'd left and not arrived home more than two hours later?

She unbent enough to apologise.

'I'm sorry you were worried.'

Her eyes glittered in the half light of the moon as it cast a silvery glow through the uncurtained window.

'I've actually been at the police station,' she said abruptly.

I sat her down on an upturned bucket, then took up a position on the floor in front of her.

'What?'

'I've been in the police station,' she repeated. 'It's a long story.'

'I've got all night,' I said, grimly.

'After I left you, I went and waited for my taxi, but when I went to get in, there was another girl already in it. The taxi driver said that this guy had asked him to take her home, given him the address and the fare and then just legged it. He didn't want to be on his own with her because she was so drunk, so he asked if I'd mind if we dropped her off first and then he'd take me home.'

'And of course, you agreed.'

'Of course! I felt sorry for him – she was completely out of it. Anyway, we got to the address he'd been given and she didn't have a key. We tried knocking on the door, but there was no answer and then she threw up in the middle of the street. He said he couldn't leave her there, so he'd have to take her to the police station, so...'

'So, you agreed to go with them.'

'Obviously. He still needed someone else with him. So, we took her to the police station and got her inside. The police assumed I knew her, which clearly I didn't, but they asked if I would mind staying with her until the ambulance came, as there were no female officers at the station.'

'And being the good citizen you are, you said you would.'

This time, my interruption earned me a small smile of acknowledgement that she would never have considered doing anything less.

'The taxi driver said to ring him when I was ready to leave and he'd take me home for free, to say thank-you. Anyway, long story short, the ambulance turned up, she got hysterical and a bit aggressive and refused to get in it, so they wouldn't take her. The police had to put her in a cell overnight to sober up and my taxi driver friend came to collect me and drop me off back here.'

I sighed.

'Olivia, how many more times are we going to have this conversation? You can't save the world on your own. Sometimes, people have to deal with the consequences of their mistakes. You weren't responsible for her – you didn't even know her for Christ's sake!'

'I'm not a child,' she said stubbornly, 'And I'm not trying to save the world, just my little corner of it. It didn't cost me anything to help tonight, so why shouldn't I have done?'

'Because anything could have happened to you!' I raised my voice again, frustrated that she couldn't, or wouldn't, understand my concern. 'The taxi driver could have attacked you. *She* could have attacked you! You said yourself she got aggressive with the paramedics. What if it had been you?'

'If you wanted a meek little girlfriend who'll let *you* behave however you want and only do what *you* want her to, Tom, then you picked the wrong girl to go out with. Maybe you need to re-evaluate our relationship!'

This time when she went to leave, I didn't try to stop her. Part of me knew she was right; I *did* need to re-evaluate our relationship, but not for the reasons she was hinting at. We were very different people with a very different outlook on life; she cared far more about others than I did for one thing. It wasn't that I *didn't* care about them, but I'd been brought up to think first and foremost about me and mine. Olivia had a far broader concept of looking out for people and it was one of the things I admired about her, even though her attitude frustrated me at times. I loved her because of who she was and I didn't want her to change, not really. I just wanted her to take a bit more care for her own safety. The other issue I knew I was innocent of and I was less sure how to resolve that. I wasn't going to stop speaking to other girls and I didn't get the impression that Olivia wanted me to either, but if we were going to be together, I needed to know that she trusted me, otherwise we were doomed to fail. Hoping that sleep might grant me a revelation to resolve this problem, I headed to bed, hoping I would still have a girlfriend the next morning.

Things were definitely awkward when we met over breakfast and although we sat together, there was almost no conversation exchanged beyond the necessary requirements for passing bottles of tomato ketchup and other condiments. For once, it was a relief to have a nine o'clock lecture and after throwing my breakfast down in minimal mouthfuls, I bid Olivia a hasty goodbye, planted a tentative peck on her cheek and flew out of the door to catch the bus, praying that I'd not delayed my departure for too long in my forlorn hope that some form of apology might have been given, or at least a level of truce reached.

My lectures allowed me to forget about my relationship woes for a little while at least. It was impossible to think about anything else when facts that needed to be recorded were being spat out at you like spraying bullets. This term I was preparing for an essay on Catherine the Great and although I was continuing with our habit of clubbing every night, I was well aware that going out drinking was not really my primary purpose in attending university. I didn't have much idea what life would hold for me once I'd graduated, but I knew that whatever else happened, I wanted to get my degree. Going to university had always been the plan and I didn't intend to waste any opportunity I was given, whether social or academic.

At lunchtime, Olivia was waiting for me outside the lecture hall. Nothing further was said about the argument of the night before and I was content for now to let it go, hoping that she'd come to her senses and accept I'd done nothing wrong. I hadn't been flirting and I'd been right to be concerned about her safety, especially when she showed such a flagrant disregard for it.

One evening Olivia was summoned to the phone and returned to the Common Room looking pale.

'That was my Dad,' she whispered. 'He's coming down to see me.'

'Will I get to meet him?'

'Of course.'

'It's OK if you don't want me to.'

'No, I want you to. It's just...oh never mind.'

She refused to say anything further on the subject and spent the remainder of the evening resolutely staring at the TV, worrying at the fringe of her scarf.

More than once over the next few days I tried to bring up the visit, but every time I did, she either changed the subject or distracted me with a kiss until I'd forgotten what I'd been saying.

'What if he doesn't like me?' I asked Eoin. 'You know what fathers are like about their daughters.'

From his comfortable position of having already met and been approved of by Sophie's parents, he was nonchalant about the whole ordeal.

'It'll be fine. Just don't be rude to him or tell him his football team's shit!'

'I'm not a bloody idiot! I don't even know if he likes football though – Olivia's not told me much about her parents.'

Mr Whitely was due to arrive on the first morning of Reading Week and Olivia and I were waiting in the Common Room when his car pulled up.

'He's here.'

'I don't know why you're so worried about your Dad coming --'

'Who says I'm worried?'

'Olivia, you've barely eaten since you found out he was coming. Do you really think pushing your food into piles cons me into thinking you've eaten it? And before you try to deny it, Sophie's noticed as well.' I smiled at her, willing her to see I was on her side, that I was trying to support her.

She remained quiet.

'As I was saying, I don't know why you're so worried about this visit, but you don't need to be. I'm sure your Dad and I will get on fine.'

'That's what I'm worried about.'

Two tears rolled down her cheeks but in a moment she'd flicked them away and gone to open the front door.

'Sweetheart!'

I hadn't known how young Olivia's father had been when she was born, so it was something of a shock to realise he was only in his mid-30s. Olivia had recently introduced me to some of the old Hollywood movies and I was struck by his resemblance to Cary Grant, even down to the immaculately tailored suit and the air of sophistication that I immediately envied.

'Dad, this is Tom,'

He shook my hand looking puzzled.

'My boyfriend.'

He recovered so well from the shock that I almost didn't realise Olivia hadn't told him about me.

'Nice to meet you, Tom.'

'You too, Mr Whitely.'

'Call me Adam. Mr Whitely always has me looking for my father.' He laughed loudly, showing two rows of very even teeth.

He looked his daughter up and down.

'You don't look too bad,' he said eventually. 'Trousers suit you better than those gypsy skirts; they're more slimming I think. And let's be honest, all men prefer Kate Moss to Sophie Dahl, don't they Tom?'

He laughed and caught my eye, inviting me to join their conversation.

'I'm more of a Jennifer Aniston man,' I smiled.

He nodded approvingly then moved beyond us to examine the antique Ottoman chair that stood in the hall. Olivia refused to look at me so I took hold of her hand and squeezed it tightly, kissing her cheek, unsure what I'd done to upset her.

'You guys certainly landed on your feet with the accommodation, didn't you?'

She pulled away and crossed her arms around herself, leaving me to respond to her father.

He asked for a tour of the campus, so we took him through the woods to the main site and although his mouth puckered slightly at the sight of the ugly brown splotches on his shiny shoes, he was good enough not to comment on it. I suggested lunch in the refectory, where at least the paths were paved and chatted to Adam all the way there as Olivia was still being very quiet. It was like talking to the older brother I'd always wanted – we had similar tastes in almost everything and I could see I'd been worrying for no reason. Whatever Olivia's issues with her parents were, I decided it must have been her mother who was the cause. Adam was so easy-going; I couldn't imagine him being the problem and I couldn't understand why Olivia hadn't wanted to live with him when she left her mum's. He was nothing like her reaction to the news of his visit had led me to expect.

On the way to lunch, we met Eoin, Sophie and Zoe emerging from various buildings. As was often the case recently, Zoe's eyes were red-rimmed and I found myself wondering who'd been the latest undergraduate to reject her, but she soon cheered up at the sight of us.

I can't believe you're Livvy's Dad,' she giggled on being introduced. 'You don't look old enough.'

'Young love,' he smiled. 'I fell for Livvy's mum the first time we met and we didn't want to wait for a family. She was beautiful in those days: legs up to her armpits. She could have been a model if she hadn't fallen pregnant. No idea where she got it from though – her parents were both short and round. Didn't even come up to her shoulder!'

We all laughed at the incongruous picture he painted.

'Livvy takes after her grandparents, don't you love? A bit short on inches.'

Olivia nodded.

'Will you join us for lunch?' Adam offered. 'I'd love to get to know Livvy's friends.'

'It's been absolutely fine,' I muttered to Eoin as we queued for our food. 'He doesn't seem like a dad at all! He's way cooler than mine.'

'It's good to see a student who understands the need to eat healthily,' Adam remarked to Zoe, as she picked at a plate of salad. 'I'd assumed you'd all be living on pizza and chips.'

She smiled at his approval, even as Eoin rolled his eyes at me and continued attacking his oversized breakfast roll.

'You know,' Adam said thoughtfully, looking at Zoe and Sophie. 'You two would make good models. Ever considered it? We might be able to use you for one of our campaigns.'

'Smarmy git.'

I elbowed Eoin, afraid Adam would hear him, but luckily he was too engrossed with the girls.

'He's just being nice.' I hissed. 'Don't be a dick.'

Fortunately for my friendship with Eoin, Zoe soon drew Adam's attention to her and they spent the rest of lunch and the return journey to the Hall like they'd been friends for years: deep in conversation about the modelling idea, arms linked and ignoring the rest of us.

'She's so selfish,' I grumbled to Eoin. 'She can talk to him about modelling another time. I wanted to get to know him today.'

'Why?'

I frowned. 'What do you mean?'

'Why are you bothering?' He basically called Livvy fat and she's barely said a word the whole time we've been with you.'

'No he didn't! He only said she took after her grandparents.'

'Who he'd just described as short and round.'

He jerked his head to where Sophie and Olivia were walking slightly ahead of us; Sophie had her arm round Olivia's shoulders, which were shaking.

'I'm taking Livvy out for dinner tonight,' Mr Whitely announced as we arrived back at the Hall. 'Would you four like to join us?'

'That'd be lovely,' I said. 'Thanks.'

'Why didn't Lisa come down with you?' Olivia asked suddenly, as the others mumbled their approval of the proposed plans.

'I'm only here for a couple of days and business is busy, so she couldn't get away. She sends her love though,' he added, frowning slightly. 'Where shall we eat?'

'Chaucer's is nice,' I volunteered.

'No! They won't have a table at short notice,' Olivia said abruptly.

'What about The Imperial?' Eoin offered. 'It's just down the road from here. You'll pass it as you drive back into town. Big red brick building on the right - lots of land around it.'

Mr Whitely looked suitably impressed. 'I'll meet you there at seven thirty then. Livvy, you can sort a table can't you?'

His daughter nodded and with that, he gave her a kiss on the cheek and swept down the drive, the sleek BMW Z3 Roadster purring away as the gravel kicked up beneath its wide tyres, the dust cloud almost obscuring the personalised number plate.

'The Imperial sounds terribly posh,' Olivia said. 'You wouldn't think it was a Wetherspoons from the name, would you?'

'No,' Eoin agreed. 'You wouldn't, would you?'

Olivia smiled warmly at him as she opened the door.

I returned to my room alone. I needed to think about what Eoin had said. I prided myself on being a good judge of character – was it really possible I'd got Adam so wrong?

A little after half past seven the five of us walked through the door of The Imperial to find Mr Whitely already at the bar, a large glass of red wine in front of him, along with two smaller glasses: one empty, the other containing a large measure of whisky. He rose to greet us, the smile I had so admired now appeared too white and too wide to appear genuine as he kissed the girls and shook hands with Eoin and me. He didn't comment on Olivia's outfit this time, but nodded at her, making a delighted look spread across her face.

'It's an interesting little place this, isn't it?' he laughed once we were at our table. 'Not quite The Ivy though.' He winked conspiratorially at Zoe who was sitting beside him. 'It's a wonderful restaurant – you really should try it someday.'

'I'd love to,' she beamed. 'It's definitely the place to be, isn't it? Tara Palmer-Tomkinson, Tamara Beckwith, Caprice – they're all so fabulous!'

'Well, it's not easy to get a table, as you can imagine, but there's always ways and means when you know people. I met Naomi there last week.'

'That's A-mazing! I'm such a fan of hers.'

None of this meant anything to me and I glanced at Olivia to ask what they were talking about, but she was too busy laughing loudly at something Eoin had said, her cheeks pink.

'It hasn't always been like that though - you remember what it was like in the early days, Livvy darling, don't you?'

Her head snapped round.

'When you first started at that school we could barely afford even the scholarship fees and the horrible little snobs didn't want to know you, did they? By the time you left though, they were falling over themselves to be your friend.'

'I remember,' she said quietly and I took her hand under the table, grateful when the waitress chose that moment to come and take our order.

'Chips, Livvy?' Mr Whitely raised an eyebrow. 'Are you sure darling?'

She flushed almost to the colour of her wine and ordered a salad instead, taking a long drink from her glass while the rest of us developed a sudden fascination for the table. When mine arrived, there were more chips than even I could have eaten and with a small sense of satisfaction I slid some of them onto Olivia's plate, hiding them under her salad leaves while her father was distracted by the smiling waitress bending down to place his plate in front of him.

As the meal continued I noticed he spent longer and longer talking to Zoe rather than his daughter. They had found a shared interest in the goings on of the rich and famous and at first she seemed enthralled by his accounts of dinners at The Ivy and The Pharmacy, but I was distracted for a moment by a chip that shot off my plate and by the time I'd embarrassedly retrieved it, she was shaking her head and her smile had become forced. He said something too quietly for me to hear and she shot a quick glance across the table at Olivia. I couldn't help envying the man's powers of persuasion because whatever he said next made Zoe blush and it wasn't long before she was nodding her head again.

Towards the end of the main course, Mr Whitely went to order some more drinks as our waitress seemed to have disappeared and I took the opportunity to go to the toilet, feeling it was safer to leave Olivia while he was absent. The toilets were on a corridor that was separated from the rest of the pub by a door. It was quite a narrow passageway and I had to push past a couple who were pressed against one wall, oblivious to anyone who might want to pass by them and I smiled to myself, remembering all the times I'd been so desperate to kiss Olivia that I too hadn't cared where I was or who might see us. I hurried through my business, anxious to return to Olivia ahead of her father, so when I re-emerged from the Gents, the couple were still there. I couldn't see their faces, which were too tightly locked together to allow for any identification, but it was with a certain amount of shock that I recognised the girl's distinctive blouse.

'Oh good, you're back,' Sophie said, as I sat down. 'We didn't want to leave Eoin on his own.' She gave her boyfriend an affectionate grin.

I panicked as I realised where they were going and tried to silently communicate to Sophie the need to wait. My efforts were in vain however and I shifted agitatedly in my seat, trying to respond to Eoin's inquiries about why girls always went to the toilet in pairs, while I waited for their return. When they came back however, they were giggling uncontrollably.

'What's so funny?'

'Someone was getting a bit friendly in the Ladies,' Olivia chuckled. 'We got in and out as quick as we could.'

I joined in the laughter at her unintended pun, but my mind was whirling. Did I tell her or pretend I'd seen nothing?

A few minutes later Zoe returned to the table rubbing her arms, which had goosebumps rising beneath the pale flesh, one corner of her blouse escaping from the waistband of her skirt.

'Where've you been? You've been ages.'

'I went to the loo and then I popped out for a fag.'

For a brief moment I envied her; Olivia had made me give up smoking and even though I knew she was right to do so, it was a habit I missed.

'You must have just avoided the couple in there then,' Sophie laughed. 'You were lucky - we had to beat a hasty retreat!'

Zoe's pale cheeks turned to a powdery rose, but she kept her composure reasonably well. Olivia had returned her attention to her meal and was devouring the remainder of her pilfered chips before her father returned, but Sophie's eyes narrowed. At that moment Mr Whitely arrived with a tray of drinks.

'Sorry about the delay folks,' he said. 'I went to the Gents and then it took ages to get served.'

Sophie's eyes slid to the bar, which had very few people waiting at it and she promptly choked on the piece of steak she'd been chewing. There was a quiet hiss beside me and Olivia spoke very little for the rest of evening, except to order a dessert that I ate most of and to say a tight-lipped goodbye to her father.

'Let's go for a walk,' I suggested on our return to the Hall.

Olivia nodded. Behind the Hall was a small, wooded area and it was to there she dragged me. As soon as we were beyond the sight of anyone walking past, she pushed me to the floor in front of a tree and straddled me. I'd never been kissed with such ferocity before and I could taste her anger, but my body reacted as any man's would and after a short time, I felt her fumbling with the fly of my jeans. I grabbed her hand, stilling its movement.

'What? It's what you want, isn't it? It's what you all want. Or am I not attractive enough for you? Would you rather it was Sophie here with her oh so perfect clothes, or Zoe with her so perfect figure? Am I too fat to sleep with or does it not matter? Will any woman do? Do you like them to know what they're doing, or do you prefer it when they're a bit more innocent? Does it even matter as long as it feels good for you?'

Her voice pitched higher with each question and her hand squirmed in my grip, fighting to return to my flies. I held her until she stopped trembling, feeling my own body relax with her.

'First of all – yes, of course it's what I want – eventually – but not like this. I don't want our first time to be because you're angry with your dad and trying to prove some kind of point. As for the rest – it's you I want, no-one else. Don't tell him I said this, but your Dad's an idiot.'

'You've changed your tune,' she said. 'You were getting on like a house on fire this morning.'

'I know and I'm sorry. I was an idiot too. I just wanted him to like me.'

'Everyone does. Do you really fancy Jennifer Aniston?'

'She's hot. But so are you.'

'Really?'

'Really.'

She leant against me and we sat listening to the silence.

'It would have been my first time,' she said eventually, her voice muffled by the collar of my coat.

'Our first time,' I agreed, kissing her hair.

'I didn't mean it like that,' she said. 'I meant my first time ever. I know it wouldn't be yours, but I'm a late starter. Everyone else I know has done it and I guess I want to know what all the fuss is about. Dad's always played around - that's why Mum's the way she is. I think he drove her to it with his affairs and his constant jibes about her weight. Him and Lisa haven't been married long, but I doubt tonight was the first time he's cheated on her.'

'I guess it must be easy to do if you're surrounded by models all day.'

She frowned at me and then unexpectedly, laughed.

'What do you think Dad does?'

'I don't know – I'd assumed a modelling agency or something, from what he was saying at lunch and in the pub.'

'He has a couple of shops! He calls them 'boutiques' 'cos it sounds posher, but they're basically dress shops. He uses pictures of people wearing the dresses on his advertising leaflets.'

It was the most forthcoming she'd been about her parents, but I was still distracted by her earlier comment.

'What did you mean when you said you knew it wouldn't be my first time?' I asked, forcing my limbs to remain relaxed.

'Oh, I know you've slept with four people: two girlfriends and a couple of one-night stands.'

'Who told you that?' My hands twitched.

'Zoe. She told me you'd all been talking about it one night in the pub when I wasn't there.'

I remembered that night well. We'd all had a few pints and the conversation had turned to our sexual experiences. It wasn't a conversation I was comfortable with and when they'd asked me I'd simply plucked a number out of the air and added as few details as possible, never dreaming it would get back to Olivia.

'It's OK though,' she said brightly. 'It's probably best if one of us knows what we're doing. I've never gone further than kissing.' She lifted her head from my shoulder. 'I'm glad it'll be you.'

I kissed her. It seemed the safest option.

We stayed cuddled under my coat until I was unable to ignore the growing cold and damp seeping through my clothing.

'Nice though this is, we can't stay out here all night,' I said, unwrapping my arms.

'Do you think we could maybe go away together?' she asked. 'Just for a weekend I mean.'

I did know what she meant and I grinned.

'I think we could probably manage that. It'd be nice to have some time on our own; I'd kill for some privacy at times.'

'Tell me about it!' she groaned. She ran her hand down my body and this time I didn't push her away. 'Let's make it soon.'

A fervent nod had to suffice as a response and I knew she could feel that I agreed with her.

We sat a moment longer and I didn't want to break the mood, but I had to check she wasn't going to kill her room-mate overnight. What Zoe had done was awful, but I couldn't help feeling a bit sorry for her and I was starting to think Olivia had been right about her all along. She gave the impression of being predatory, but there was something unnatural about the fact she was so brittle, jumping in less than a heartbeat from overflowing self-confidence to a snivelling wreck.

'What are you going to say to her?'

'I don't know,' Olivia admitted, her face troubled. 'She was stupid and I hate her for it, but...'

'You know what your Dad's like,' I finished.

She nodded. 'He's charming and good-looking and he knows how to flatter women and make them feel special. That's what Mum used to say anyway; it's why she always forgave him and took him back. To be honest, I'm hoping she'll be asleep when I go up; I'm not sure I can face her tonight. Can I think about it tomorrow?'

I smiled and kissed the tip of her nose.

'Of course. See you in the morning.'

As I passed by the library window on the way back to my

own building I heard muffled sobs coming from within and paused, listening as they broke the silence that surrounded me. I had a feeling I knew who was inside and although my warm, soft bed was calling my name with all the insistence of an ardent lover, I was suddenly angry that she was the one seeking sympathy when it was Olivia who'd suffered. I squared my shoulders and made my way to the tiny room affectionately but rather pretentiously referred to as the Hall's library. In reality, there were very few books in there and the single computer screen illuminated the small corner it occupied as it winked and blinked in the darkness. It was supposed to be shut down at night, but whoever had been on it last had obviously not expected to be its final user of the evening and had failed to power it down. I was grateful for the dim blue glow that spotlighted the miserable figure on the floor.

'Zoe?'

The sniffing stopped and the ball uncurled enough to show a dark head of cropped hair.

'What do you want? If you're coming to tell me what a shit roommate I am or how awful Olivia feels, you can save your breath. I know all that and you can't make me feel any worse than I already do.' Her tone was defiant, but it was a boldness I suspected would quickly crumble back into tears if I tested it.

'I'm not here to have a go,' I sighed, sitting down next to her. 'I heard you crying through the window and I came to see if you were okay.'

'Why?'

'You're upset.' I pointed out the obvious. 'You obviously regret it, so why the hell did you do it in the first place? You must've known Olivia would find out. For Christ's sake, Zoe – she's meant to be your friend!'

She stared at me for a moment, then swallowed deeply.

'I have shit taste in men. I get suckered in by the charm

every time. There was a guy back home,' she bit her lip and looked away. 'If anyone had found out, he'd have lost his job and I'd have been expelled, so it was all terribly romantic – we were risking everything to be together, so I figured it was love, right? He broke it off the day of my final exam. *I don't want it to end Zoe, but you have to think of your future.* By the time term started, he was already seeing a girl in the year below me.'

Tear swollen eyes met mine. 'You won't tell anyone will you? I don't want to get him into trouble.'

'You should report him,' I told her. 'He took advantage of you.'

'I'm not sure they'd even believe me.' She smiled sadly at me. 'Why can't I find someone like you? Olivia doesn't know how lucky she is.'

She kissed my cheek and left, merging into the darkness beyond the circle of light from the computer screen, the damp spot on my cheek the only sign she'd ever been there. I stood for a moment, wondering if I was now allowed to seek the comfort of my own bed and banish other people's problems at least until the morning. My bed renewed its offer of relief and I rushed to answer its call, eager to put some distance between them and me.

'She wasn't there when I got to the room last night,' Olivia told me at breakfast the next day. 'I was in bed when she came in, so I just pretended to be asleep. This morning she was already gone when I woke up.'

Moira, the Hall Warden looked grim when she met us leaving the dining room. 'I need a word.'

She was a short round woman, who by all stereotypes of her kind, should have been jolly and motherly, but neither of these adjectives could be reasonably applied to Moira. Her face, which was always pinched as though she were in pain, now gave the distinct impression that it was vinegar flowing through her veins and she spoke through thinly pursed lips.

'I assume I don't need to enlighten the pair of you about last night's events?' she inquired, looking at Olivia for all the world as though what had happened had been her fault in some way.

'How did you...' Olivia's voice trailed off beneath the unforgiving stare.

'I had an early morning visit from Zoe, asking to swap rooms,' Moira answered, her stern features not relaxing an inch. 'She was somewhat upset and inclined to ramble, but I eventually got the story out of her. It wasn't pretty listening.'

She let the last point hang in the air for a while before she continued.

'However, other, more serious matters came to light during the course of the interview and that is why you two are here. Oh, it's nothing you've done,' she said waspishly as Olivia and I exchanged bewildered looks. 'I just wanted to ask you not to give her too hard a time about what happened.'

Finally, her face lost its rigid appearance and the taut lines that criss-crossed her forehead relaxed into their natural folds.

'I imagine this isn't easy for you either,' she addressed Olivia, 'But Zoe's had a pretty tough time of it. She's agreed to tell her parents about what happened last year and we'll get her some help here as well. All I ask is that you don't make life harder for her.'

'We won't,' Olivia was quick to say. 'Will you...will you tell her I don't hate her? I can't talk to her at the moment, but I don't want her to think that.'

Moira nodded and opened the door to her apartment to let us out.

'What was all that about?' Olivia let out a low whistle between her teeth.

I shrugged. 'Search me.' I didn't want to lie to her, but it wasn't my secret to tell.

'I think I'll make myself scarce this morning,' Olivia said as we reached the bottom of the stairs. 'Come into town with me?'

'Why don't we see what's on at the cinema?' I suggested. 'That'll keep us out of the way for a few hours.'

She nodded and we spent the walk to my room to collect my coat and wallet engaged in a friendly argument about what we were going to go and see. Olivia won of course and I sat through 'Fools Rush In' wondering if it might not have been better just to have stayed at the Hall instead.

I hadn't forgotten about Olivia's suggestion of a weekend away together, but I couldn't quite bring myself to book a hotel. I told myself it was only because I wanted to get the right location and the right hotel, but it was nothing to do with that. The truth was, I was terrified. I knew what she was expecting from the weekend away and although I wanted it just as much as she did, I was also scared almost out of my wits. I didn't want to mess it up and she was expecting me to take the lead because as far as she was aware, I'd done it before and therefore must know what I was doing. I knew the sensible thing to do was to tell her the truth, but that would mean admitting that I'd lied about it and then not taken the opportunity to tell her the truth when it was offered to me. I wasn't worried she'd tell anyone else, but I was concerned about how she'd react if she found out.

'I've booked us a hotel in Plymouth,' she informed me one morning, as we walked to the bus stop. 'I got fed up of waiting for you to do it, so I've booked one night at the Travelodge. We're going this weekend.'

I forced a smile to push down the sick feeling rising from my stomach.

'You don't mind, do you? You did say you wanted to.'

I tried to make my expression look more genuine to remove the anxious look from her face.

'Of course not, don't be silly. Why would I mind? It's a good idea.'

I had to keep reminding myself of this over the next few days as I found myself thinking of little else but the upcoming weekend. Despite my copious note taking, my lecture notes made no sense when I read them back – my mind had obviously not been as focused on the lecture as I'd thought. Olivia, ever practical, assured me that she had bought an ample supply of condoms and would make sure they were safely in her bag before we left.

The train to Plymouth only took about an hour and so we arrived just as the clock struck twelve, with time to kill until we could check into our hotel. Fortunately, Olivia had planned for this and she led us to the seafront. The red and white stripes of Smeaton's Tower rose majestically to greet us, but she ignored the towering edifice and led us through the park and onto the seafront to The Dome. The curved glass winked at us, reflecting the winter sun as it chased the waves in the harbour, bouncing off the cross-Channel ferries that glided through the water.

Inside were a multitude of rooms depicting parts of Plymouth's long history. I liked the Elizabethan street scene, even though I had to cover my nose to protect it from the insidious smell. The pungency of it made me wonder exactly how they had managed to artificially create such a vile odour. However, it was the Blitz section that captured Olivia's interest and it was here that we lingered the longest, watching the video that described with painful volume the noise and terror of those nights in 1941 when the city shuddered and quaked under the onslaught of German bombs. It was a sobering thought that much of the city we'd just walked through had been built up from the destruction to begin again. I'd experienced the same feeling of horror when I had gone to Hamburg on a school exchange trip and seen the St.

Nikolai memorial and it *should* have put my own worries into perspective.

Late in the afternoon, we made our way to the hotel, threading our way through rival university students on their way home from lectures and suited office workers rushing to collect their children from childcare centres and a part of me envied their ordered lives; married, jobs, children. I wondered if this was what the future would be like for us, eager to get home at the end of the working day to see each other and spend time with our children. I happily daydreamed about our children until the blue sign above the entrance brought all my worries rushing back to the surface. What if I was no good? What if I hurt her? We'd booked a table for dinner so I still had a few hours in which to try to get my head together about it, but with the anxiety bubbling away in my stomach the thought of food made me nauseous.

The room itself was typical of its kind; a large white bed occupied the centre of the room and a desk, a wardrobe, a couple of chairs and a television were the only other furniture. The modestly sized bathroom opened off to one side and it was into there that Olivia disappeared almost as soon as we entered. I didn't have much unpacking to do, so once I'd hung up my shirt and trousers, I settled onto the bed to watch TV. The nights I had lain awake worrying must have all caught up with me because the next thing I was aware of was the sound of the hairdryer.

I opened my eyes to find Olivia drying her hair, clad only in her underwear. It was an electric blue concoction, with a black lace trim and body reacted viscerally to the curves of her hips and then again to the swell of her breasts above the satin and lace when she turned to face me. I tried to swallow, but it stuck in my throat and came out as a kind of guttural groan, which alerted her to the fact I was no longer asleep.

'Sorry,' she said. 'I didn't want to wake you, but if I don't do it now, my hair won't dry in time for dinner. Can you pass me the bag with my straighteners in?' She gestured to the bag beside me. 'Oh, never mind, I'll get it myself.'

She turned the hairdryer off and leant over me to get the bag, her body briefly pressing against me. I couldn't help myself; I put my hand on her waist, my palm spanning the smooth skin and it was as if flames were racing over me in a frenetic game of chase. Her lips sought and captured mine and I kept her confined in the circle of my arms, my hands tracing over her body. It was some time before I could bring myself to let her go and even more until she moved to continue getting ready.

'I did think about getting a Princess Leia outfit,' she said as she pulled the straighteners through her hair, still clad only in her underwear, 'But I'm happy to see it won't be needed.'

I swallowed. She wasn't helping matters.

'I'm not so obsessed with Star Wars,' I stammered.

'Oh no,' she said, smothering a smile. 'You can just quote most of the films and get all flustered when Carrie Fisher's in that tin bikini. I thought it might help things along, you know?'

She grinned and I knew it must have been the expression on my face that caused it. What was she trying to do to me?

Dinner was a necessary interruption and the wine helped to calm me down, as did the drinks in the pub afterwards, but the moment couldn't be delayed forever, nor did I truly want it to be, although I was puzzled when Olivia took a towel out of her bag and laid it on the bed.

'I don't want them to know what we've been doing,' she flushed.

'Try to relax,' I said, as much to remind myself as to reassure her.

I pulled her towards me, then ceased to think and just let things happen. I couldn't begin to describe precisely how it felt, even to myself. It was strange, clumsy, awkward and wonderful, but most all it felt right. Afterwards, we lay quietly together.

'Are you OK?' I asked. 'Did it...did it hurt?'

'A bit,' she admitted, 'But I'm fine. Really.'

It was once I switched the light back on that panic set in.

'You're bleeding!' I pointed at the towel, horrified at the thought that I'd damaged her in some way.

'It's perfectly normal,' she laughed.

I panicked. 'Are you sure? It didn't happen last time!'

'It wasn't me last time!' she snapped and rolled away from me.

The body that had so recently been like liquid beneath me now held itself with the rigidity of a corpse.

'I'm sorry,' I said, kissing her shoulder. 'That was a really stupid thing to say.'

'Yes it was. I accept that there's been others before me, but it doesn't mean I want to be reminded of them,' she snapped.

I still couldn't tell her the truth; I'd already done enough to spoil our first time. I held my tongue until her body signalled that I'd been forgiven, then I rolled her over into a warmer embrace and watched her while she slept, a slight crease marring the smooth skin of her forehead. Even in slumber she seemed to chastise me for my careless words. How could I have hurt her so badly? I hadn't meant to; I'd just been so terrified I'd done something wrong and damaged her. I should have confessed there and then, I supposed. I'd almost decided to wake her up and tell her my secret, when her hand slid down my back and warm kisses covered my chest and I reasoned that postponing it for a few more hours was not an unreasonable decision to make. It was a night of interrupted sleep, but I eventually awoke the next morning with her arm and leg dead weights across my body and her hair tickling my nose. We returned to Exeter different people to when we had left thirty six hours earlier, but even to Eoin and Sophie we would only acknowledge that it had been a pleasant weekend and Plymouth was well worth a visit. In public we continued much as we had prior to our weekend away, but when we were alone I found it impossible not to reach out for her, even if it was just to rest my hand on hers. I needed her more than ever and there were several nights out where we arrived late and dishevelled. Many such arrivals were at Olivia's instigation (although I had no objection) and she would often appear at my door in the middle of the days when Peter had a lecture and I didn't. Having discovered the joys of a physical relationship we were reluctant to pass up any opportunity to explore each other further and we had some narrow escapes from discovery as we came up with increasingly inventive places to snatch some time alone.

After our weekend away, the weeks flew past and before long the Christmas holidays were looming large and I faced the prospect of being separated from Olivia for several weeks. Despite what had happened with Zoe, she still planned to go to her Dad's for Christmas; not that she really had much of a choice. She said she'd have preferred to go to her grandmother's, but her mum was going there for Christmas and not knowing what kind of state she would be in apparently made visiting quite difficult. I still wasn't totally sure what the issue with her mum was, as although Olivia had let slip a few hints that her mother was a bit unstable, I hadn't liked to press the issue too much – we'd still only been together a few months after all and Olivia repeatedly assured me she'd tell me when she was ready. I knew by now not to disagree with her if I wanted a quiet life and had accepted that on this matter, I was just going to have to be patient.

We continued to sneak away for moments of solitude in the weeks following our weekend in Plymouth and this was made easier by the fact that Sophie had moved in to replace Zoe as Olivia's roommate and the girls seemed to have worked out some sort of rota system that meant we could all rely on some time alone when we wanted it. None of this meant that I'd owned up to my lies though. As time went on it got harder and harder to find the right moment to tell her the truth and the longer I delayed it, the more scared I was of telling her and the more of an issue it became in my head. I kept telling myself that I'd tell her the next time, or I'd tell her over lunch the next day, but I never wanted to break the mood, or spoil her lunch. I came up with a hundred different reasons, each as flimsy as the last, as to why I couldn't break my silence on this subject.

In some ways, having that guaranteed time together made life much easier, but it also meant that the temptation to abandon the essay I was meant to be writing and seek out Olivia instead, was much greater and increasingly difficult to ignore, especially when she'd knock on my door and an inquiring eyebrow would be raised as her face appeared in the gap between the door and the frame. My desk was covered in ink splatters where I'd thrown my pen down so often in my haste to leave.

Zoe had offered Olivia a tentative but heartfelt apology one morning when they'd unavoidably met on the stairs and this had resulted in a thawing of their relationship, which Olivia professed herself to be very relieved about.

'I don't like there to be bad feelings between us,' she said. 'It's not really her fault, is it and she seems better now.'

Consequently, Zoe became part of the clubbing crowd again. There were still drunken moments when she launched herself at the nearest single male, but there were noticeably less tears afterwards and on the whole she was a calmer, more toned down version of the girl we'd first met. I'd heard she'd been having sessions with the campus counsellor and they seemed to be having a positive effect on her, so it was a surprise on a night out some time later to see her out of control again. I'd been to the toilet and seen her pinned to the wall with her tongue down the throat of the man she'd been dancing with earlier in the evening.

'Normal service resumed,' I thought to myself as I passed them. 'Well, that didn't take long.'

It was only because of the split second of quiet when the DJ switched tracks that I even hear her muffled, 'Stop it!'

Knowing what she was like, I almost ignored it and carried on walking, but the memory of her vulnerability that night in the library flashed through my mind and made me stop and turn round. He was pushing her towards the door, his hands all over her. The bouncers looked disinterested, even as Zoe tried to right her clothes and release herself from his grasp. I caught up and stepped in front of them.

'There you are!' I slurred. 'We've been looking everywhere for you! Sorry mate,' I flashed him a conciliatory smile and rolled bleary eyes at him, 'She's needed elsewhere.'

I shepherded Zoe back towards the safety of the inner room.

'Sorry!' she shouted in my ear. 'He wouldn't leave me alone after we danced and I thought if I kissed him he might be satisfied with that and then I could tell him to bugger off. It kind of backfired.'

It seemed that he really was that slow on the uptake, or that the drink had addled his brain to the point at which he no longer cared if his partner was willing or not, because he came after us again.

'Whassamatter babe? I reckoned you was up for a good time. Come on. Leave the wanker and let's go.'

She was more able to defend herself now that he was in front of her and Zoe let fly with her right hand, leaving a livid red handprint like a birthmark on his cheek.

'Fucking cock tease!' he roared, grabbing her wrist and pulling her towards him again.

In a matter of seconds, Zoe's knee had made contact with his groin and he was rolling on the floor, the cries of rage turned into ones of pain and humiliation. The bouncers appeared as if out of nowhere; one checked that he was okay, while the other clamped a hand on Zoe's shoulder to forcibly eject her from the club. In vain, I protested that she'd only been protecting herself, but they were adamant that she'd caused the trouble and had to leave.

'Wait for me by the door,' I told her. 'I'm just going to let the others know. Don't go without us!'

I'd expected that Olivia would be full of indignation that Zoe had been blamed – she was always telling me that women were punished for the actions of men – but she was strangely quiet beyond agreeing to leave with us all. As we exited the club a sudden rush of wind to my left made me instinctively jerk my head back, so the blow grazed the corner of my mouth rather than landing fully on my jaw, as had been the intention. Still, it was enough to split my lip open. Dazed from the first blow, I didn't see the second one coming and would have had far worse than the black eye I ended up with, had Eoin not pulled me out of the way.

As an amateur boxer, he'd sized up the situation and the man straight away. One sharp jab, well placed, was all it took to bring him to his knees and then we left him in the care of the bouncers, to whom I took pains to point out that surely this proved they'd ejected the wrong person from the establishment they were supposed to be guarding.

'Maybe next time you won't be quite so quick to judge.'

My dazed state and the knowledge that I'd been defending a female was making me feel quite self-righteous. I was about to tell them that perhaps they should consider doing their job better, for if they had, I wouldn't have been injured, but Eoin dragged me away before I could begin my speech. I decided he was probably right and discretion was the larger part of valour.

'Tom, you're hurt,' Zoe exclaimed as we joined the girls,

who had scuttled out of the way as soon as I'd been hit. She dabbed at the blood on my lip with a tissue.

'I'll do that!' Olivia snatched the tissue out of her hand, eyes blazing.

I'd preferred Zoe's gentle touch to the fierce pressure of Olivia's blotting of the wound but thought it wise to stay silent.

'I'm so sorry, Tom. I never meant for you to get hurt.'

Zoe's eyes were shimmering under the sulphurous street-lights and I reached out to squeeze her hand.

'I'm OK, honestly. It's not as bad as it looks and it's certainly not your fault.'

'Not her fault? I assume that was the guy you slapped?'

Zoe nodded; her expression guarded.

'Well maybe if you hadn't led him on and then humiliated him he wouldn't have hit Tom. So, it kind of is your fault, isn't it? Once again, people suffer because you don't think!'

Sophie threw an apologetic look at Zoe, then hurried after Olivia as she stormed off down the street, linking arms as she caught her up, her calm tones carrying further than her words did.

'She doesn't mean it, Zoe. She's just upset.'

'Aren't you going to talk to her?'

'No chance!' I laughed. 'I'll wait until Sophie's calmed her down first.'

'He doesn't want a broken nose to add to the collection!' Eoin laughed.

'She'll be fine by the time we get back.' I said. 'She's a bit shaken I think. I'm sure she'll apologise when she's had time to think about things.'

I'd reassured Zoe and by the time the three of us arrived back at the Hall, she looked much happier, even laughing at Eoin's appalling jokes.

'Thanks for rescuing me tonight,' she said, as we said goodnight. 'And again, I'm so sorry you got hurt.'

'Stop worrying,' I said, giving her a hug. 'I'm fine.'

I could have done with a similar reassurance myself as I saw Olivia standing in the shadows watching us, but there was no-one to give it to me by the time Zoe had gone up the stairs towards her room, as Olivia had vanished.

I found her in the laundry room, folding up her clean washing.

'What was all that about?'

She glared at me.

'You can't see it, can you? This is how people like her operate. She gets you feeling sorry for her and you let your guard down and the next thing you know, she'll be in your bed.'

'Olivia, that's ridiculous! You think she set the whole thing up tonight just to get to me? I'm flattered you think I'm worth all that trouble, but really? You're mad!'

'That's right. I'm paranoid and imagining things. I know you love me and so why would you cheat on me? I've heard it all before, Tom. I heard Mum and Dad screaming it at each other for years. Don't treat me like an idiot!'

'I will if you insist on behaving like one!' I'd defended myself over and over again against the same accusations and I'd had enough.

'If you don't trust me when I've given you no reason not to, then I don't see how we'll ever work together. I'm not your Dad, Olivia and it's not fair to punish me for his mistakes! I can't be the man you want me to be and never speak to other women – that's not who I am and I don't want it to be! You were out of order tonight. You're being completely unreasonable. I actually thought you might be proud of me for stepping in, for not making assumptions and walking away! I can't win. You're the one who said she wasn't truly to blame for what happened with your Dad and the minute that version doesn't suit you, it's all her fault again.'

I brushed my hand wearily across my face.

‘I’m going to bed. I’ll see you tomorrow.’

I closed the door behind me, ignoring the sobs I could hear and walked across the grounds to my room. *What am I going to do?* Again, I’d been found wanting, again I’d done the wrong thing and we’d had a row that could have been avoided if I’d just apologised. *Why couldn’t you have bitten your tongue?* A part of me that I didn’t want to listen to, replied. *Because you weren’t in the wrong.*

Things were a little strained the next day. I was angry with Olivia and angry with myself for not knowing how to put things right. Sophie had tried to talk to me, to explain how Olivia was feeling, so I knew they’d discussed what had happened, but I cut her off.

‘I know you’re trying to help, Soph and I appreciate it, I really do, but if Olivia wants me to know all this, then she needs to tell me herself.’

I then made it impossible for her to talk to me by avoiding all the usual places I could be found. I was confused about everything, but most of all I was frightened. I was frightened I was going to lose her, frightened that if I did, it might not matter. I was trying to be a better person for her, trying to do the right thing and it was exhausting. Every time I thought we were making progress with her trust issues, something would happen and we’d have to go through the whole cycle again. It was starting to get me down and I had no idea what to do. Eoin and I were close, but talking about our feelings isn’t something men are very good at and I was always conscious that Sophie and Oliva were good friends. I didn’t want to risk making the situation any worse.

That night was the termly formal dinner and it was with great reluctance that I pulled on my tuxedo. These dinners were organised by the Hall’s student committee and the seating plans were prepared well in advance, so it was inevitable that I would be seated next to Olivia. It was also likely that we would be nowhere near Eoin and Sophie as the committee apparently liked to sit you with a partner, if you had one, but also with people you didn't normally socialise with, in a bid to encourage new friendships to form. Of course, what normally happened, or so we had been told, was that you endured each other's company as best you could during the meal, making polite but forced conversation and then as soon as the last plate had been cleared, made a beeline for your friends, with whom you spent the rest of the evening's entertainments.

As I'd predicted, Olivia was on one side of me, but the seat to my right was occupied by Kate, a dark-haired girl from the West Midlands who was a fellow smoker and who still let me have an occasional sneaky drag on her cigarette, following Olivia's ban on my habit. On the far side of Olivia was Matt, also a member of the Oxbridge Rejects club. We were reasonably friendly with both of them, so dinner was not so much of a chore as I had feared, although neither Olivia nor I ate very much. By the middle of the evening, having consumed more than my fair share of wine during the meal and then moved on to spirits, I couldn't even remember what the menu had been.

Olivia had gravitated to Sophie's side at the conclusion of the meal and Kate had dragged me into the smoking room. Once seated on the ageing sofa it was beyond my capabilities to get up again, so I decided to remain there, chatting to the girls. After all, if my girlfriend had abandoned me, there was no harm in talking to anyone else, was there?

'So, what's going on with you and Liv?'

I shrugged.

'Dunno. We had a bit of a row yesterday.'

'So, you still together then?'

I shrugged again.

'Dunno. Haven't really spoken today.'

I lapsed into silence. I didn't want to talk *about* Olivia. I wanted to talk *to* her. I felt ungrounded and I didn't like it. It didn't feel like freedom, it simply felt dangerous and unsafe. I was vaguely aware of people talking and moving around me and then it all fell silent and I was alone. At least that was how it felt. Virginia, one of the second years, stood in the doorway observing me. I squinted at her. *Vir-gin-ia*, I thought. It was a difficult word to say. *No wonder she pre... pre... likes Ginny better. S'far easier.*

'I heard you say that you and Livvy had split up,' she said, moving to sit next to me. 'It's a shame; she's a nice girl.' She patted my knee. 'But you can't sit here feeling sorry for yourself. You have to move on.'

I gave her a considered look. Had I said we'd split up? I couldn't remember. I didn't think I had. I didn't think we had split up. Not officially anyway. Did she know something I didn't? Had Olivia said something to her? She swayed a little and I wondered if she was as drunk as I was, or if it was the spinning of the room that caused her to lean over. She put her arm on the back of the sofa to steady herself and then lurched towards me again. I thought she might be trying to kiss me and wasn't sure how I felt about that. I panicked and misjudged the amount of sofa between me and the floor. Arms came up between mine and hauled me to my feet. I squinted at the figure trying to work out who to thank for putting me the right way up. It was Zoe.

'Go to bed, Tom,' she sighed.

That seemed like an excellent idea. Perhaps my room had not been afflicted by the same spinning disease as the rest of the Hall and I might find some peace there. Halfway there however, I was beginning to suspect that perhaps it was me doing the spinning. I tested out my theory by turning round on the spot and then wished I hadn't.

Oh dear. I looked at the steps. *I'm sure they used to be grey.*

I wasn't entirely sure why the steps were suddenly a different colour but suspected I might be to blame and I knew they needed cleaning. The last time something like this had happened, the Common Room had been 'Closed for Cleaning' one morning, leading to a lot of unhappy students who missed their daily dose of Teletubbies. Watching this had, for some unknown reason, become something of a ritual for those of us who didn't have nine o'clock lectures. I hadn't been responsible for the disruption on that occasion, nor did I want to be held to account this time. Therefore, cleaned the steps must be. I found an empty carton of washing liquid in the laundry and filled it with water, returning to the path to throw it at the steps.

Why are the bottoms of my trousers wet?

I stared accusingly at the empty carton. The steps still weren't the right colour. I staggered back to the laundry room to refill it. Olivia was there.

'Hello.' I hung my head and shuffled my feet. I felt like a naughty child confronted by its parent.

'What are you doing?' She pointed at the limp cardboard carton in my hand.

'I think I might've been sick on the steps. I'm cleaning it up.'

She frowned. 'Why didn't you just use the bucket?'

What bucket?

She picked up the bright orange bucket in front of me and waved it at me.

Ah that bucket.

'I was outside. Wouldn't have got inside in time.'

'What? No, I mean, why didn't you use the bucket to clean it up? You can barely get any water in that box.'

Ah. Yes, that would have been more useful. My head hurts.

She pushed me down onto the step at the side of the sink.

'Wait there,' she instructed filling the bucket at the tap.

She disappeared and returned a few minutes later swinging the now empty bucket.

'All sorted.' She hauled me to my feet. 'Come on, let's get you to your room.'

The spinning had subsided to something resembling the motion of a cross-channel ferry in the harbour while I'd been sitting down, but it returned like a top in a force ten gale the moment I was on my feet again and I leant heavily on Olivia's shoulder as we walked down the path.

'The stairs are the right colour again,' I observed happily as we mounted them.

'That's what happens when you clean them properly,' Olivia remarked drily.

Once she'd undressed me and got me into bed, she perched on the edge of it and stroked my forehead. Her hand was cool and it kept things in focus as long as it was there.

'I'm sorry,' she said. 'Not just for ignoring you tonight, but for last night as well. You were right. I am trying, but it's hard for me. I don't let people in easily and it scares me how much I need you.'

'Stay,' I whispered, trying to lift my hand to her face. I smiled seductively. 'Peter won't be back for ages.'

'I can't,' she said, kissing my forehead. 'Go to sleep. I'll come and see you in the morning.'

The hangover the next morning was the most painful one I'd ever had and it was only the painkillers Olivia dispensed at regular intervals that made it bearable. She was a welcome sight every four hours and by dinnertime I was able to get dressed and face having something to eat.

'Did I do something to upset Ginny last night?' I asked as I said goodnight to Olivia later that evening. I didn't remember much of the evening before being sick on the stairs and I was worried I'd somehow offended the rather upright treasurer of the committee, who'd been rather off with me over dinner.

Olivia's eyes sparkled with suppressed mirth.

'No. She was pretty drunk herself last night and I gather from Zoe that she made a bit of a fool of herself.'

'You two made up then? I'm glad.'

'Yeah, we're cool. I apologised to her last night as well.'

I hugged her and went to my room, wondering what on earth Ginny had done that had made Olivia so gleeful. Whatever it was, it had brought her and Zoe back together, so I wasn't going to question it too much.

After Christmas the months flew past as quickly as the evenings lightened. Formal dinners and the summer ball came and went with little to disrupt our routines and Olivia and I had settled into our relationship more comfortably. She had stopped accusing me of flirting with everyone else and now simply rolled her eyes when I denied that anyone ever flirted with me. We'd put all our date nights on hold for a while as we were deep into exam season. Not only was it difficult to arrange an evening where neither of us had an exam the next day, but we both had a lot of studying to do and so we had to be content with whatever time we could snatch together.

Nevertheless, as with everything else, the exams soon came and went and then Olivia's birthday arrived. I'm hopeless with presents – I always have been – my mother has a whole box of jewellery and ornaments I've bought over the years that she never wears or has on display. For Christmas I'd bought Olivia a mug with a chocolate bar on it. She'd bought me a pair of solid silver cufflinks with my initials engraved on them. She said she loved the mug, but it seemed so inadequate when I realised how much thought had gone into her gift to me. I was determined to get it right this time and had even resorted to quizzing Sophie in a desperate bid to get some kind of hint about what she might like. It couldn't be too extravagant – it was almost the end of term and funds were running low – but it had to be carefully chosen. It had to show I cared.

Wandering through the back streets of Exeter one day I found it: the perfect present. It sat in the window of an antique shop nestled between a baker's and a shop selling cameras. In between ugly china figures and William IV port glasses sat a ring; small diamonds clustered around three sapphires. The price tag made me gulp a little, but I had my credit card to make up the difference between the cost and what I could afford and I thrust my card at the salesman before I could have any second thoughts. It was worth every penny to see Olivia's face when she opened it.

'It's not an engagement ring,' I warned, 'I just thought it was pretty, that's all.'

She smiled. 'It's beautiful,' she said. 'I love it. And I never imagined it was anything more than a birthday present. It's far too soon to think of anything like that!'

The topic came up again a couple of weeks later on the last evening of term, when we were in the pub and she pulled me to one side.

'I don't want you to freak out,' she said, showing me her left hand. 'I'm only wearing it there today because I wanted to wear my other ring and I didn't want to take yours off altogether, so I moved it onto my other hand. I'm not pushing to get engaged, but you know what people are like; they'll jump to conclusions, so I just wanted to you be warned in case.'

'Why don't you leave it on there?' I suggested gently, brushing a stray hair from her face.

'Because we're not engaged. I told you – I'm only wearing it there for today.'

'But if you leave it there, people will know you're taken.'

She raised an eyebrow.

'I have got a tongue in my head you know. I can tell them.'

'But if you're wearing a ring they won't need to ask, will they?'

I'd never intended the ring to be any kind of marking my territory symbol, but somehow it suddenly seemed terribly important that she wear it.

'Now you're the one being ridiculous!' she snapped. 'You made it very clear when you gave it to me that it was not an engagement ring, so why the sudden insistence that I wear it like one? I'm not a possession, I don't belong to you. And even if we were engaged – which we're not – you still wouldn't own me. I'm not even sure I want to get married. Ever!'

She had kept her voice low, presumably as aware as I was that we had an audience ever eager for gossip, but her words bounced around my head. *She's not sure she ever wants to get married?* I saw that without even realising it I had begun to plan for our future together. I had a year abroad to come and I had briefly looked into whether it might be possible for her to come with me. I hadn't spoken to her about it, had just assumed that she would want to. *If she's not planning for the future, does she even love me?*

'I need some air.'

I walked the streets for hours, thoughts buzzing around my head like bees bumping from one flower to the next, constantly busy, never pausing for long enough for me to collect and organise them. I eventually returned to my room exhausted and depressed, not sure I wanted to face the next morning. The note on my pillow with its scrawled 'I'm sorry' was screwed up and abandoned to the bin.

I managed to catch Olivia alone after breakfast the following morning.

'Let me go first,' I interrupted her before she'd had a chance to say anything. 'We're obviously in different places right now and I'm sorry that yet again I'm falling short of your expectations. I think it's probably best if we take a break for a while to decide what each of us wants.'

She looked at me in silence, tears filling her eyes and trickling down her face. She made no attempt to wipe them away.

'Have a good summer,' I said. 'I love you, but I'm not sure that's enough for either of us.'

'I know what I want,' she said, choking on the words. 'Let me know when *you* decide. You've got my number.'

She walked away and I just watched her go. I felt numb.

GRACE

My phone rang and I debated for a moment whether to let it go to voicemail. I'd done that the last time Grace rang though and it seemed rude to do it a second time, especially when I'd already ignored one message. Reluctantly, I slid my thumb across the screen.

'Hello?'

'Hi Tom, it's Grace. How are you?'

'Good thanks. You?' I winced at the stilted conversation.

'Plodding along, writing, the usual. Listen, I was just ringing to see if you got my message about the dance next week?'

'I did, yes. Sorry I've not rung back; I've been trying to finish translating that novel – they moved the deadline up by a week and I've been flat out trying to get it done in time.'

'No, it's fine. I understand if you're too busy, it was only a thought.'

'No, I'd love to come.'

I clapped my hand over my mouth too late to stop the words escaping. Where had that come from? I'd had every intention of giving a polite but firm refusal. It was too late to wish it unsaid now though. It was on a Friday evening, so I'd have to make an excuse and ask Mum to babysit. It wouldn't be a problem, but I hated lying.

In the end, I settled for a half-truth when she asked about my plans.

'I got chatting to a couple when I was out a few Sundays ago,' I told her, 'And they rang to invite me to join them at some charity thing they're going to.'

I eased my conscience by reminding it that the dance was partly to raise money for charity. I told myself I hadn't lied. Grace and her brother were a 'couple' – it was a word to describe two people. She hadn't said Ashley wasn't going to be there. Admittedly, she also hadn't said he would be, but I wasn't going to quibble over a technicality.

Luckily, Mum didn't ask further questions. I think she was too relieved that after months of having me mope around the house I was finally taking an interest in something outside of the children. She didn't care what it was, she was just grateful it existed and had lifted my spirits a little.

Mum and I had always been close and she understood much of what I'd been going through, having suffered with the same depression herself a few years earlier. I hadn't told her that at my lowest I'd considered a way out – only rejecting that option because of the children – but I had a feeling she knew without my saying a word. It was there in the way she looked at me from time to time and the way she would often appear at the door at odd times of the day. These visits usually coincided with the times I was really struggling. I talked to Olivia of course, even though there wasn't much she could do to help, but it was Mum's practicality and sometimes her mere presence, that helped me through the worst of it. Having her move in with us was one of the best decisions we'd made and I was even more grateful now to have her close.

'Have fun,' she said as I kissed her cheek in farewell a few days later. 'The kids have chosen their film and I'm armed with popcorn and sweets.'

'Don't let them stay up too late, will you?' I said.

'Do I ever?'

I looked at her and she laughed.

'I'm their grandmother, I'm supposed to indulge them. Don't worry though, I'll be good and so will they.' She pushed me towards the door. 'Go on, or you'll be late.'

Holding my hands up in surrender, I said goodbye to the children, who barely turned away from *Wreck It Ralph* long enough to say goodbye.

'You're spoiling them,' I told Mum, nodding at the film. 'When you suggested a film night I thought you meant some popcorn and sweets, I didn't realise you were going to buy them a brand new DVD.'

'Stop complaining. Stop worrying so much and just go and enjoy yourself. A new DVD isn't going to turn them all into spoilt brats overnight. You turned out all right, didn't you?'

I gave up and left her to it. She was right after all: the kids deserved a treat. The atmosphere at home had been pretty awful for the last few months and much as we tried to shield them from it, we couldn't entirely protect them. Nor in many ways would we want to entirely. Olivia always said that life wasn't all flowers and rainbows and the children had to learn how to deal with the unpleasant parts as well as enjoying the nicer bits. I wasn't sure I agreed with her but bowed to her better understanding and trusted that – with the help they were receiving – the children would cope.

The traffic was light and I found a parking space more easily than I'd anticipated. I hadn't spent much time in Fleetwood in the evenings, but it seemed it wasn't such a night-time hotspot as Blackpool was. I had some time to kill so, not wanting to appear too eager by arriving early, I wandered down the road to the boating lakes.

The early evening sun glittered on the surface of the water as I stood on the little bridge that divided the two lakes, watching the last of the day's sailors packing their boats away. A couple of model boats floated lazily, their sails bending away from the slight breeze that aided their progress across the lake and I was reminded of a previous visit when I'd stood in this exact spot with my family.

Olivia and I had driven to Cleveleys with the children, our bikes strapped to the rear of the car, then cycled up the promenade to Fleetwood. As it was five miles each way, in spite of Theo's protests that he could cycle himself, we'd attached the trailers to the back of the bikes and fastened all three children into them, along with a picnic lunch. We ate it sitting on the grass in the Marine Gardens and then took the children for a walk around the nearer of the two boating lakes to allow them to stretch their legs before we put them back in the trailers for the return ride. As we reached the hump of the bridge, we heard someone shouting.

'Don't touch the propeller, don't touch it!'

We looked down to see a middle-aged woman sprinting around the edge of the lake, waving her arms at a group of children who had gathered on the far bank. On the near bank, where she had presumably set off from, a man stood, frantically jabbing at a remote control, a look of panic on his face. On the concrete path that circled the lake, a sleek white boat lay on its side, its propeller still spinning wildly and a full-throated roar was coming from its engine. The children who had congregated round it were obviously torn between the excitement of seeing the boat launch itself out of the water onto the surrounding path and the alarm of having it land so close to them. It was to this group the woman was shouting. Just as she reached them, her husband – for so we assumed the man to be – managed to get the remote to respond and the engine sputtered and fell silent. The woman sank to the floor in evident relief and gave her husband a weak thumbs up. The orange flag bearing the boat's name hung limply as the man, who had by now walked round to join his wife, tucked the boat under one arm. The other went round her and they returned to their car, all the while carrying on an animated discussion.

'Well, that was an unexpected bit of excitement,' Olivia laughed.

'That was brilliant!' Xander said.

'Really cool,' Theo agreed. 'Did you see how fast it was going?'

'Were you watching it?' I asked.

Theo nodded, his eyes ablaze.

'One minute it was sailing along and the next it shot off, hit the side and bounced up onto the path. Can we get a boat like that? One with an engine I mean. Those sailing ships are okay, but the motor one was awesome.'

We told him we'd think about it and for a few days it was all he talked about, but then he lost interest and by the time it came round to his birthday there were other things he wanted far more than the model boat and the subject was dropped.

As I stood watching and reminiscing, I wondered if we ought to buy a boat. I felt sure the kids would enjoy sailing it and it would remind us of happier times. Olivia and I had laughed a lot in those days, but there had been a singular lack of that sound of late. Maybe a boat could help restore some of the joy that had gone missing.

By the time I'd mulled over this idea, it was time to head back the way I had come and make my way to the dance. And to Grace. I dismissed all thoughts of the boat and strode through the gardens, now worrying that rather than being ridiculously early, I was in danger of being unfashionably late.

The Art Deco architecture of the Marine Hall never failed to make me smile. Although not as imposing or spectacular as the Tower Ballroom, it had more than enough charm of its own to compensate. The domed roof added the finishing touch of classical elegance to the white building and perfectly complimented the beautiful gardens in which it sat. Appreciation of its architecture was another thing I had to thank Olivia for. She loved anything to do with the 1920s and 30s and I had come to admire the building style of the period thanks to being dragged around innumerable Poirot filming locations.

The first year after we moved to Poulton, Olivia and I had brought Theo to Fleetwood for the Heritage Tram Day and as we wandered around the town afterwards, it struck me that all the council's money appeared to have been poured into the Esplanade. The rest of town looked a little shabby and had an air of self-pity about it as it remembered its glory days as a holiday resort. The seafront, however, was beautiful. It was completely at odds with the surrounding area and the disparity reminded me of the Midland Hotel further up the coast in Morecambe. Like the Marine Hall, the hotel was a stunning Art Deco building set against a backdrop of empty B&Bs and boarded up windows. I'd taken Olivia there for afternoon tea when she was pregnant with Elodie and she'd spent the whole afternoon telling me about the episodes of Poirot which had been filmed there and trying to spot which bits she recognised from the programme.

Perhaps it should have made me sad that the preservation of these pockets of 1930s glamour had been at the expense of the surrounding areas. After all, as Olivia pointed out, people were more important than buildings. But part of me couldn't help feeling glad their architectural value had been recognised and taken care of. So much of Blackpool's heritage was being lost due to neglect, mismanagement and lack of funds and it made me all the more grateful that Fleetwood was not following the same path.

Grace was waiting for me at the bottom of the steps that led to the main door and she waved as she caught sight of me.

'Sorry I'm late,' I said. 'I was down by the boating lake and I lost track of time.'

'Oh, it's beautiful down there, isn't it?' she said, her smile widening. 'Ash and I used to sail boats on it when we were kids. I haven't done that for years.' She laughed and pressed her teeth into her bottom lip. 'You've made me all nostalgic now.'

I couldn't help returning her smile before I asked the all-important question.

'Is your brother inside?'

Grace looked puzzled and, I thought, just a little guilty, then the moment passed and she shook her head.

'No. Sorry, were you expecting him to be?'

'Not really.' I tried to disguise the wobble in my voice, 'I just wondered, that's all.'

Again, the panic closed around my throat and I fought against it. I was doing nothing wrong. I hadn't known her brother wasn't coming and it was only dancing. I was breaking no promises, even if this did suddenly feel more like a date. Deep lungfuls of sea air helped and by the time my foot hit the top step I had regained enough control to be able to open the door for Grace. She smiled again as she passed in front of me, leaving a pleasant cloud of perfume behind her.

'Can I let you into a secret?' she whispered, leaning into me during the first dance.

I nodded, conscious of how her body pressed against mine as we moved around the floor. I didn't trust myself to speak.

'Ash was going to come tonight, but I told him not to.'

I risked looking at her and she gave me a sheepish grin.

'I heard some of what he said to you in the Tower and I told him that if he was going to grill you like that again, I didn't want him to come.'

'I hope you didn't fall out on my account,' I said quickly. 'I wasn't offended.'

'He's a bit overprotective at times and it's suffocating. It's like he thinks I can't make decisions for myself anymore.'

'I'm sure he doesn't mean to,' I said, as the music ended and we returned to our seats. 'He did imply you'd been through a bit of a rough time and that's why he was more wary than usual of new people in your life.'

She banged her drink down on the table and some of her Coke spilled onto the plastic surface. Automatically, I grabbed a tissue out of my pocket and started mopping it up. She stared at me for a moment, as though about to say something, then seemed to change her mind and returned to the conversation.

'He had no right to tell you anything. Did he say why?'

I shook my head and she sighed, dragging a hand through her curls.

'I can't be too cross with him, I suppose. I'd have told you eventually and he only does it because he cares. I just worry that when I do meet someone I really like, he'll scare them off.'

She paused for a moment and I kept my face carefully neutral until she continued.

'At the start of my third year of university, I met Ian and fell head over heels in love. He seemed to feel the same way and so when he asked me to reconsider my career choices, I did. He said he couldn't bear the thought of me being away from him for long periods of time, so he wanted me to do a job where I wouldn't have to travel. That's how I ended up at the local library. The truth of it is, he wanted me to be at home when he was, so I worked part-time so I was always there when he got home from work. I enjoyed the job at first, especially on the days where we had primary school groups in, but I've got a degree and helping kids decide between the latest David Walliams and *The Diary of a Wimpy Kid* wasn't exactly taxing my brain: I wanted something more challenging.

By that time Austin had proposed and when I said I wanted to do something else, he argued that it wasn't the best time for me to leave my job. We were supposed to be saving for a wedding.

"Besides," he said, "Once we get married, you won't be working for long anyway. You'll be at home with the kids." We'd never discussed it before and I had no idea he was expecting me to give up work when we had children. As the wedding got closer, he became more and more demanding about everything. The slightest little thing was enough to put him in a raging temper and if I ever questioned his reaction, he just said it was only because he thought I deserved to have the very best of everything. I wanted so much to believe him and it was never directed at me, so I convinced myself it was only pre-wedding stress and that he'd be back to himself once it was all over.

Then one night we went out for dinner and I was too friendly to the waiter. I mean, I wasn't, but he said I was and he locked me out of the house without my bag. I had to walk to Ashley's and ask him to let me stay the night. The next day, Austin came round first thing in the morning to apologise. He said he'd realised after about ten minutes that he was massively over-reacting and opened the door, but I'd already gone. I'd been outside for at least half an hour pleading with him to let me in but he persuaded me I'd been muddled about the time because I'd had a drink.

Even in the lead up to the wedding I knew I was making a mistake. There were lots of incidents like that where he'd do or say something and then make out I'd imagined the whole thing or misinterpreted what he'd said. For a time, I honestly thought I was going crazy, but my parents had spent a lot of money on the wedding and I didn't feel I could call it off without letting everyone down, so I told myself I was just anxious and it would be all right. The honeymoon was awful – nothing I did was right: the hotel wasn't good enough, the resort was too busy, we should have gone outside of the peak holiday season. When I tried to tell him that he'd made all the choices, he looked at me as if I was mad and denied he'd had anything to do with it. He even suggested I should see a doctor about my memory issues.'

She shuddered.

'I still don't know if he was actually planning to get me committed, but he certainly threatened it enough times.

When I fell pregnant I was delighted but it only caused more problems. We had a row about me not wanting to give up work and he hit me. He apologised straight away and it wasn't particularly hard on that occasion, but it was enough to leave a mark. I told Ash I'd had a dizzy spell and knocked my face on the open fridge door, but he told me later that was the point from which he started to get suspicious.

The day before I was due to have my first scan, he got mad at me because I hadn't ironed the particular shirt he wanted to wear. We were stood on the landing and the next thing I knew, I was at the bottom of the stairs, with Austin standing over me shouting at me for not being more careful. I didn't even protest that I'd felt him push me.

I knew then that things were never going to improve. He'd hurt me twice while I was carrying his child and if he couldn't be trusted then, things were only going to get worse. I waited until he went to work, then phoned Ash to come and get me. When I lost the baby I was devastated, but I'm ashamed to admit I was relieved as well. A child would have tied me to him forever. At least without one I could make a clean break. Austin kept insisting he'd done nothing wrong and begged me to take him back. It took two years and a restraining order, but I got free of him in the end. Since then, Ash has insisted on vetting any man I meet, even if it's only a friend. He blames himself for not realising sooner what was happening. He says that as a policeman he should have recognised the signs long before he did, but Austin was good – he was charming and caring. Unless someone else caught him out in a lie, there was no way they'd ever have known what he was doing to me. On the face of it, I was just easily confused. I should've called the wedding off, but I thought I could change him if I was the perfect wife, which at the time I had every intention of being. Naïve and stupid I know, but I was only twenty-two when we got married.'

She took a deep drink, then set her glass down and grinned at me.

'So now I've bored you senseless with my life story,' she said, 'Why don't you tell me yours, starting with why you wear a wedding ring, but haven't mentioned that you're married.'

I answered her question. I told her about Olivia, how we'd met at university, got married and had three children. I told her all about the ups and downs of our relationship and in a bid to match her honesty with my own, confessed to feeling that no matter what I did or said, it was never enough to banish Olivia's demons entirely. I explained how it made me feel inadequate because I could never make her as happy as she made me. I told her about the problems it caused between us and I laid out all the difficulties of the last few years, which had resulted in me agreeing to meet up with her – a woman I barely knew – and in the process, lying to my family about what I was doing.

'The truth is,' I said, 'I love my kids and they will always come first. I still love Olivia as well, but it's not enough anymore and I'm lonely. Is it wrong to want someone to share it all with?'

'I don't think so,' Grace said slowly. 'You said it yourself: you want your kids to be happy and you want to protect them for as long as you can, but you also deserve to be happy. Until I got married, I believed in love that lasts forever and that there was one person for everyone, but marriage to Austin taught me all that stuff is okay in fairy tales where everyone lives happily ever after, but it's not real life. Love in the real world is messy and people sometimes get hurt by it. There's first loves and last loves and all kinds in between, but in the end you have to take care of yourself, because if you don't no one else will.'

'Do you honestly believe that?' I was curious – she hadn't come across as cynical before. Her expression softened.

'Not really,' she said, 'I think there are good people out there, but they tend to get trodden on. I'm not as self-interested as I make out, but at the same time I do believe if you have a chance for happiness, however fleeting it is, you should grab it with both hands. It doesn't matter if other people wouldn't approve. If a relationship is over, at some point you have to move on. You might not be ready straight away, but you will be eventually, it's inevitable.'

'What if your happiness would hurt someone else?'

'Then you have to weigh it all up I guess,' she said with a shrug of her shoulders. 'How important is your happiness compared to how badly they'd be hurt? At the end of the day, you shouldn't ever set out to hurt people. If you can avoid it, you should, but not at the expense of your own feelings. I have no doubt I hurt Austin when I walked out on him. In his own way, he did love me, but should I have sacrificed myself just to keep him happy?'

'No, of course not!' I said firmly, 'But that's a totally different situation. If the relationship is fixable, don't you think you should work on it rather than running away?'

'That depends on whether you both want to fix it, I suppose. If it's worth saving, then yes you'd fight for it, but love on its own isn't always enough. Like you said, sometimes it's difficult to accept that a relationship is over and sometimes it's not worth even starting one. That said,' she added slowly, 'If I thought the man was worth waiting for, I might be prepared to be patient.' She laughed and grimaced. 'I've made myself sound terrifically hard and I'm not, I promise. For the right man I'd let my guard down. Sometimes though, when you see a chance potentially slipping away, it's a challenge not to grab on and simply refuse to let go, especially when you've experienced the alternative. I'm not interested in playing games. If I get involved I'm in it for the long haul.'

My head was spinning. I knew I'd been given a message, but I wasn't completely clear what it was.

'Anyway, that's a terribly serious talk for only the third time we've met. Shall we dance?' Grace held out her hand and I allowed her to pull me to my feet.

On the floor I forgot about trying to puzzle out what she'd meant. I could only concentrate on one thing at once and I was fully occupied for the remainder of the evening in counting the beats of the music and trying not to step on Grace's toes.

When the evening ended I discovered Grace was parked in the opposite direction from me, so I walked her back to her car.

'Jump in,' she said. 'I'll run you round to yours. No sense in you walking all that way back when I've got to go that way anyway.'

She pulled into the now empty space behind my car.

'Don't go yet,' she said, catching hold of my arm as I made to leave the car. 'I just wanted to say thank-you for a lovely evening.'

'It was my pleasure,' I said and I meant it. I couldn't remember the last time I'd enjoyed myself so much.

'And no panic attacks this time.'

I grimaced, thinking about the one I'd narrowly avoided at the start of the evening.

'Well, I like to limit the entertainment I provide for the general public.'

'I'm sorry, that was insensitive. I didn't mean –'

'It's fine.'

'Even so,' she took my hand. 'I'd hate you to think I was making light of it.'

My hand tingled where hers covered it.

'I don't, don't worry.' My voice came out as a whisper and I felt rather than saw her lean a little closer.

'I'd never want to hurt you, Tom. Do you think we could do this again?'

It wasn't a good idea. My brain was screaming at me to get out of the car, while my body was rooted in the seat, paralysed into inaction by the fear she was going to kiss me. If she did, I couldn't have sworn that I wouldn't kiss her back. Luckily for my conscience, she didn't.

I opened my mouth to say I couldn't possibly. It wouldn't be right. It wouldn't be fair to anyone. I still loved Olivia.

'That would be lovely,' I said. 'Next Sunday in the Tower?'

She leant over fully this time and kissed my cheek.

'Perfect.'

I scrambled out of the car and watched as she drove off, leaving me standing on the edge of the kerb but feeling as if I was about to step over a precipice. This was not who I was. I loved my wife. Why was I even thinking about meeting Grace again and worse, actually looking forward to it?

I'll text her tomorrow and cancel, I thought as I got into my car and set off to return to my family. *I'll make some excuse. I'm not ready for this.*

III
OLIVIA 1998-2001

I spent the whole summer trying to make it up to Olivia. I'd hurt her badly and I had to pay for it. She didn't do anything directly to make me suffer; she wasn't as petty as that, but she was understandably cool with me when I rang. It was entirely my own fault. I was the one who'd given her a ring but freaked out at the thought she might think I was proposing to her. Then I'd tried to bully her into an unofficial engagement. It was no wonder she was confused about how I felt. If I wasn't sure about my feelings for her, how could I expect her to be?

'I do love you, of course I do,' I told her the first time I rang. 'I just got scared by it all, you know? I'd started planning our future in my head and when I realised that it made me aware that however I see my future, you're in it. We're only nineteen and I lost the plot a bit.'

'Tom, we had a row because I said I *didn't* want an engagement ring.' She sighed.

"I know. That freaked me out as well because then I panicked that you weren't sure about us anymore. Look, I know I'm making a mess of this. I'm trying to explain something I don't understand myself. I really am sorry though.'

'I know. I'm sorry Tom, but I've got to go. I'm back on duty in five minutes.'

She was spending the first half of the summer working for a residential kids club, so our conversations were hurried affairs, conducted between my work shifts and hers. We'd survived, but barely and I was anxious to see her again. I needed to hold her; to prove to her how sorry I was; to show her I loved her, despite my own stupidity doing its best to prove otherwise.

For the second half of the summer, she was staying with her grandmother and had secured a job temping in an office. I'd worked a double shift at the wine bar and was just sinking into the sofa when the phone rang.

'It'll be for you,' Mum said, raising an eyebrow. 'No-one we know would ring this late.'

'Tom?'

A cold ball of fear formed in the pit of my stomach. I could hear the tears in her voice. Was this it? Was this the phone call where she told me she'd decided it wasn't worth it anymore. That I wasn't worth it?

'What is it? What's happened?'

A noisy sniff answered me. Then she cleared her throat.

'Nan's got cancer.'

A huge feeling of relief rushed through me and I instantly felt guilty. I knew how important her Mum's mum was to her and I didn't know what to say. It was Nancy Roberts who'd supported her granddaughter through her parents' divorce and the anorexia, even offering to help when Olivia decided she could no longer bear to live at home. The distance between them had been the only thing that prevented Olivia moving in with her instead of the council flat and her grandmother had phoned her every week. She'd even sent food parcels she knew her proud and independent granddaughter needed but would never ask for.

'I'm so sorry.'

It was utterly inadequate, but then everything seemed inadequate under the circumstances. In the end I booked a few days off work and went to stay with them, holding Olivia in the early hours of every morning while she sobbed in my arms. In the light of her grandmother's illness, our disagreement suddenly seemed infantile and trivial and the breach healed much quicker than it might otherwise have done.

I was doing the washing up on my third morning there when the doorbell rang and I heard Olivia begging someone not to come in. Drying my hands, I wandered casually into the hall, trying not to appear too curious but eager to seize any opportunity to demonstrate to Olivia that I could be relied on to support her.

'Mum...please...Nan doesn't need this. Just go home!'

'Don't be ridiculous, Livvy! She's my mother. Of course I'm going to be here. Obviously she wants me at a time like this. I'm here to help.' She ran the back of her hand across dry eyes and sniffed emphatically. 'I can't believe you'd turn me away from my own mother on her deathbed. So cruel. I know I've made mistakes in the past, Livvy, but this is too hard!'

The woman in the hallway puzzled me. Her clothes were clearly expensive, even to my ignorant eyes and she obviously spent a lot of time and money on maintaining her appearance. I knew she was in her mid-thirties, but her skeletal frame made her look several years older. Her face, when she turned it in my direction, was frighteningly reminiscent of the villain from the He-Man cartoons I'd loved as a child. I took an involuntary step back. The frown, which had given her the demeanour of a petulant toddler, disappeared the moment she noticed me and she tottered unsteadily towards me. Her heels click-clacked across the wooden floor and she beamed at me as though I were a long-lost friend.

'You must be Tom,' she purred, leaning forwards to plant a highly scented kiss on each cheek.

She was much taller than her daughter and in bending to kiss me I was awarded an ample view of her cleavage. It struck me as odd that her breasts were so out of proportion with the rest of her. There was a hissed, '*Mother*', from behind me and I dragged my eyes up to her face and smiled weakly. I suddenly realised that for all her posturing, Zoe was an amateur at this game: here was a true professional. Even with an awareness of this fact, I could feel how easy it would be to be drawn in by her.

'Livvy's told me all about you and I'm so pleased to finally meet you. I'm Laura. Livvy,' she scolded her daughter with a vulpine grin, 'you didn't tell me how good-looking he was. You've done well for yourself.'

I took a step backwards to escape the cloud of perfume that saturated my lungs and moved to Olivia's side.

'I'm glad to meet you too,' I lied, gripping Olivia's hand tightly.

'Come and sit down,' Laura said, pulling me away from Olivia and into the living room. 'Tell me all about how you met. Was it love at first sight?' She leant into my shoulder and sighed. 'I do love a good love story.'

She'd seated herself on the middle cushion of the sofa, insisting that Olivia and I sat on either side of her and then refused to relinquish our hands, exclaiming over the ring I'd bought Olivia for her birthday. Despite all the trouble it had caused, I was pleased to see she was still wearing it.

'This is beautiful! Such exquisite taste. Your father always had a good eye for jewellery, you know. Mind you, it wasn't the only thing he had a good eye for but he always bought a decent apology present. Not that that's what this was, I'm sure. You wouldn't do anything to hurt my girl, would you Tom? You seem like such a nice boy.'

She stroked my cheek, sharp fuchsia nails pressing into my flesh, her gaze intense and focused.

'Hello Laura.'

The voice of Olivia's grandmother came from the open doorway and I was amazed at how much disapproval she managed to pack into two words. The hand on my face convulsed and I gasped and pulled away as two beads of blood appeared on my cheek.

'Tom why don't you and Olivia go and make us some tea. I could certainly do with a cup. Sleeping during the day always makes me so thirsty.'

We scuttled into the kitchen where our clinking of cups and the hiss of the kettle masked all but the slightest murmur of voices from the living room, Nancy's firm tones cutting through the higher pitched protests of her daughter. When we returned, carrying the tray of mugs and a plate of biscuits, it was to find that Laura had removed herself to one of the armchairs and the slightly sulky expression had returned.

As you can see, Olivia's doing a wonderful job of looking after me and you said yourself you're too busy to come and see me as much as you'd like, so there's really no need to put yourself out.'

'And what about when she goes back to university? How will you manage then?'

'I can always defer for a year.' Olivia's voice was quiet.

'Absolutely not!' Nancy snapped the words out and I clamped my jaw together so hard I could hear my teeth squeaking in protest. 'You'll go back in October, exactly as planned. If I need help then I'll arrange it. I may be dying – yes I am, let's not dress this up.' She waved their protests away impatiently. 'I may be dying but I'm not going gaga and I will be the only person making decisions about either my future or my care. Is that clear?'

I could see where Olivia's stubbornness came from and I had to suppress a cheer of support as Nancy's glare encompassed her daughter and granddaughter.

'Just because I let you pack me off to bed this morning doesn't mean I'm going to let you make all my decisions for me. And as for you,' she paused and levelled a long hard look at her daughter. Laura shifted in her chair and made a careful study of her manicured hand. 'You can start to make decisions about my life only once you can make them about your own. My decisions are influenced solely by my brain – can you say the same about yours?'

She continued as the silence became awkward.

'I don't want to hear any more talk about deferring university. There is to be no interfering with any plans I might make for what's left of my life. And Olivia, if you plan to marry that boy, you might want to start talking to him before you make decisions that affect him as well as you.'

She softened her last pronouncement with a gentle smile directed at both of us.

'And now, if you don't mind, I'm still feeling rather tired, so I'm going back to bed. Laura, I'll see you whenever you're next down here. If you'd like to come and stay once Olivia's gone back to university, then you can arrange the dates with her when you leave.'

She continued swiftly, but I had no doubt she'd heard her daughter's murmured 'thank you' and seen the single tear that escaped before Laura had the chance to sweep it away.

'Tom love, would you mind getting the sausages out of the freezer so they'll defrost in time for dinner?'

Nancy levered herself out of the chair, waving Olivia away impatiently when she tried to help. As soon as her mother had disappeared up the stairs, Laura grabbed her bag and wobbled out of the house with barely a goodbye between us, the echo of her heels lingering far longer than she did. I remained glued to my seat, uncertain of how to behave.

'So, Nan thinks we're getting married,' Olivia said eventually, not looking at me.

'Well, I suppose it does look like an engagement ring.'

'I guess it does.'

She held out her hand, twisting it this way and that, looking at the ring from different angles.

'We'd better get those sausages out.'

Nothing more was said on the subject and I returned home a couple of days later, but our phone calls over the remaining weeks of the holiday were less frosty and I had the definite sense I'd passed some kind of test. Having now met Olivia's parents, I was infinitely more appreciative of my own. They may not have been the most adventurous of people, but they were safe and stable and I knew that in a crisis they would come through for me.

'Why don't you invite Olivia to come here for the weekend?' Mum suggested one day. 'We'd love to meet her.'

'I could do,' I said cautiously. 'You're not to give her the third degree though: she doesn't talk much about herself or her family.'

'We'll behave,' Dad promised, grinning at Mum.

'You'd better,' I muttered, going into the hallway to use the phone.

As I'd expected, Olivia was a bit reluctant at first, even when I pointed out that I'd met most of her family and she'd yet to meet any of mine.

'Exactly,' she said. 'You've seen my family: we're not exactly the Waltons. I don't do the whole happy family thing.

'This is important to Mum and Dad and actually, it's kind of important to me as well. We've been together nearly a year now and I'd like to introduce you to them. They've promised not to ask too many questions.'

I wasn't sure I believed their promise, but I wasn't going to tell her that. She sighed and there was a long pause before she eventually agreed to come down the following weekend.

I met her at the train station and kissed her cheek. Her skin felt papery to my lips and I was shocked by the difference a week had made to her appearance. Her plain jumper exposed the angular peaks of her collar bones and her face was drawn.

'It'll be fine, you'll see.'

As soon as we stepped through the front door, she was enveloped in a bear hug from my mother, while Dad hung back a little, waiting for Mum to release her.

'Come on upstairs, I've cleared some space in Tom's wardrobe for you to hang your things.'

With that, she propelled Olivia upstairs.

'I'm so sorry about your grandmother. It must be very difficult for you. Is there any way that your Mum would be able to help?'

'Dad, she promised!'

He shrugged. 'You know what your mum's like. I'm sure it'll be fine.'

His words echoed my own to Olivia and I wondered if they'd sounded as hollow to her as they did to me. Dad disappeared into the kitchen to make tea. It burnt my throat when I took the first gulp and I yelped.

'You need to relax and trust your Mum.'

'I'm going to kill her.'

"It'll be OK.'

'They've been ages.'

'Mum wanted to get to know her.'

"She's got two days to do that; she doesn't have to do it all in one go.'

'Hobnob?'

By the time they came back downstairs I'd almost cleared the plate.

'What did you say to her?' I demanded, jumping up and sloshing my tea over the arm of the sofa.

'Sshh. I'm fine.' Olivia helped herself to a chocolate biscuit and accepted the now cooled mug of tea from my dad before sitting down. Her eyes were red-rimmed, but her smile seemed genuine. I sat down, confused.

'I've booked a table at The Rainforest Café for tonight,' Dad said into the silence.

'Isn't that in London?' Olivia asked, eyes widening. 'Is it posh?'

'Not particularly,' Mum laughed. "It's more quirky than posh, but even if it was, that floaty dress is perfect.' She leant over and patted Olivia's hand gently. 'It'll look lovely.'

Olivia's head dropped but not quickly enough to prevent me seeing the tears in her eyes again. I glared at Mum, who merely raised an eyebrow at me and calmly helped herself to a biscuit.

'We'll need to leave here at about six o'clock,' she said, 'So you two will need to entertain yourselves until then. Just make sure you're back in time to get ready.'

I didn't get chance to speak to Mum until after I'd seen Olivia back onto the train on Sunday afternoon and I wasn't totally sure what I wanted to say to her. Part of me was furious with her for the way she'd interrogated Olivia, but to my surprise, Olivia herself hadn't seemed to mind. In fact, the last thing she did before boarding the train was tell me how wonderful my mother was. The hug they'd shared when they said goodbye had been warm and longer than I would have said was normal for a first meeting. I was utterly bewildered.

'I like her,' Mum informed me on my return home. 'It's a wonder she's done as well as she has with her background. You told us what her dad was like and from what she said about her mum, I'm not surprised she left home. The bigger surprise is that she didn't do it sooner.'

'Her Mum seemed OK when I met her,' I said. 'Just a bit over the top about everything – too enthusiastic, too sad, you know?'

'Well, I would imagine the highs are easier to cope with than the comedowns. That's when the paranoia sets in as I understand it.'

'What do you mean?'

'Well at least when she's taken it she's happy. I gather it's pretty horrific when she's craving it and doesn't have any to hand.'

'What are you talking about? Doesn't have what to hand?'

'Tom darling, what exactly do you think is wrong with Olivia's mum?'

'She's not said much about it, but from what I saw, I wondered if she was maybe schizophrenic or something.'

'Oh sweetheart! I love you dearly, but I do wonder sometimes if we kept you a bit too sheltered. Laura Whitely's a drug addict. Olivia moved out of her home because her mother's dealer was starting to get a bit too friendly with her.'

'Did Olivia tell you that?'

We'd been together for almost a year and she hadn't breathed a word to me about any of this, but after less than an hour with her, my mum had apparently been given her entire life story.

'How do you do it?'

She shrugged and gave me her infuriating 'it's a mum thing' look. It wasn't a mum thing though; it was *my* mum's thing: two minutes with her and complete strangers would share their innermost secrets. She had a knack of getting people to open up to her that I was in awe of. As a teenager, my friends had confided all their worries to her without even realising they were doing it. It was impossible to hide anything from her, although I did still try on occasion just to see if she'd lost her touch.

The rest of the holiday sped past and it wasn't long before I was back on the train heading down to Exeter ready to start my second year. We'd moved out of Halls and were sharing a house with Eoin, Sophie and Zoe, so Mum sent me off with fifty quid and a detailed shopping list of all the essentials I needed to stock the cupboard with.

Olivia's train had arrived an hour or so before mine, so by the time my taxi pulled up outside the mid-terrace house that was to be our home for the next nine months, she'd already met the landlord and collected the keys.

'Come in and choose your room,' she said as she opened the door. 'Kettle's on and the others should be here soon.'

Once we'd all arrived and unpacked, the house looked a little bit more like a home. After we'd dealt with the flea infestation – allegedly caused by the previous tenant's cat – it felt a bit more like it too. We spent the first day of our tenancy scratching at the raised red lumps that patterned our limbs and the second avoiding the aftermath of the resulting fumigation. By the third day we were keen to settle in.

Although we were still just about within walking distance of the campus, it was much easier to do it by bus and while we were happy to walk the downhill path into town, the slog back up the hill laden with heavy bags of shopping was a far less appealing prospect. We were soon on first name terms with most of the local bus drivers.

We'd been back less than three weeks when Olivia got the phone call to say she needed to go and see her Nan to say goodbye. She'd deteriorated quicker than expected and had asked to see her granddaughter for a final time before the end. I offered to travel with her, but Olivia said she preferred to go alone. After promising to be back by the end of the week when our housewarming party was scheduled, she kissed me goodbye and jumped into the waiting taxi.

I'd had no word from her by the time Saturday arrived, other than a brief call to say that she'd arrived safely and by eight o'clock the party was in full swing: music pulsated out from the speakers; the red, amber and green glow of the traffic lights Eoin had 'liberated' from Islington High Street – now re-wired – were flashing a steady rhythm of their own.

I lost count of the number of drinks I'd had; I remembered the beers with Eoin at the start of the party and the vodka and oranges with friends who'd shared Halls with us the previous year. After the Sambuca shots with people from my course, things got a little hazy. I stumbled into the kitchen aware that my glass was disappointingly empty and in search of something with which to fill it.

'Looking for this?'

A bottle with a red label was waved under my nose and I peered at it.

'Yes... Maybe... Fill 'er up!'

I proffered my glass, attempting to keep it steady as the clear liquid danced and sloshed its way from bottle to glass.

'You're Tom.'

'Am I? Yes, I suppose I am.'

'I'm Vicky. I'm on your course.'

I peered at her, trying to decide which of the three people had spoken.

'You're hot.'

She leant forward, over-balanced and landed on my face.

'The middle one,' I thought. 'Definitely the middle one.'

My brain finally caught up and I leaped backwards crashing into the kitchen table. Somehow I ended up on the floor tangled in one of the chairs, unsure quite what had just happened and wondering if involuntary unfaithfulness counted as cheating.

'There you are!' Sophie's disembodied head appeared, floating mid-way up the side of the door. 'I've been looking all over for you. Olivia's back.'

I jumped to my feet and promptly fell over the chair again. Impatiently kicking it away and losing my trainer in the process, I dashed upstairs.

'You're home!' I crossed the room in one giant step and grabbed the girlfriend I'd never been so happy to see.

'Stop it, Tom!'

She turned away from my kiss and took a step backwards.

'But I've missed you!'

'I missed you too, but I've had a long day and I'm not really in the mood.'

Then I remembered.

'Shit.'

I sat down with a thump on the bed and pulled her down next to me.

'How was it?'

'Awful. I...Actually, do you know what? I'd rather not talk about it now.'

I put my arms around her and rested my chin on her head.

'I'm so sorry, darling. Is there anything I can say?'

I felt her shake her head and squeezed her even tighter.

'Why don't you go to bed? Get some rest.'

She lifted her head and raised an eyebrow at me. 'I wanna have sex on the beach' pounded out from the speakers below us.

I waggled my eyebrows at her.

'I'm game if you are. Nice and romantic in the moonlight.'

She smiled. 'Oh yes, very romantic; all that sand getting everywhere!'

I shuddered at the thought and we chuckled quietly together.

'It feels wrong to laugh,' she said suddenly. 'Like I'm not sad enough if I can still laugh.'

'What would your nan have said to that?' I asked.

She thought for a moment. 'Probably something unrepeatable in polite company.'

'Exactly.'

'Go downstairs. Give me fifteen minutes and if I'm not down come and get me.'

She pushed me out of the room and I went down the stairs more steadily than I'd ascended them, then went in search of my missing trainer. It was offered to me as soon as I entered the kitchen.

'Figured you'd be back for this at some point.'

She smiled and used the brief moment where we both had hold of the trainer to pull me closer.

'Thought we maybe had some unfinished business.'

Her voice was steady, but up close I could see her eyes were glazed and she was working hard to focus on my face.

'No,' I said firmly, moving away from her. 'No unfinished business. I have a girlfriend.'

'She wouldn't have to know.'

'I'd know.'

I cursed my trainer, which was refusing to go back on my foot and sat down to unlace it.

'I'm sorry,' I said, although I wasn't quite sure what I was apologising for. 'You're really nice, but I'm not interested.'

'Well, that's just charming!'

She swept out of the kitchen, righteous indignation radiating from her.

'What was all that about?' Olivia asked, coming in and pouring herself a drink.

I shrugged.

The neck of the bottle crashed against the side of the glass and Olivia swore under her breath as she grabbed a towel to mop it up.

'Honestly, it was nothing.'

She looked at me, waiting.

'Just before you arrived she kissed me and I fell over when I tried to back off.'

'She kissed you.'

I nodded.

'Did you kiss her?'

'No! I told you. She sort of planted herself on me. I

jumped back and fell over the chair. Sophie can tell you – I was on the floor when she came in. That's how I lost my shoe.'

I waved the offending footwear at her, its laces flapping pathetically.

'I still can't get it back on,' I said sadly.

'Well, you can either claim it's a fashion statement or you could maybe ask for help?'

I waved it at her again.

'Will you put it on for me?' I asked hopefully.

She bent down and shoved my foot unceremoniously into the trainer, then pulled the laces a little tighter than was strictly necessary I felt. I yelped.

'Was it good?'

'Huh?'

'The kiss. Was it good?'

'No. I don't know. I fell over pretty much straight away.'

I realised too late that this was probably not something I should be joking about. Olivia knotted the laces, the knot pushing into the top of my foot.

'Ow! OK, I'm sorry. There was no time to think about whether or not it was good.'

'Hmm. How quick was it? This quick?'

She brushed her lips fleetingly against mine.

'A bit longer I think.'

More pressure this time, but still brief.

'That's about right.'

'So not as long as this then.'

When she released me to come up for air, I shook my head.

'Definitely not.'

'And that was good?'

'Oh yes.'

She nodded and gave me a satisfied smile.

'Don't forget that, will you?'

'You might have to remind me occasionally.'

'Oh, don't worry, I will,' she called over her shoulder as she picked up her drink and walked out of the room.

The next morning, I woke up to find the bass notes of the music still beating below me. I groaned.

'Get Eoin to turn that off, will you?'

I pulled the pillow over my face. Olivia tugged it away.

'Turn what off?'

'The bloody music. I can hear the bass from the speaker from up here.'

'The music's off. The party finished about midnight.'

That meant the thumping I could hear was in my head. It was going to be a long day. I opened my eyes and the room lurched alarmingly. I clamped them shut again but it didn't help.

'I made you a bacon sandwich,' Olivia said. 'And there's orange juice on the desk, but you're going to have to sit up to get it.'

As hangover cures went, it was a decent one and once the plate was clean and the glass emptied, I was beginning to feel like something that at least resembled a human being.

'You're an angel,' I told her.

Over the next few months, I had plenty of opportunities to return the favour as Olivia slowly came to terms with the death of her grandmother. I held her tightly while her sobs soaked my shirts, listened while she ranted about the unfairness and injustice of the world; was understanding when she locked herself in her room to study for the degree she had faithfully promised to gain and held my tongue when she shouted at me for no reason or blamed me for things I had no control over. It was a testing time, but gradually I got her back, regaining the old Olivia; a little sadder, a little more mature, but more like herself than she had been since the night of the party.

It was the realisation that things were pretty much back

to normal that prompted my decision to reveal the lie I had allowed her to believe for almost a year. I'd actually made the decision to come clean the morning after our house-warming party, but I'd excused my inability to begin the conversation by persuading myself that it wasn't fair on Olivia to dump such a major revelation on her so soon after her Nan had died. Consequently, my mouth had stayed shut. The days had turned into weeks and inevitably, into months. I knew if I didn't tell her now, I never would and it would always be hanging between us. It wasn't, I reasoned, as bad as if it had been the other way around and actually, she might be quite pleased to find that we had come together in the same state.

'What do you mean, you lied?' she demanded when I prepared the ground for the rest of the story.

'Well, not 'lied' exactly,' I said. 'I didn't tell you the numbers, I just didn't correct you when you said you knew there'd been four before you.'

'So how many had there been?'

Her voice had taken on an edge I didn't like and it was making me uneasy. When I'd rehearsed this in my head, her voice had been less brittle.

'None. You were the first.'

'Then why did you let me think I wasn't?'

'At first I was stunned you knew what I'd said and then I was embarrassed that I'd lied and then you started saying it was a good thing because I'd know what I was doing and I couldn't tell you!'

'So, it's my fault?'

I liked to think I'd learnt something about being a boyfriend over the last year and a half and I knew the answer to this one.

'Of course not! I'm only saying that you seemed pleased and I didn't want to disillusion you.'

'I was trying to convince myself it didn't matter, that it was okay: you wouldn't be comparing me to the others.'

'Oh Olivia, why didn't you say something?'

'Why didn't you?' she countered.

We sat in silence for a moment.

'The thing is, Tom. If you've lied to me about this, how do I know you've told me the truth about anything else? Did whatsherface kiss you, or was it the other way round? Are you telling the truth now, or is this another lie? Have you really slept with hundreds of women?'

It had never occurred to me that this was how she might see it.

'I promise I'm being honest about this and I promise I haven't lied to you about anything else. I'm telling you now because I want you to know the truth. I'm sorry I let it go on for so long, but I never know how you're going to react to anything. You're so passionate about everything and I love that about you, I honestly do, but it does make it hard to admit to making mistakes.'

'I don't know what to say,' she said quietly. 'It just seems that whenever things are going well between us, something else crops up to throw a spanner in the works. I'm starting to think maybe we're doomed to failure. Relationships shouldn't always be this difficult, should they?'

There was nothing I could say.

'I'm going out,' she said eventually. 'I need some time to think.'

I let her go and waited until I heard the front door close before I allowed the tears to fall, muffling their sound with the pillow. She hadn't returned by the time I stumbled into bed that evening, but when something disturbed me in the early hours of the morning, I could feel the comforting weight of her arm across my chest and the tickle of her breath on my neck. I smiled at the familiar annoyances, breathing in the welcome scent of her shampoo and relaxed back into sleep.

‘I’m coming with you,’ Olivia announced, throwing her bag on the floor and dropping in an exhausted heap onto the sofa.

‘Where?’

‘Vienna. I’ve seen my tutor and got it all sorted this afternoon.’

I sat up, startled out of the somnolence that had crept over me the moment I’d walked through the door. We’d been discussing this for months and had argued it backwards and forwards, with Olivia refusing to commit to join me on my year abroad.

‘What are you talking about? When did you decide that? We’ll need to arrange some intensive German tuition for you ASAP. You’ll need at least a basic grasp of the language before we go. How have they even given you permission without it?’

Much as I wanted her to come with me, I didn’t want to jeopardise her degree in order to achieve it.

‘I’m going through Erasmus. The language isn’t an issue. I did an intensive course with a tutor in the summer and I’ve been going to classes all year. I wasn’t sure I was going to come, but Nana said I should learn the language in case. I’ve got more than enough to get by and I’m sure I’ll pick it up fairly quickly when I’m hearing it every day.’

‘I don’t believe you,’ I said admiringly. ‘You did all that just in case you decided to come? You’re insane.’

‘No – I like to be prepared. Besides which, Nana said it would always be useful to have a language.’

I offered up a swift silent thank you to Nancy who seemed to have decided that I was the man for her granddaughter.

‘I love you so much. Marry me.’

The shock on her face was, I’m sure, reflected in my own. I hadn’t intended to propose, it had slipped out. I’d always have done it eventually, but I'd planned on a far more romantic version that involved Piccadilly Circus, the statue of Eros and a lot more of a build-up to actually asking the question. On a battered sofa with the springs poking through to jab us in the leg was not how I wanted to remember this moment.

'What?'

'Marry me. Say yes and let's go choose a ring.'

'OK. Yes.'

She seemed dazed and her mood didn't change all the time we were looking at rings, until she found the one she was looking for. She rejected the big stones and ostentatious settings I picked out and instead opted for three small diamonds set between curved bands of white gold.

'It's not that expensive,' I said dubiously. 'Are you sure that's the one you want?'

'I'm sure. I love you, not what you can buy me. We're students; we have the rest of our lives for you buy me expensive jewellery if that's what you feel the need to do. I don't need a ring worth thousands to know you care.'

I handed over my credit card and we walked into the nearest pub, Olivia twisting her hand so that the sun caught the diamonds, reflecting her happiness into the eyes of every passer-by.

'I think we should celebrate,' I said, ordering a bottle of champagne. My credit card could take the hit again. It's not every day you get the woman you love to agree to spend the rest of her life with you.

As we clinked our glasses together, I had a sudden vision of us repeating the action over the years: on our wedding day, at the birth of our children, on their wedding days and again at the birth of our grandchildren. The enormity of what we had signed up for was overwhelming, but it felt good. This was it now, no going back no matter what the arguments, uncertainties or difficulties. We were forever a team.

We decided to have our engagement party at the Cowley

Bridge Inn – it had been our local the year before when we'd been in Halls and stood not too far from the site of our first kiss. It was a mock Tudor building with whitewashed walls and exposed beams and for such a large building, the inside had a deceptively cosy feel, reinforced by the open fire that filled the pub with a warm, sweet scent throughout the winter months.

My parents had expressed some concern when I'd phoned them – not objecting to either Olivia or our engagement, merely sounding a note of caution about our youth and inexperience. Once reassured we weren't planning to rush into the marriage itself they were far more congratulatory in their reactions. By contrast, Olivia hadn't wanted to tell her parents I'd proposed but I insisted they had a right to know. They may not be in the running for any Parent of the Year awards, but they deserved to be told about such a big event in their daughter's life. I'd wanted to speak to her father, to ask him formally for his permission, but Oliva forbade me from doing so.

'The only person whose permission you would have needed was Nan's,' she told me, 'And you'd have had that in an instant. My dad doesn't get to give permission for anything.'

We argued about it, but in the end I conceded that she was right. It wasn't just her determination which forced the issue; a large part of me knew her argument that he'd forfeited any right to make decisions for her was justified and correct. It was only my own sense of what was the 'right' way to do things that made me keen to approach him. In the end, we settled on a compromise where she would inform her parents in writing that I'd wanted to ask for her hand officially, but that she'd informed me it was unnecessary as she intended to marry me with or without their permission.

Her father had written back about a week later saying congratulations and enclosing a cheque for fifty pounds to buy ourselves an engagement gift. There'd been no reply from her mother, either to congratulate or condemn the engagement, but when I asked if this was a bad sign, Olivia dismissed my concerns out of hand. It didn't matter one way or the other, she told me. She didn't care if her parents approved or not. I had no reason to disbelieve her.

We were soon caught up in the business of exams again and as Olivia had given herself the added pressure of a GCSE in German, alongside her university exams, there wasn't much time to think about anything other than our studies. Consequently, almost without us noticing, it was all over and we were looking forward to the long summer break before we flew out to Vienna for our year abroad. We'd got jobs as teaching assistants and already had a flat sorted out, so once we'd done our weeklong induction course, we'd be ready to go. I was considerably less nervous about the whole thing now Olivia was coming with me, although I knew my parents were still worried about me being so far from home.

We hadn't planned to make a big fuss about our year abroad, so it was something of a surprise to come home one day during our last week in Exeter, to find the house full of our friends: Eoin, Sophie and Zoe had decided to throw a Bon Voyage party for us and had somehow managed to keep the whole thing a surprise.

The party had been in full swing for a couple of hours when I noticed Olivia had gone missing. Having searched unsuccessfully through the downstairs rooms, I eventually found her sitting under the desk in our bedroom.

'What are you hiding under there for?' I laughed. 'Come and join the party.'

I held my hand out to her, to help her out from under the desk, but she shook her head.

'I don't feel like it. You go back and have fun.'

'Don't be silly. Come downstairs.'

'I don't want to, Tom. Just leave me alone. Go back to the party.'

I shrugged and left her to it, cross that she was being so difficult. A few drinks later however, she still hadn't emerged from her self-imposed isolation and I was swinging between anger and concern. I decided to have one more attempt at making her join our friends. After all, they'd gone to a lot of effort to arrange the party and she was being rude by refusing to join in.

'You need to come downstairs,' I announced as I pushed open the door. 'All these people are here for us and...'

I stopped mid-sentence as I saw she'd been crying.

'What's happened?'

She gestured to the scrunched up ball of paper that was half hidden behind the open door. Smoothing it out, I read it, shock and anger consuming me as I did so. It was from her mother.

Dear Olivia,

My darling girl, how can you be so naïve? I wasn't much younger than you when I met your father. He filled my head with talk of how much he loved me – how he couldn't live without me. Filled it so much that he drove out every ounce of hope and ambition I had for myself. Before I knew it, I was lumbered with a baby and a husband with a wandering eye – it wasn't ME he wanted, not the person inside, just the doll he wanted to have dressed up on his arm. I would have *been* somebody, *done* something with my life if I hadn't been stupid enough to get myself pregnant. That was the end of all *my* dreams. I never thought I'd be counselling you against making the same mistake. I know Tom seems lovely now and I'm sure he believes himself to be in love with you, but at the end of the day, my darling, he'll let you down. They always do. Don't think you can go into this believing that he'll be faithful. He won't be. As soon as your looks start to go, his eyes (and his hands and other body parts) will wander. Even if you resign yourself to this fact and tell yourself that it's a price you're willing to pay to be with him, it won't be enough and he will break you. He won't know he's doing it and if he does, he won't care.

Step away from this now, before it's too late and you end up pregnant with a baby you don't want and husband who doesn't want you. I only want what's best for you.

Your loving,
Mum x

I looked at Olivia, unable to trust myself to say anything rational.

'I know.' Her voice shook.

She crawled out and on her hands and knees made her way to where I'd dropped to the floor, my legs made wobbly by suppressed rage. She laid her head on my shoulder.

'You won't, will you?'

It came out as a whisper: a doubt she didn't want to give voice to. A doubt, it seemed – no matter how hard I worked to dispel it – would always plague her. I knew she hated the power it had over her as much as I did and all I could do was patiently reassure her over and over again.

'Never,' I said, kissing the top of her head. 'I promise.'

It was the innocuous action of pulling her sleeves down that drew my eyes to her wrists and the horizontal red lines that tracked across them, scorching the pale skin. I tightened my grip on her and kissed her hair again in an attempt the stem the rage that, if it was allowed to erupt, would be directed at the wrong person. This time, the 'never' I said to myself was different. Never again would I allow her parents to inflict such damage on their daughter and if that meant cutting them out of our lives completely, then that's what we would do.

In spite of my protests, Olivia had replied to her mother's letter, although she refused to let me see what she'd written and I could only hope that whatever the letter contained, it was enough to ensure her mother didn't repeat the accusations she'd levelled at me. Whatever doubts she might harbour about the speed of our engagement – which wasn't actually that quick in the grand scheme of things – and whatever bitterness she held onto from her own experiences, she had no right to make assumptions about my character or to make her daughter suffer. Her words had been cruel, whether she had intended them to be or not and I found it hard to forgive her for the hurt she had inflicted on Olivia.

The beginning of our year abroad and its consequent physical distance gave me the opportunity to start putting some metaphorical distance between Olivia and her parents. My fury towards her mother hadn't dissipated over the summer holidays, which Olivia had spent living with us. She'd managed to secure a job temping in the local council offices and I'd gone back to my regular holiday job at my Dad's wine bar. Before we left the country, I even went so far as to write to Mr and Mrs Whitely, setting out my conditions for continued contact with Olivia. I didn't expect anything to change, but I had to try for her sake. I understood her love for them and why she couldn't make the break herself, but someone had to protect her from them. Confrontation and ultimatums weren't in my nature, but for Olivia I was prepared to be strong. We heard nothing more from her mother, but it was only as we boarded the flight to Vienna that I felt my fury dissipate a little, as though by leaving the country we could also leave behind her mother's negativity and my anger about it.

When we arrived at the tiny flat we were renting for the year, I had a sense that our adventure was truly beginning. The week of induction and orientation had been interesting and useful, but I was keen to get settled into our new home and begin exploring the city that was to be our playground for the next nine months.

Built on a much smaller scale than London, Vienna soon proved itself easy to navigate around. The U-Bahn system was logical and cheap, while the S-Bahn allowed you to see much of the city as you rocked and rolled along the noisy tracks. At the beginning of our time in the city we were happy to walk across the bridge which covered the wide expanse of river separating our district from the main body of Vienna. As winter drew in however, and the mornings became darker, we soon found ourselves grateful for the rickety tram that pulled up not too many metres from our building: it was worth the extra few schillings to start the day marginally warmer. It felt as though our bridge was the first solid structure the wind hit as it blew down the Danube from the Waldviertel. The iciness of that blast shot through innumerable layers of clothing and skin to chill our organs so thoroughly that we didn't fully recover from the shock until we were back at home each evening, with the heating on full, not caring about the cost of our gas.

Despite the cold, we fell utterly and completely in love with the city, spending our weekends walking miles through its streets finding new places to eat and drink and new architectural wonders to gaze in awe at. There was a style to suit everyone, from the Gothic-Romanesque Stefansdom, through the Baroque Karlskirche to the modern Expressionism of Hundertwasser Haus and we loved them all. At various points throughout the year, we even talked about the possibility of not returning to the UK at all and remaining in

Vienna, although we almost always instantly dismissed the notion.

As we got used to living together free from any outside influences or housemates and with both of us working almost full time, there were the inevitable arguments about whose turn it was to cook dinner or wash up, or who should take the rubbish out on bin day, but we managed tolerably well on the whole. Eoin and Sophie flew out for a couple of short stays, as did Zoe. My parents visited for occasional weekends and Olivia's telephoned now and again, but otherwise our year abroad was spent with little communication with the world outside Austria. Colleagues took us skiing at the weekends – a new experience for us – and introduced us to the joys of après-ski, Olivia joined a book group run by one of the teachers and I played football every week. It was a tiring, but fairly blissful existence.

'I think my German's definitely improved while we've been here,' Olivia remarked one day towards the end of our time there. 'I can certainly join in the discussions about the books a bit more than I did at the beginning.'

I looked at her and laughed.

'What?' she said, instantly offended. 'You don't agree?'

Still laughing, I shook my head.

'It's not that,' I said. 'Did you realise you said all that in German?'

She looked disbelieving for a moment, then laughed herself. 'I guess it's improved more than I realised if I didn't even notice I was speaking it.' She dug her elbow into my ribs. 'At least I don't dream in German though, unlike some people I could mention!'

It was my turn to look confused.

'You woke me up the other night shouting in German. Honestly, I don't think I've ever been so scared. I thought there was someone else in the flat!'

I smiled ruefully.

'Sorry.'

She nestled into my shoulder and tucked her arm through mine.

'Don't be. Once I got over the shock I was quite pleased to realise I understood most of what you were shouting.'

All too soon, we said goodbye to our Austrian friends and boarded the plane back to England and almost before we knew it, we were back in Exeter ready to start our final year. Most of the people we'd begun our degrees with had graduated the previous summer and departed either back home or onto jobs elsewhere, so it was only a handful of our old friends who were still around. There were a few like us, who'd spent the previous year abroad, but most of the familiar faces who were still studying were now doing Master's degrees. Numbered among them, to our delight, were Eoin and Sophie with whom we had agreed to share a house.

It was strange being back in Exeter. The city felt familiar and yet very different all at the same time. We also had to adjust to sharing our living space with other people again and it almost felt like we were taking a step backwards in our relationship. While we'd been away, Olivia's insecurities seemed to have faded into the background. We worked at the same school, we lived together and the only time we were apart was if she was at her book group or I was playing football and she'd seemed content. I'd rarely had to worry about her eating, but our return to university had thrown her all out of kilter again and I couldn't help but wonder if it was because her parents were once again within driving distance.

A few weeks into term, once we'd established a routine, she settled down again and having Sophie to talk things over with banished some of her more irrational fears. The house we'd chosen for our final year overlooked the Exe and like the river, time flowed steadily on through lectures and exams until it was suddenly our graduation week. My ceremony was the day before Olivia's and my parents came down for it, sitting next to Olivia in the darkened auditorium, wide smiles splitting their faces as they watched me collect my scroll.

'I'm sorry you can't stay for mine tomorrow,' Olivia said as we sat in the dining room of The White Hart. 'I'd much rather have had you there.'

Mum patted her hand.

'No apology needed,' she said. 'It's only right your parents see you graduate. We're celebrating with you today. Speaking of which,' she paused and reached into the shopping bag by her feet. 'They're nothing much, but we want you both to know how proud we are of you.'

She handed us each a brightly wrapped gift and watched anxiously as we opened them. Inside, the small packages were identical silver Cross fountain pens with our names engraved on them.

'I know you'll probably be changing your surname soon, Livvy,' she said, 'But you got your degree in your own name, not Tom's and we thought it would remind you of who you are when you start getting talked about as "Tom's wife" or "so-and-so's mum". It's important not to lose your own identity when you get married and have children.'

'No chance of that with you love, was there?' Dad laughed and Mum blushed.

'Don't take any notice of him,' she said.

'Thank-you so much. It's beautiful,' Olivia leant over and hugged Mum, her eyes full.

I echoed her thanks and squeezed her hand when she sat back down.

'We have something to tell you actually,' Olivia said, once she had control of her voice again. 'We've been talking about the wedding and we've decided we'd like to get married next summer, unless you have any plans for then?'

'If we had, we'd cancel them!' Mum declared firmly, running round the table to kiss us.

'I wondered if I could ask you a favour,' Olivia said hesitantly.

We'd discussed this the night before and I'd tried to reassure her that Mum would be delighted, but I knew she was still nervous about asking.

'Of course,' Mum's face was immediately full of concern. 'What is it?'

'Would you come and look at dresses with me? I know it's meant to be my mum, but...' her voice trailed off and her hands twisted her napkin into tortured origami.

'You'd rather show your mum once you have a better idea of what you want? Of course, I'll come with you. I'd love to! We can make a couple of nice days of it – wedding dresses, lunch, champagne, the full works. When you've got a better idea of what you're looking for, we can do it all again with your mum. Unless you'd rather go on your own with her?'

Olivia laughed and shook her head, the tension suddenly released.

'That sounds perfect,' she said. 'I like your way of shopping.'

The following afternoon I met Olivia's parents and her stepmother at the door to the auditorium. I'd sent Olivia in to collect her robe and mortar board before they arrived, trying to delay the moment of their meeting as long as I could. When they eventually turned up – her dad and Lisa thankfully arriving first – I couldn't help but draw comparisons with my own parents. My dad had worn a sober suit and tie, while my mum had opted for a summer dress with a jacket – smart enough for the occasion, but not drawing attention to themselves. By contrast, Olivia's mother and step-mother seemed to have agreed on a competition to see which of them could wear the most fake tan and the most make-up. Lisa's dress, while it hugged every one of her curves, at least covered her from shoulder to knee, whereas Laura was clearly subscribing to the maxim of 'if you've got it, flaunt it' and had more than an ample amount of her cleavage on display for anyone who cared to see it. I had to admit though, she looked far healthier than the last time I'd seen her. Her attitude towards me was still curt – she'd never really forgiven me for the letter I'd sent prior to our departure for Vienna – but I was content with that if it meant she curbed her tongue in front of Olivia.

I plastered a smile on my face and ushered them all inside, sending up a quick prayer that they'd all refrain from sniping at each other until the ceremony was over. God, or luck, was clearly feeling beneficent that day, as by the time we'd found our seats and Laura had apologised for sitting on the knee of another parent as she tried to squeeze through the gap between his knees and the seat in front, the lights had dimmed and the ceremony began.

Once we were released from the need for silence however, it was a different story and arguments started before we'd even left the auditorium. As the lunchtime sun hit my face I took a deep breath and turned to face my future in-laws.

'Okay you two, listen to me for a moment.' I took another steadying breath, reminding myself I was doing this for Olivia, as they turned startled faces towards me.

'This is Olivia's day and you will not ruin it for her. You will behave like civilised human beings and you will be nice to her. Do you understand? If either of you can't manage that, feel free to leave now and I'll take her to celebrate on our own. If you want to be part of today, you play nice. Got it?'

To be fair to them, they nodded and fell silent, while Lisa mimed applause at me. I was in shock myself though perhaps I shouldn't have been. Mum's advice was usually spot on and it was her counsel I'd sought about what to do if Olivia's parents started arguing. Laura still looked like a sulky child when Olivia emerged, blinking, onto the bright terrace, but her father seemed determined to play his part.

'Photos and then we'll celebrate properly darling,' he said, kissing her cheek. 'Why don't you and Tom stand over there where those flowers are and then I'll take one of you and your mum. Is that all right Laura?'

Laura stopped sulking and nodded. Clearly the thought of posing for photographs cheered her up and I silently praised Adam Whitely for thinking of it. Despite the years they'd been divorced, he obviously still remembered how to appeal to his ex-wife's better nature.

Dinner that evening – at Adam's insistence – was booked at The Thistle Hotel on Queen Street. It was far posher than our lunch at The White Hart, but he'd insisted that nothing but the best would do for his daughter's graduation. I took consolation from the fact it was near to Exeter Central so we had a quick escape route if we needed it.

The meal was more pleasant than I'd expected. The food was excellent – which I had anticipated – and the company well-behaved – which I hadn't. Once we'd eaten, Adam called for a bottle of champagne and once we all had a glass in our hands, he tapped his lightly with his coffee spoon.

'I'd like to propose a toast,' he said, 'to my...to *our* wonderful daughter Livvy. We're all very proud of you darling. To Livvy!'

We raised our glasses and drank while Olivia turned scarlet.

'While everyone's in the mood for celebrating,' she said, 'Tom and I have some news for you. We plan to get married next summer. We haven't talked about any details yet, except the date, but we wanted to let you know.'

'I'll check my diary,' Laura said, 'But if you could avoid the end of August that would be lovely, as I'll probably be on holiday then...'

I shot her a glance across the table and she immediately

swallowed the rest of whatever she'd been about to say. 'But obviously your wedding comes first, so I can always switch it to an earlier week if needed.' She gave me a quick glance, then took a gulp from her champagne flute.

'How big a cheque do I need to write?' Adam asked.

Olivia choked on her drink.

'I wasn't expecting you to pay for anything,' she stammered. 'We weren't planning on anything big.'

'Rubbish,' he said. 'Of course, I'm paying for my girl's big day. You and Tom have a think and then let me know how much you need. Just don't go booking Westminster Abbey!' He laughed, as dutifully, did Laura and Lisa. Olivia and I smiled politely.

The subject of the wedding was dropped and the conversation moved onto other matters, like what our plans were for the future.

'Olivia's got a job in the university library,' I said proudly, as she excused herself to go to the bathroom, 'and I'm doing a Master's in Translation Studies.'

'So, she's going to be working while you carry on loafing around?' Laura said. 'Is that why you want to marry her, so she can support you while you carry on being a student all your life? My mother's money and house are paying for you to not get a job?'

I leant forwards, resting my elbows on the table, my hands clenched tightly together.

'I'm going to say this once and once only and I'll say it slowly so you understand me. I'm marrying Olivia because I love her and for no other reason. To suggest otherwise is both offensive to me and insulting to your daughter. If you'd said that in her hearing, we'd be leaving now and you would not be coming to the wedding. If you continue to run her down and make her doubt herself or our relationship, you will not be a part of our lives. Don't think for a moment that I'll let any child of mine be exposed to someone who clearly thinks so little of me.'

'Who do you think you are to speak to me like that?' Laura cried, almost knocking over her drink, so great was her agitation. 'What would Olivia say if she heard you speaking to me like that?'

'She'd probably give him a round of applause,' Lisa remarked drily, sitting back and toasting me with her glass. I suppressed a grin.

'And rightly so,' Adam added. 'He's quite right, Laura. You're out of order and you know it. As for who he is, he's the man who's about to become your son-in-law and he's perfectly within his rights to ban you from seeing their children, although don't tell Livvy I said that,' he muttered to me, 'So I'd pipe down if I were you. I for one am glad to see our Liv with someone who's prepared to fight her corner for her. And before you say anything,' he added, turning back to look at me, 'I'm well aware of my own shortcomings as a father.' His shoulders slumped. 'But I am trying,' he continued. 'I want to be a part of her life. I know I've made mistakes, but I do love her and I want her to be happy.'

'And I am Dad,' Olivia said, overhearing the last part of his speech.

She dropped a kiss on his head then resumed her seat at my side.

'We all want you to be happy darling,' Laura said. She glanced sharply at me then continued. 'We do love you, even if we're not very good at showing it.' She threw her hands in the air and a tear escaped, leaving a furrow in her make-up. 'Oh, I don't know why I'm trying to hide it. It's not like you don't all know about it. I'm clean, Liv,' she said, holding out a hand. 'I have been for a few months now. I don't mind admitting it's a struggle, but I am trying.'

Olivia tentatively took her mother's hand and gave her a weak smile.

'That's great, Mum. Really great.'

After we'd said goodbye to her family and were walking home, I turned to Olivia to raise the issue that had been bothering me since her mother's little speech.

'You didn't seem too pleased about your mum kicking the drugs. I thought you'd be delighted. It's a good thing, isn't it?'

'It would be if I believed her.'

'You think she was lying?'

'No, I believe what she said, I don't believe it will last, that's all. Trust me, I was a lot more enthusiastic the first few times I heard it. But she'll relapse in the end. She always does.'

Again, I realised my naivety when it came to the kinds of problems Olivia had faced growing up. Even after almost four years together, I was still learning about her childhood and trying to understand the lasting damage it had caused.

'Dad's trying though,' she said. 'It wasn't easy for him today – it never is when he's with Lisa and Mum and they managed not to fall out, which was a first.'

I kept quiet.

'What do you think about what he said about the wedding?' she continued. 'It would certainly make it easier financially if he helped with the cost, but...'

'But you want it to be the wedding we want, not some overblown display of wealth.'

'Exactly.'

'Well, you heard what he said, just let him know. Why don't we work out what we want and the costs and then decide what to let him pay for? That way he feels involved, but we don't lose control. My parents have said they'll help as well, so we can tell him they want to pay for part of it.'

'We'll need to decide soon,' she said. 'Places get booked up really fast and we've only got a year.'

'It will be the first thing we organise once we've moved,' I said. 'Let's get that out of the way first. Once we're settled in the new place, the wedding will be the next job, I promise.'

'A house of our own and a wedding,' Olivia said, resting her head on my arm for a moment. 'It all makes us sound terribly grown up, doesn't it?'

A week later we were cursing the need to grow up as we heaved boxes in and out of the car and dragged them into the relevant rooms of our newly rented house. But despite the cursing and the bruised and aching limbs, it was with a quiet sense of satisfaction that we sat down to dinner that evening.

'Here's to us,' Olivia said, raising her wine glass to mine.

'To a bright future and whatever it brings,' I agreed.

We bumped our glasses together and smiled. Just as I had on the day I proposed, I felt the security of our togetherness wrap itself around me. We'd taken another step in our journey and the next big milestone – the wedding – was not far off. For a moment I allowed myself to see again older, wrinklier versions of this scene, children and grandchildren around the table with us, but always with Oliva and me at the centre. I leaned over and kissed her.

GRACE

I tried several times to text Grace to cancel, but I never got more than halfway through the message before deleting it and jabbing the phone back into my pocket. She had done nothing to warrant my rudeness and it seemed to me to be both childish and churlish to cancel our date purely on the basis that I felt more for her than was logical on so short an acquaintance. I kept telling myself the word implied more than it should have, but I couldn't help referring to our upcoming meeting as such. Yes, she was a very attractive woman but we were just friends who happened to be of the opposite sex. We'd each had a difficult time of late and found the other easy to talk to. There was nothing wrong with our supporting each other, nor was there anything underhand about our meeting, even if it did feel slightly clandestine to not have told anyone that my trip to the Ballroom was not being made alone.

As had been the case previously, being unencumbered by children who could never say goodbye quickly, Grace was already waiting at the entrance when I arrived. That she had waited for me bothered me slightly – it removed any lingering doubt that we were not going to the Tower together. It made it explicit that we were not simply meeting there and the distinction made me uncomfortable. This was confirmed at the end of the day when we arranged to meet the following week and then again the week after.

'Tom, you enjoy dancing, don't you?'

'Of course.'

It was true. Having been reluctant at first, I was enjoying it more and more. There was a sense of freedom in flying around the floor in a Quickstep and I was discovering that it was difficult to feel depressed while you moved to good music with a beautiful woman in your arms. Although I still struggled with the idea of dancing with someone other than Olivia and had to sit down if certain songs were played, I had noticed an improvement in my mental health over the last few weeks and I could only put it down to my return to the ballroom floor.

'Why do you ask?' I continued.

Grace flushed.

'Well, I just wondered – and feel free to say no if you don't want to, I won't be offended – if maybe you wanted to make it a bit more official?'

Fiery hot fingers of panic clawed their way up my throat until she continued.

'I thought maybe we could find a dancing school and do some of the medals, or competitions or something. It's only an idea though,' she hastened to add. 'It's probably a silly one, but I figured it might be fun. I miss all that since Ash hasn't been able to compete and I wondered if it might be something for us to do. I'm happy to carry on as we are though if you're not interested.'

I put an end to her babbling by laying a hand on her arm.

'I don't think it's silly,' I said. 'I'll have to check at home first, but I think it's a great idea. Did you have a particular school in mind?'

She shook her head.

'Not really. I mean, I know a couple of places, but you never said where you'd gone with Olivia and I assumed you wouldn't want to go back there?'

She was absolutely right of course and it was typical of her thoughtful nature to have considered my feelings. I named the school Olivia and I had attended, but assured her that particular place aside, I didn't much care where we went. I promised to give her a definite answer the next time we met, but I knew I needed to talk it over with Olivia first. It was time to talk to my wife about the situation, but it wasn't a conversation I looked forward to.

In the end it was much easier than I had anticipated. I asked Olivia what she thought of the idea and I got the distinct impression she considered it utterly ridiculous I'd even considered it might bother her. I took comfort from that and from the fact that even if I had not been wholly forthcoming about my feelings for Grace – how could I be when they weren't clear even to me – at least Olivia now knew of her existence.

The lessons, when they started, came as something of a shock. I'd believed I was in reasonable shape, but I soon learnt there was a huge difference between dancing for pleasure and dancing for the purpose of passing exams and training for competitions. The lessons I'd had with Olivia had been sedate affairs conducted at our pace with no pressure. This time, instructions were rattled out and every little mistake pounced on.

'Slow-slow-quick-quick-slow. Heel turn. Bend your knees more – you're meant to be gliding elegantly across the floor not doing a cockney walkabout.'

It was all delivered with a smile and I knew Liz, with her

gruff voice and no-nonsense attitude, was helping us to make massive improvements, but it was exhausting.

'Can you show us that one more time please?' I mopped my face with the towel I'd soon learnt to bring with me. I knew the step inside out by now and could have done it backwards, but I needed a few more seconds rest before attempting it again.

We ran through our routine from top to bottom, then looked at each other and grinned. That had definitely felt better, but the grins slid away when Liz shook her head in mock exasperation.

'Again!'

Despite these frustrations, I looked forward to our lesson each week. I loved the challenge of learning something new and Grace and I worked well together. If I forgot the next step of our routine and led her into a different one, she just followed me with nothing more than a raised eyebrow and a smothered giggle. She did take it seriously, as did I, but we couldn't help laughing at each other when things didn't go to plan. Ultimately however, we wanted to do our best and improve. On occasion however, Grace's high expectations of herself and her desire for perfection did sometimes hamper the speed at which we picked things up.

'I've been dancing all my life, why can't I get this right tonight?' She half stamped her foot in irritation. 'What's the matter with me? It's not even the most difficult step we do.'

'Why don't we leave it for now and come back to it later?' I suggested. 'Maybe give our brains a break for a few minutes?'

Grace just looked at me as though I'd suggested she tap dance naked round the studio car park.

I bit my lip, sharing her frustration. We'd spent the last fifteen minutes trying to master this part of our rhumba and every time we came out of the fan and into the turn, Grace bumped into me.

‘Come here Tom and do it with me,’ Liz instructed.

I went through the motions with her, stopping when she dropped my hand and nodded.

‘Shift your weight a bit to the right on that step and put more pressure into that arm. If you do that, it will give Grace more space on the turn.’

This time we managed to get through the whole routine without making a mistake and even Liz was happy with it.

‘You’re doing so well,’ she said. ‘I think it’s time to put in for your first exam and you could think about a competition or two as well.’

‘Really?’ I said, looking at her in surprise. ‘Do you think we’re good enough?’

‘I’m not saying you’ll win,’ Liz replied, turning the CD player off, ‘But the experience will do you good. It’ll give you a chance to see the kind of standard to expect when you start doing them seriously.’

Grace tucked her arm in mine as we walked out to our cars.

‘What do you think? Should we do it?’

I considered it for a moment. Most of the competitions were on a Sunday anyway, so I didn’t need to worry about the children and although it was scary, I could already feel the excitement bubbling up inside me.

‘I think we should,’ I said at last. ‘Like Liz said, it will give us some experience before we start aiming to win.’

‘You think we’ll win?’

‘Not now, but in the future, why not? That’s why you enter competitions, isn’t it, to win? What’s the point of entering if you’re not trying to beat everyone else?’

She laughed.

‘What monster have I unleashed with this? I had no idea you were so competitive!’

‘I’m not,’ I protested, laughing myself. ‘Well maybe I am a

little bit, but I don't see the point of entering competitions if you're not ultimately aiming to win one.'

'Okay, so we're agreed, yes? Next week we'll ask Liz to enter us for our medal test and we'll enter the next competition we can.'

Although the medal test went well, our first competition was an unmitigated disaster. Grace forgot her shoes, having brought her practice bag instead of her competition bag, prompting a frantic call to Ashley. Fortunately, he was off duty and used his spare key to retrieve the correct shoes from her flat, then raced across the county to Southport to deliver the shoes to her. They arrived well ahead of our scheduled dances, so the minor excitement had nothing to do with the disaster that followed, but it didn't stop Grace blaming herself for it.

'It was our first comp; we knew it was going to be tough. We learnt loads, so don't worry,' I said in the car on the way home. 'Liz did say there'd be a lot of gamesmanship.'

'I know,' she said, wiping a tear away, 'But it's not like I've not done this before. I should have just let it go, but I was still thinking about the shoes when we did the rhumba and I let us get boxed into a corner. I should've been paying more attention to the people around us.'

'I forgot half our cha-cha-cha routine,' I said, 'And I promise you I wasn't thinking about your shoes then. Was that your fault as well?'

'No, I suppose not, but I'm more experienced at this and having all that stress at the beginning didn't help, did it? I should be guiding you through these first few competitions, not causing problems for you.'

'Well at least we'll always remember our first comp and no matter what happens now, they can only get better, can't they? Or do you want to give up on the idea of the comps and only do the medals? If it's going to upset you this much when it goes wrong, is it worth it?'

She dashed away the remaining tears and glared at me.

'Absolutely not do I want to give up. I didn't have you down as a quitter, Tom Blythe.'

I laughed.

'That's more like it. I'm not, but there's no fun in doing it if you're going to get upset when we don't do well.'

She stared at me for a few seconds before replying. 'You genuinely don't mind that I messed up do you?'

'We both messed up and of course I don't. This is meant to be something fun. I don't care about being the best, it's just a little challenge for us. The important thing is that we enjoy it.'

She shook her head with a sad smile. 'If that had been Austin, he'd have been furious. Sometimes I forget that not everything is my fault anymore. I do enjoy it and I won't get as upset next time; I promise. It's only that I'd been looking forward to it so much and it was an utter disaster.'

'The next one won't be,' I said. 'I know the tricks to look out for now as well, don't I and I won't be as nervous in future because I'll have done it all before.'

'I can't promise that,' she laughed. 'I've done loads of them and I still get terribly nervous.'

From then on we seemed to have a competition almost every week and we steadily improved, until we reached a point where we even managed a few podium finishes, although the top step always eluded us. However, as the number of competitions rose, so did the amount of time we spent practising. I had no objection to this, as it was always a pleasure to spend time with Grace, but I could no longer pretend to myself that I felt nothing more than friendship for her. It had been months since our first meeting and the feeling I had been unwilling to name on that occasion had only increased in the intervening time. I was still just as reluctant to give voice to it though. In spite of everything that had happened, I still loved Olivia. To admit I was also in love with

Grace would have been a betrayal. It was hard enough to acknowledge the fact to myself; to speak it out loud was unthinkable. Dancing with her, I swung between the pleasure of having an excuse to hold her close and the torture of having her so close and being unable to act on the desire to kiss her. It felt like an eternity since I'd last had any kind of intimacy with Olivia. In the last few months, she'd been truly apologetic, but I didn't blame her; I hadn't been in the mood either. None of that however, changed the fact I desired Grace in every way and it was becoming increasingly difficult both to hide it from her and to deny myself the luxury of indulging in fantasies of moving our relationship from the ballroom to the bedroom.

Through a desire to spend more time away from the temptations of the dancefloor, but unable to not have my weekly fix of seeing her, as one of our rare Sundays without a competition coincided with Tram Sunday, I asked Grace if she'd like to go with me. Ordinarily, I would have forfeited my day alone to take the children, but Mum had already arranged to take them to see *Despicable Me 2* and in a competition with the Minions, the poor heritage trams stood no chance. I saw them off, over-excited and giggling and then left to collect Grace, who would – I hoped – be pleased to see me but be far less giggly and excited. It was the first time I'd suggested doing something together outside of dancing and she had seemed very keen at the time. I'd been careful to stress I was only asking casually if she'd been thinking of going, as if she was it would make sense to go in one car. Parking was often difficult on the Open Days.

It was a warm day and consequently the streets around the tram depot were particularly crowded. It wasn't just the number of people who had turned out and were compacted into a relatively small area. That space was simultaneously occupied by various small stalls as well. There was the usual array of sweets, cakes, handmade soaps, crocheted characters and everything else you would think of as being sold at such events. Grace and I ambled our way along, stopping occasionally as some sale item or other caught our eye. I bought sweets for the kids, then reconsidered and promised myself I'd hide them in the cupboard until later in the week. They'd have ingested more than enough sugar for one day by the time they returned from the cinema. I also bought an arrangement of silk flowers for Olivia. Neither of us were particularly fond of artificial flowers, much preferring the real thing, but this was a particularly pretty arrangement that reminded me of her wedding flowers and I felt sure she'd approve.

'They're lovely,' Grace said as the stallholder handed over the bag she'd placed them in. 'I'm sure she'll love them.'

I smiled at her, grateful she understood. I knew how fortunate I was that she was so understanding about my situation, simply accepting without complaint how things were. Not many women would have been prepared to do that; they'd have pushed and demanded I make a choice, but so far, Grace had done neither. It was a fact for which I was very grateful. I knew I couldn't put off a decision forever, but I wasn't ready yet. I was slowly getting better and the stronger I felt, the nearer the moment of choice came, but for now I was content to leave the issue alone. I could still, with a clear conscience, say I had crossed no line and for the present, that was enough.

I'd parked the car in Victoria Street – not in a car park as such, but where the road had parking spaces painted in the middle of it. By the time we got there, the crowds had thinned out considerably and instead of the noise of people chattering, we could hear the sound of music. As we turned into the street we were met by the sight of what looked like a family group gathered around a car with its doors flung open. The music we'd heard was coming from its stereo. As we paused by my car, curious to see what they were planning, they got into a line and started dancing down the street, laughing to each other at the absurdity of their behaviour.

'That's a Balmoral Blues, isn't it?' I asked Grace.

The non-dancing member of the group turned around at the sound of my question.

'That's right. Join in if you want to. It's not a private party – they won't mind.'

I was about to decline politely, but Grace spoke before I was able to get a word out.

'Could we, Tom? Please?' Her eyes were dancing with merriment and I couldn't bear to refuse her, so we threw our bags onto the back seat and dashed over to join one end of the line.

'It'll be good practice,' Grace assured me as we crossed over in the dance and I valiantly tried to pretend I wasn't dying of embarrassment.

'How do you figure that?' I asked. 'We don't do sequence except for fun.'

'Well, if you can dance on a public street in Fleetwood on Tram Sunday then panels of judges and examiners should hold no fear for you!'

I laughed with her and pushed away the feelings of discomfiture. She was right. So what if it was in public? So what if we looked a bit odd? What did it matter what anyone else thought? I was doing something I loved with the woman I – I pushed that thought away too.

Towards the end of July, we had a competition in Blackpool, which gave us a respite from the usual three stops we had to make on route to a competition in order for Grace to go for what she termed a 'nervous wee'. This had become something of a running joke between us, as even a relatively short car journey to a competition inevitably involved several stops at the motorway services. Although we had learnt to channel our nerves into something more constructive once the competition started, Grace still got worked up beforehand and had usually transferred her nerves to me by the time we reached the venue. Mercifully, there wasn't time for any of this on the twenty minute journey to our latest competition, although Grace did dive into the Ladies the moment we arrived. However, it also meant we didn't have the usual exhaustive discussion about our routines, so it was no surprise to either of us when our rhumba didn't go quite to plan. It wasn't exactly disastrous – we managed to cover the mistake we made – but it certainly wasn't as polished a performance as would normally have given. We knew we had no chance of being recalled for the final, so we settled back to have our lunch and wait for our next dance.

I'd just taken a huge bite out of my sausage roll when they called our number. I nearly choked on it as I tried to swallow it quickly, knowing we only had a few minutes to take our place on the floor. Grace looked equally perplexed and as we waited for the last few numbers to be called, I noticed she had a flake of pastry clinging to the corner of her mouth. Without thinking I gently wiped it away with my thumb, knowing she'd be mortified if it was spotted by the judges or other competitors.

Her skin was warm and soft and the gesture felt more intimate than I had intended it to be. The seconds following my careless action stretched out into an eternity. I couldn't tear my eyes from her face and Grace seemed similarly afflicted. The pad of my thumb burned and the heat from it spread outwards in concentric circles, while Grace pressed the tips of her fingers to the spot where I'd touched her.

Fighting against my body, I forced my mind back to reality as the music began and the final got underway. I moved through the routine automatically, my feet doing steps of their own accord. All I could think about was Grace and how much I loved her. My eyes tracked every movement she made. When the steps took her away from me it felt like a physical pain and I was glad to pull her in close again. I couldn't have claimed with any certainty that we'd done the right steps in the right order, but it didn't matter. Whatever we had done, the judges obviously liked it because they awarded us our first ever win. Standing on top of the podium I put my arm around Grace and hugged her as she battled to contain her tears. We'd worked so hard and after what we considered a disappointing performance in the heat, to have actually won it was beyond our wildest dreams. We'd finally reached the top step. We were no longer individual dancers who just happened to dance together, we were a partnership.

Whatever it was that had happened during the rhumba remained unspoken and I was glad of it. After our rocky start to the day, we ended up coming home with a nice haul of medals. As well as our first place in the rhumba, we came second in the Jive and the Quickstep and third in the Foxtrot and the Waltz. It was our best overall performance so far and we were in the mood to celebrate. Grace made me pull over on the way home and she emerged from the shop with a bottle of champagne, which she waved at me.

'I know you can't have too much as you've got to drive,' she said, 'But you have to come in and have a drink with me. We have a duty to celebrate our first victory.'

Laughing, I acknowledged she was correct and agreed to have one glass with her before returning home.

It was the first time I'd been inside Grace's flat and I was surprised to discover it was much larger than I'd imagined. A narrow corridor from the door opened out onto a double bedroom and a bathroom on one side and a second bedroom opposite. Beyond that was a sizeable lounge and an open-plan kitchen diner. Everything was painted in very neutral tones, but the furniture in the living room was a deep teal and bright modern art prints adorned the walls, adding splashes of colour that avoided the whole thing having the feel of a show home. I couldn't help contrasting the orderliness with the comfortable chaos of my home. With three young children, I couldn't remember the last time our house had looked this tidy. Even when the children had put their toys away and I'd been motivated enough to clean it properly, it still looked lived in. Here, I was afraid *I* made the flat look untidy and took my shoes off, returning them to the mat by the door. Grace laughed at my evident nervousness.

'Make yourself at home, I'll get the glasses.'

I perched on the edge of the sofa, my hands clasped tightly together until Grace handed me a filled champagne flute and I immediately started looking round for a coaster, not wanting to leave a ring of condensation on the unmarred glass top of the coffee table.

'Well done us,' Grace said, clinking her glass on mine before sitting down in the armchair and tucking her feet beneath her.

'To many more triumphant dances,' I replied, relaxing a little as the first cold bubbles slid down my throat.

We sat in silence for a moment, sipping our drinks and savouring the taste of the champagne and the victory. I tried to think of something to say to fill the silence. Then Grace grinned at me and leant forward to top up her glass and suddenly everything felt normal again, our conversation flowing as naturally as it usually did. We somehow got onto the topic of families and after a few more top-ups of her glass I persuaded Grace to show me photos from her childhood.

'You've got to promise not to laugh,' she warned me. 'You have to remember the late eighties and early nineties were the times that fashion forgot. And you have to promise to show me yours at some point. It's only fair.'

She left the room and returned, rather wobblily, a few minutes later with a large photograph album clasped in her arms. She dropped heavily onto the sofa next to me and laid the album in my lap. The photos were nowhere near as embarrassing as she'd intimated, or not the ones of her at any rate. I wisely forbore to comment on the ones of her brother.

Ashley had definitely been a dedicated follower of all the fashions: the curtain haircut, the plaid shirt, the baggy jeans – they were all there. Grace, on the other hand, had been a very cute child with tumbling red curls that fell almost to her waist.

'What happened to all that hair?' I said, gently tugging one of her short curls.

She frowned slightly.

'Austin insisted on me keeping it long, so when I left him, the first thing I did was go and have it all chopped off.'

'Oh God. Grace, I'm so sorry, I–'

She laid a finger over my lips.

'Don't apologise.'

Then she leant over and kissed me. It was a just a light, gentle kiss that brushed my lips, but when I didn't object, she deepened it, leaning into me. She tasted of champagne and my fingers found their way into the curls that had prompted this unexpected event, pulling her closer still. The movement unbalanced her and she knocked the now empty bottle off the table. The shock was enough to bring me to my senses and I pulled away from her abruptly.

'I'm sorry, Grace. I can't do this. I thought I could, but I can't.'

She looked at me sadly, but I wanted to believe there was understanding in her expression as well.

'It's Olivia, isn't it?'

I nodded.

'No matter what, she's going to be there between us. I thought you were coming round to the idea of us, but you still love her so much.'

I nodded again and a single tear rolled down Grace's cheek.

'I wish someone loved me the way you love her.'

'I'm so sorry,' I whispered.

'Don't apologise for being a good man. You can't help how you feel.'

'I know. But I'm sorry all the same.'

I left the flat at a run, pretending not to hear the stifled sobs I left behind me. They tore me apart, but what could I do? I couldn't just stop loving my wife, no matter how much simpler it would make things if I could.

I had to speak to Olivia. I needed to confess what I'd done and hope she could forgive me.

IV

OLIVIA 2002-2005

The year between our moving in together and the wedding flew past quicker than I had anticipated. Between study and work there were days where we hardly spoke more than a handful of words to each other and it was only thanks to Olivia and Sophie's organisational skills that everything came together in time. Alongside my lectures I'd found work with a translation service and this, although it paid well, often kept me up until the early hours of the morning trying to meet my various deadlines. Olivia's hours – although more regular – were long and she'd often stay at her desk past the official end of her day if there was still work to be done, which there inevitably was.

It was a tiring year, but we knew it had purpose. Olivia's dedication showed she was capable of taking on more responsibility when the opportunity arose and my work gave me invaluable experience. It also enabled me to make contacts in the industry and build up an impressive portfolio to take to interviews.

The venue for the big day was easily chosen – Powderham

Castle had been the location of our graduation ball and we felt it was the perfect choice. We decided to hold the ceremony in the American Garden rather than the house itself as, according to Olivia, the Gothic Pavilion would provide the perfect romantic backdrop for our photographs. I was happy to leave that to her. I was more interested in what food we were going to have. Similarly, our choices for best man and bridesmaid – Eoin and Sophie – were made speedily and with no fuss. The guest list, however, proved a little more problematic. The heart of the matter was that while we wanted something small and intimate, our parents had other ideas. We were forced to compromise in the end and given that we'd managed to get our own way about everything else, we couldn't really complain.

'What do we do about Zoe?' Olivia sighed as we addressed the envelopes for the invitations.

I paused in the middle of licking the one for my aunt and uncle.

'It's been a few years, surely it won't be a problem now?'

She pulled the envelope out of my hands, sealed it and slapped it onto the 'to be posted' pile.

'I don't want our wedding to be one of those where it ends in a punch-up,' she said. 'Mum and Lisa can barely tolerate each other. Can you imagine the chaos it will cause to throw another of Dad's conquests into the mix?'

I shrugged rather helplessly.

'Do you want to not invite her?'

'No, she's our friend. I just... is it too much to hope they'll all behave?'

'Surely you don't think Zoe would –'

'Oh of course not! Don't be silly. I know she's happy with Dean, I don't want her to be upset or for it to be awkward, that's all.'

I moved to sit next to her and put my arm around her shoulders.

'Look, if I know Zoe she'll stay well clear of your dad and I'm willing to bet he'll pretend nothing happened. They won't be sat anywhere near each other at the reception and even if they do bump into each other in the evening, neither of them will want to do anything to spoil our day. It'll be fine, trust me.'

I could see she wasn't wholly convinced, but unless we didn't invite one of them, there wasn't a lot we could do except hope. In the end, the lead up to the day was so busy we had no time spare to worry about errant guests. There were last minute meetings with the florist, a final fitting of Olivia's dress, morning suits to collect and a hurried visit to the Castle to finalise the details of the day. It was only on the evening before that we were finally able to relax. Everyone who had already arrived or lived locally, gathered together for a meal. I sat at one end of the extended table, leaning into the back of my chair and watching with pleasure as friends and family alike chatted happily.

'Nervous?' Eoin asked, taking in a large mouthful of his pint.

I shook my head. 'Not in the least. As long as she turns up I don't care about anything else.'

'Hey Liv!' he shouted down the table. 'You planning to do a bunk tonight?'

She rolled her eyes at him and turned back to her conversation with Sophie and Zoe.

'You aren't really worried about her not turning up, are you?' he asked, serious for a moment.

'No. It's just one of those things you're meant to worry about, isn't it?'

'God I hope I'm this calm when my turn comes,' he said. 'If I'm not, I'll be relying on you to talk me down.'

I looked at him for a moment as he stared at his pint.

'Mate, you and Sophie... are you...?'

He looked up and a guilty expression flashed across his face.

'Shit. I wasn't meant to say anything tonight.'

'Whyever not?'

'You're getting married tomorrow. We didn't want to steal your thunder.'

I clapped him on the shoulder and shook his hand.

'Well, we appreciate the thought, but congratulations all the same.'

'Thanks. You'll be my best man, won't you?'

I laughed at the worry on his face. 'Of course. I'd be honoured. So, when are you going to tell everyone?'

'We've told our parents already, but we were planning to invite you guys round for dinner when you get back from your honeymoon and tell you then.'

'Well, as you let the cat out of the bag early, you can feed us anyway and tell us what your plans are instead!'

He grinned and I sat back in my chair and contemplated the scene again. Everyone in the room had come together – travelling miles in many cases – to wish us well on our wedding day. My parents were sitting with Olivia's and miraculously they all looked happy. Laura, much to Olivia's surprise and delight, had stuck to her programme of getting clean and I was beginning to realise what Adam must have seen in her when she was younger, before all her problems started. Various friends and relations were scattered throughout the bar and it was all for us. It felt a little overwhelming and for the first time I became aware of the nerves lurking in the wings. They were ready to burst onto the stage the minute I allowed them to, but I had no intention of giving them the spotlight. There was no need for them: everything was going to be fine. Olivia and I were going to stand in front of the registrar and say our vows and then live happily ever after. I caught her eye and she smiled, sending my nerves back to their dressing room to sulk.

The day itself passed by in something of a blur. I'd spent the previous night in Eoin and Sophie's spare room and woke to the smell of coffee wafting up the stairs. Sophie handed me a Costa takeaway cup the minute my foot hit the bottom step.

'I've done a coffee run for everyone, there's a chocolate twist on the table in the kitchen,' she said, waving the hand that wasn't clutching the cardboard cup holder and paper bags. 'Eat it before you put your suit on please. Speaking of your suits, they're both hanging up in the dining room. The buttonholes are in the fridge, the rings are in Eoin's trouser pocket, your mum and dad are coming at ten thirty to collect your bag for tonight and the wedding car is due at eleven. *Don't* be late.'

With that, she kissed me on the cheek, whispered, 'See you soon' and flew out of the door. A moment later I heard the purr of her car engine as she set off to join Olivia at our house. I just hoped my fiancée was ready for the whirlwind who was about to descend on her. Eoin emerged from the kitchen, grinned and shoved the pastry into my hand.

'If you don't eat it, it will be me that gets an earful.'

In a matter of minutes all that was left were the dregs of the coffee and the flaky bits of pastry that clung to my fingers. Eoin followed it up with a mug of tea and a doorstop of a bacon sandwich.

'God knows what time we'll end up sitting down to eat,' he said, 'And if you keel over in the middle of the ceremony my life won't be worth squat!'

Despite our best efforts, when the blue and cream vintage limousine pulled onto the drive – Olivia was travelling in the matching 1920s Rolls Royce – we were still attempting to tie our cravats. We were on our third attempt when the chauffeur stepped in to assist us.

'You're not the first men I've had to help with these,' she

assured us, laughing at the dismay on our faces. 'No-one will be able to see the crumpled bit, don't worry!'

At last, we were ready to go.

'Rings?'

Eoin patted his pocket and grinned.

'When you get in the car, make sure you tuck your coat tails under you so they don't crease,' the chauffeur reminded us.

Olivia didn't keep me waiting too long after the official start time of the ceremony, a fact for which I was very grateful. My first glimpse of her made my breath catch in my throat. Her dress was medieval in style with wide sleeves and a low waist. The cream satin seemed almost alive, shifting and changing with each step she took towards me. It wasn't particularly traditional or fashionable, but it was one hundred percent Olivia. It was the perfect choice for her and she looked more beautiful than ever. I barely registered Sophie behind her, other than to see that her ice blue dress matched almost perfectly with our cravats and the swirled pattern on our waistcoats.

I was so entranced by the picture Olivia presented that I can only assume I managed to repeat the vows without stumbling and got her name right. When the registrar gave me permission to kiss the bride, all I could think was, *She's not 'the bride', she's my wife.* My Olivia. My wife.

By some standards the reception was a very sedate affair. The meeting we had feared between Zoe and Olivia's dad passed without incident, no one got drunk enough to embarrass themselves, there were no punch-ups and the day ended as pleasantly as it had begun. Eventually, guests began to leave and those who were staying overnight at the venue, drifted off to bed. Having said goodnight to the last few stragglers, Olivia and I took a stroll through the grounds on the way to our room.

'Well Mrs Blythe, have you had a nice day?'

'It's been lovely. But not as lovely as hearing that name and knowing it's mine.'

'It doesn't seem quite real yet, does it? Mr and Mrs Blythe. It sounds like it's Mum and Dad we're talking about.'

'Or Anne and Gilbert.'

I laughed at the reference to one of her favourite books, as she continued.

'Mind you, if we're as happy as either couple in twenty years' time I'll be satisfied,' she said.

'Have I told you how beautiful you look?'

'Only the odd ninety-nine times.'

'Let's make it a round hundred then. You look beautiful.'

I stopped and pulled her close for a kiss.

The next afternoon we boarded our flight for New York. Of all the decisions we'd made about the wedding, our honeymoon destination had caused the most debate. Initially we'd toyed with the idea of returning to Vienna, but even the locals don't stay in Vienna in the summer months if they don't have to. Beyond that, we'd had vastly differing ideas about where to go. Olivia had suggested Egypt – a short stay in Cairo and then a romantic cruise down the Nile. That was too long to spend in close proximity to other people for me. My contribution to the discussion had been a trip to Iceland or Norway. I'd even been prepared to do two or three days on a river cruise to the fjords as part of it, but they were deemed unromantic locations. In the end, we'd compromised on a ten day trip to America with five days in New York and five in Washington. The events of the previous September had made it something of a challenge to book and consequently the only flight we were able to fit into the timeframe we had available were ones that left the day after the wedding. It wasn't ideal but we couldn't face the thought of starting again with no destination we could agree on.

We embarked on the lengthy flight armed with tips to avoid jetlag and numerous recommendations for places to eat and 'must-see' tourist spots. We had a whirlwind trip: a baseball game, a Broadway show, the Statue of Liberty, the Empire State Building and a rather expensive trip to Tiffany's. Washington followed with its monuments and museums and then, it was over. Time to come home and resume normal life. Olivia had to get back to work and I was due to start my new job the following week, having sat my final exam just before the wedding. The honeymoon had been almost perfect, but I think by the time we boarded the plane to return to England, we felt ready to get back to Exeter and start our married life. Unlike when we had flown home from Vienna, there was no sense of stepping back. We'd already taken the biggest leap forward and we were keen to see what the future held for us.

In fact, the future was cloaked in the mundane. Not boring so much as simply being the same as that of any other newly married couple. There was no great change in our relationship because we'd exchanged rings. Life continued just as it had previously, punctuated only by small excitements like Olivia's new passport – this one in her married name – arriving. Over the next few years Olivia got her promotion to Senior Librarian and I built up a more regular stream of work through clients with repeated assignments. Although we were saving for a house deposit we managed to still make the most of our time together.

'Best to get some travelling in before you have kids,' Mum told us. 'Once they arrive, going abroad is twice the expense and ten times the hassle.'

The first Christmas after we got married we returned to Vienna for a few days to see old friends and to experience again the beauty and festivity of the Christmas markets. Rathausplatz was the most spectacular by virtue of being the one most oriented to tourists. Schönbrunn was the prettiest, taking place as it did in the grounds of the palace: the beautiful butter coloured building provided a picturesque backdrop which formed a perfect contrast to the bright gaudiness of the stalls. But it was the little Spittelberg market that was our favourite. Nestled away in the narrow cobbled streets, the stalls there held more traditional Austrian wares including a pretty pair of glass earrings I secretly purchased, intending to give them to Olivia on Christmas morning. With cheeks reddened by Glühwein we revisited our old haunts and reminisced our way around the city.

Eoin and Sophie got married almost a year after we did – an intimate service with just close family and friends, followed by a party of epic proportions that went on well into the early hours of the next morning. Even Eoin and Sophie admitted to not being entirely sure who half the guests were, only that they might be vaguely related to Eoin's Irish grandfather on his mother's side.

We went on a boating holiday on the Thames with them not long after the wedding. It was a far cry from their honeymoon in Antigua, but we all agreed life on the river held a certain charm of its own.

'There is nothing - absolutely nothing - half so much worth doing as simply messing about in boats,' said Olivia with a smile, as she leant against the rail that surrounded the rear deck.

'Wind In The Willows?' I asked, handing her a drink.

She nodded, pleased. 'Not bad for someone who's never read it.'

I kissed her cheek. 'No, but I do know it's your favourite book and it's set on a river.'

'I love you.'

'I know,' I replied with a grin and we both laughed.

Mum and Dad took us to France with them and we explored the chateaux of the Loire Valley. Olivia was filled with wonder – so she told me – at the sight of the buildings she'd read so much about the history of. It was with much reluctance that she returned to our gîte each evening, only to get excited again when she learnt of our destination the following day. We even managed to squeeze in a visit to Paris for our anniversary. My parents dropped us off on their way home, leaving us to follow a few days later on the train. Dinner at the top of the Eiffel Tower and a moonlit cruise on the Seine seemed the perfect way to celebrate. There was something about Paris by night that spoke to the soul and it wasn't hard to see why it was dubbed the romantic capital of the world. Even there though Olivia continued to confound my expectations, declaring the dinner had been lovely, but her favourite part of the three days had been our evening at the Moulin Rouge.

The most exotic of our trips abroad however was to Macchu Picchu. We talked about it for a long time prior to booking it as it made a sizeable dent in our savings account, but it was somewhere we both really wanted to see – a rarity in itself – so we booked it before we could talk ourselves out of it. We did however spend the next month feeling terribly guilty and irresponsible for putting a holiday ahead of our first house. To make ourselves feel better we promised each other that this would be our last holiday abroad until we'd paid all the money back. In spite of our feelings of guilt and the stress of almost missing our outward flight – a closed lane on the M5 due to an oil spill and an accident near Heathrow – once we were in the air and heading south, we felt nothing but anticipation. It was by far the biggest trip we'd done and the thought of all the history waiting for us at the other end of our flight delighted us.

I'd expected to be blown away by the sight of the ancient Incan city, but I fell in love with the area almost as soon as we arrived. The train snaked through the Urubamba Valley, the electric blue livery complementing the azure of the sky and vivid green of the Andean mountains that rose on either side of us. The river flowed alongside the tracks and I couldn't help wondering whether the people of Machu Picchu had navigated around the rocks and stones within it. I had scant knowledge of the ancient civilisation beyond what little I'd read in preparation for our trip and I determined that when we returned, I would ask Olivia to scour the library shelves at work for anything that would give me the information I was lacking.

The bus that ferried us from the hotel to the site entrance was old-fashioned but looked serviceable. As the road narrowed however, I prayed the brakes had been regularly overhauled. A sheer drop, only populated by the odd plant or sapling, fell away to one side of it and I couldn't see the edge of the road from my seat by the window. Olivia's nails dug into the palm of my hand as she opened her eyes just long enough to take in the view. The climb from the point of admission was steep and in places I had to haul Olivia onto the next step, so it wasn't hard to understand how it had managed to remain hidden until the early years of the twentieth century.

Our arrival at the city itself left me speechless. I'd thought the historic buildings in London, Vienna and Paris were impressive, but nothing I'd seen in the past could compare to the ruins before me. The sun rose behind them, bathing the whole site in a warm rosy glow. The lush terraces, designed to prevent the buildings sliding down the mountainside, had an aesthetic quality of their own as well as fulfilling their more practical purpose. It wasn't difficult to picture the feather bedecked priest raising his hands to the sky to welcome the sun god, whom I assumed the Incans – as with other ancient civilisations – worshipped and I knew from the rapturous expression on my wife's face, a similar vision was presenting itself to her.

'Quite something, isn't it?' I whispered.

Olivia nodded and slipped her hand into mine. In companionable silence we watched the sun climb higher in the sky.

'I think we should have a baby,' she said as we returned to the minibus.

'Right now?' I laughed, then stopped when she looked hurt.

'I'm being serious. When we get home I think we should start trying for a baby.'

'What's the hurry? Bored of my company already?'

She smiled, but her eyes remained serious.

'Not at all. It's just that we'll have been married two years this summer and I want to have all our children before I'm thirty.'

'All our children?' I repeated, slightly alarmed. 'How many do you plan on having?'

'Oh at least three,' she said lightly.

I swallowed, the sudden dryness in my throat having nothing to do with the heat of the day.

'Three?' I managed eventually.

'We're both only children, Tom. Don't tell me you were never lonely as a kid. I don't want that for our children.'

I gave her a fierce hug.

'Three it is then. I'd better see if I can get some more clients to pay for them!'

When Olivia set her mind to something, she allowed nothing to get in her way and it should have been less of a surprise than it was when she fell pregnant within a few months of our return from Peru. It seemed even nature itself could not withstand her determination.

'We've got some news for you,' she said one evening, as Eoin and Sophie relaxed on our sofa after dinner. 'How do you two feel about being godparents?'

In her excitement about sharing our news, I knew Olivia had missed the worried look Eoin directed at Sophie.

'Are you pregnant?' he asked, moving to hug Olivia when she nodded. 'Congratulations. That's wonderful news, isn't it, Soph?'

Sophie looked miserable, but she forced her face into a smile.

'Of course, wonderful news,' she echoed. 'And we'd be honoured to be godparents.'

Then she burst into tears.

Immediately, Olivia dropped to her knees at Sophie's side, gathering her close. I looked to Eoin for an explanation as Sophie was incapable of further speech beyond gasping out apologies for her poor reaction to our news.

'We've been trying for a baby since before the wedding,' Eoin said. 'The women in Sophie's family have all had trouble conceiving and we knew it might take some time, but it's starting to look like it may not happen for us at all.'

'I imagined it would have happened by the time you guys got around to starting a family and that we'd be able to go through it all together,' Sophie sniffed, having regained control over her emotions. 'I'm so sorry, Liv. I didn't mean to be miserable – I'm really pleased for you, honest I am. It was just a bit of a shock, that's all.'

We reassured her she hadn't cast a shadow over the happy occasion but changed the subject anyway and spoke of other things.

'Promise me you'll still talk to me about it all,' Sophie said as they were leaving. 'Even if I can't do it myself, I want to support you while you go through it. Don't shy away from the subject with me, will you? I won't get upset again; I promise.'

We gave our word that we wouldn't and closed the door behind them. Olivia put her arms around my waist and laid her head on my chest.

'We're so lucky, aren't we?'

I murmured my agreement and held her closer.

Pregnancy was not easy for Olivia and it seemed to me as though she spent the first three months locked in the bathroom. She only emerged to drink such quantities of ginger tea and eat so many packets of ginger biscuits that she swore she never wanted to see anything containing ginger ever again.

The first scan however, not only reassured us that baby Blythe was growing well, but also marked the end of the incessant sickness. Olivia finally developed a small bump - which she took great delight in caressing - and was able to keep more food inside her. The best news, however, came when we called in to show the scan picture to our friends.

'Are you sure?' Olivia asked, gripping Sophie's hands so tightly they turned white.

Sophie nodded, her whole face glowing with happiness.

I wrung Eoin's hand and hugged Sophie.

'How long?' I asked.

'It's early days, but we couldn't wait to tell you. Eight weeks or so, we think. It might even be the reason I was so over-emotional the night you told us you were expecting. Ironic, isn't it?'

Olivia laughed and hugged her again. 'Delightfully!'

'How've you been so far?' I asked, conscious of how Olivia had suffered in the early months.

'Fantastic! I've had none of the sickness yet,' she said, casting an apologetic glance at Olivia, who stuck her tongue out. 'I feel really well. It's partly just the relief I think.'

Over the next few months Olivia seemed to expand at an ever increasing rate, although I would never have told her so. Our second scan revealed we were about to become parents to a little boy and many of our evenings were taken up with discussing potential names while Olivia shifted restlessly on the sofa, attempting to find a position in which she could be comfortable.

I'd been prepared for bizarre cravings, but towards the end of the second trimester the only ones she'd exhibited so far were for oranges and cheese on toast, which wasn't unusual for her, even pre-pregnancy. What I hadn't anticipated were the wild mood swings in the third trimester. One moment she'd be wildly excited about becoming a family of three, the next she was panicking about her expanding waistline and questioning whether she'd ever fit into normal clothes again. Then, in a heartbeat, she'd be a puddle of tears, convinced she was going to be the worst mother in the world and our son was going to hate her. On those occasions, I could only try to reassure her she was worrying unnecessarily and hope that it was just the hormones playing havoc with her head.

It was in the early hours of a cold January morning that a sharp elbow in my ribs woke me with a start.

'Get up.'

Olivia sounded urgent and I shook my head, trying to clear the last vestiges of sleep from my brain. Again, the elbow made contact with my ribs.

'We need to go. Help me get dressed.'

I jumped up and ran round to her side of the bed, grabbing a jumper and jabbing it over her head.

'There's no need to panic,' she said, wincing as I stuck my thumb in her eye for the second time. 'We've got plenty of time.'

I had a vague feeling of unease as I threw her bag onto the back seat of the car and ran back inside to help her down the driveway. What had I forgotten? As soon as I started the car, I knew. The petrol light had come on the evening before on my way home from the supermarket. I'd been in too much of a hurry to get Olivia's cheese home to stop off at the garage, knowing I had enough to get me home and back to the petrol station the next day. The RD&E was a bit further though. I glanced at Olivia as she breathed through another contraction. If I went to get petrol now she was going to kill me, having reminded me repeatedly of the importance of keeping the tank full once we got past Christmas. On the other hand, if I didn't stop and we ran out I risked having to deliver our son on my own on the back seat of the car. On balance, I decided the first option was less risky – she'd probably forgive me and it would be something we could laugh at in the future… as long as we made it to the hospital in time.

I sprinted across the forecourt and thrust my card at the startled attendant in the shop, then hurried back to the car and pulled back out onto the road, trying to avoid looking at my wife.

'What's this?' she asked, holding up the Mars Bar I'd dropped in her lap.

'An apology.' Silence. 'What?' I said, not needing to turn my head to feel the heat of her glare. 'You love Mars Bars!'

'Tom,' she hissed. 'I'm in labour. I'm about to push a baby out into the world. I don't want a bloody Mars Bar!'

The chocolate bounced off the side of my head.

At the hospital, we were taken straight to the delivery room where, a mere three hours later, Theo Joseph Blythe entered the world, red-faced but silent. I just had time to reassure Olivia his silence was not a sign of anything being wrong before the midwife put him in my arms and I laid him on Olivia's chest.

Theo opened his eyes and looked at us for the first time. Deep blue eyes regarded us steadily as we gazed anxiously down at him. I blinked furiously as his little face blurred and swam.

'I'm so proud of you,' I told Olivia, then touched my finger to the tip of Theo's nose, as though to assure myself he was really here. Immediately he let out a cry of rage.

'Someone wants his breakfast,' the midwife said. 'Do you need some help or can you manage?'

I moved out of the way while she assisted Olivia in getting Theo into the right position, drinking in the sight of my wife and my son. My son. I could scarcely believe he existed. I was a father. I felt the responsibility settle over me and I knew that no matter how much I loved Olivia, nothing else could touch what I felt for the tiny human being in her arms.

Looking at him as he fed, I wondered how my parents had been able to let me go off to university without begging me to stay at home. I couldn't ever imagine myself waving Theo off – how had they borne it? How would I when my time came?

'Stop inventing trouble and come and give your son a cuddle while I have a shower,' Olivia said gently. 'And don't look so grim or you'll scare him!'

I took Theo and sat down in the chair while Olivia shuffled into the adjoining bathroom.

'Hello little one,' I said, as he gripped my smallest finger. 'Welcome to the world. Mummy and Daddy love you very much already and we'll always keep you safe, I promise.'

He blinked at me in a soporific milk-induced hypnosis, as though he understood the solemnity of my words and accepted the truth of them. Each blink was slower than the last until his eyes fell shut and remained so, the long lashes sweeping over the pudgy cheeks. He was warm and he fitted so snugly into the crook of my arm that in that moment I felt I would be content to sit there for the rest of the day just watching him sleep.

In the days that followed, there was a stream of visitors to the house. Each visit left Olivia exhausted, but most came with useful gifts and good intentions. There were the usual sleepsuits and cute outfits, but the most welcome ones were the lasagnes and casseroles that meant we didn't have to think about what to cook for dinner that night. Eoin and Sophie came to see their godson and took over our kitchen, cooking huge batches of meals which they portioned up and froze for us. My parents came down for a few days but stayed in a hotel and Mum cleaned the house from top to bottom so it was one less thing for us to worry about.

My dad was completely entranced by Theo and Mum confided that although he wouldn't say anything, he'd been moved to tears that we'd given his name to Theo as his middle one. He held his grandson for hours at a time, ignoring our entreaties to put him down while he slept.

'You prefer Grandad's arms, don't you, Theo? They're much more comfortable than the silly old Moses basket.'

Mum just laughed at him.

'Who are you and what have you done with my husband?' she said, on finding him pacing up and down the hallway trying to get Theo to sleep. 'You were always the one who insisted Tom had to sleep in his cot and nowhere else. 'Let him cry it out' you said and here you are, the first on your feet if your grandson so much as whimpers.'

Dad smirked.

'We're grandparents. Isn't it our job to spoil him and then give him back to his mum and dad?'

Olivia rolled her eyes and bit her lip to hide her smile.

Her parents came to visit separately and made all the appropriate comments about Theo. Laura was keen to hold him, but he roared every time she picked him up and Adam, although he insisted he wanted a cuddle, was at a loss what to do with him. I took pity on him in the end and made him sit down while I placed Theo very carefully into his arms. When I withdrew, the expression on his face surprised me.

'My little girl's a mother,' he whispered. 'I can't quite believe it.'

He looked across the room to where Olivia sat, her feet curled up at her side.

'I'm so proud of you, you know,' he said, the usual bluster absent from his voice. 'Your mum and I did our best to screw you up between us but look at you now. You're going to be an amazing mother – Theo doesn't know how lucky he is yet, but he will.'

Olivia flushed. She said nothing, but a smile spread across her face and I knew how much it meant to her to finally have her father's unqualified approval. He'd been proud at her graduation, but this was different. It had taken becoming a grandparent to make him fully aware of what I'd known the first time I laid eyes on her – his daughter was an amazing human being.

When Olivia first fell pregnant we'd discussed our child-care options and decided that as my job was the more flexible of the two, I would start working from home and fit work in around Theo's naps. When Olivia finished work she would take over with Theo and I would have the time to get on with whatever I'd not got done during the day. Only if that didn't work would we look at other settings, as we were keen to keep Theo at home if we could manage it.

Consequently, after six months Olivia resumed her job at the university and I found out precisely how difficult it was to make accurate translations while simultaneously trying to stop an inquisitive baby chewing the laptop cable, pulling things on top of him and refusing to nap at the times Mummy said he had to. In short, it was a nightmare, but as we settled into a routine I found I was able to get more work done during the day.

In the summer we spent a week with my parents and they came down to us for another one. We'd bought our first house, having finally saved enough to top up the money Olivia's grandmother had left her to be used as a deposit, but it needed some work doing to it. Although I'd had a go at doing it myself, eventually I'd been forced to swallow my pride and ask Dad if he could come and sort out the mess I'd made. He and Mum had jumped at the chance to spend more time with Theo and it was lovely to hear him giggling with Mum while Dad hammered and drilled in the spare bedroom. I was concerned that Dad was overdoing it, but he waved away my concern.

'I'm fit as a fiddle, Tom. Just not used to doing this much DIY anymore. I'm finished now, so a couple of days with Theo and I'll be right as rain. You don't need to worry your mum with it.'

He was right of course and by the time they got in the car to drive home he was his usual unflappable self, waving wildly out of the car window as they pulled off the drive. Two months later, Olivia had just come down from putting Theo to bed when the phone rang.

'Tom? It's Mum.'

Her voice sounded odd, as though she was talking through a blanket.

'I'm so sorry, love. It's your dad.'

Her voice broke.

'He's dead.'

GRACE

'Tom, I'm so sorry. I don't know what I was thinking – well, clearly I wasn't thinking, was I...'

The message Grace had left on my voicemail was about five minutes long, but the essence of it was very simple. She was sorry about what had happened. It was all her fault. Please could we continue dancing together. The trouble was it wasn't that simple. For a start, it wasn't all her fault. There had been two of us in that kiss. She might have initiated it, but I had been an equal and willing participant and what was more I'd thoroughly enjoyed the experience. Despite being ashamed of my lack of self-control and in spite of the guilt that kept me awake at night, I couldn't bring myself to wholly regret our kiss. She at least, had the excuse of having drunk most of a bottle of champagne. I had no such mitigation.

Not for the first time, I cursed whichever god or quirk of nature had decreed that I would instinctively identify the women I was to fall in love with on first meeting them. I wanted to be like normal people who got to know someone first and then fell in love gradually. It was all very well knowing you wanted to be with someone, but if they, or you, were not ready for that kind of commitment, it did make life difficult. Grace's life had been hard enough in recent years and it wasn't fair for me to string her along. The truth of it was, I still loved my wife and I couldn't see that fact changing any time soon. The kiss had, I suppose, been inevitable while I continued to pretend I was almost ready to move on with my life. In some ways it had done me a favour by showing me that Olivia still had first place in my heart. Talking it through with her had helped, but I knew it was a decision I needed to make on my own. It hadn't been easy, but I'd done it. I decided I would continue dancing with Grace, but I would make it clear there could be nothing more than friendship between us. I needed to take some time for myself to sort out my priorities and I couldn't do that while stringing Grace along. If I was going to let Olivia go, I had to do it in my own time. It had to be when I was ready, not because I'd met someone else. To do that would make a mockery of the decade and a half we'd been together. I also had the children to consider. How might they react to being told I was replacing their mother? I'd read enough on the subject to know that was a likely reaction and I definitely wasn't ready for that conversation.

The next time Grace rang, I answered the call and agreed to meet her for coffee.

'Before you say anything,' I said, as we sat down with our drinks, 'You need to hear me out first. We share the blame for what happened – insofar as there is any blame to be apportioned – but ultimately it was only a kiss. Nevertheless, it did make me realise I'm not ready to make changes in my life at the moment. At the risk of sounding arrogant, I know you were perhaps hoping for more, but I'm not ready to leave Olivia behind just yet and I think deep down you know that. There's so much more I want to say to you, but I can't. It wouldn't be fair on anyone.'

'Are you telling me there's no hope for us, ever?' Grace asked quietly.

'I'm telling you it's not worth your waiting to find out.'

She nodded and laid her hand over mine. 'I would have waited you know.'

'I do and that's precisely why you mustn't. You deserve someone who's completely yours.'

'What about the dancing? Will you give that up as well?'

'Not unless you don't want to dance with me anymore.'

Her head shot up and some of the animation returned to her face. 'Do you mean that? Really?'

I nodded.

'Oh, I'm so glad. I don't want you to disappear from my life completely.'

It was only a month later that Grace confessed she'd agreed to go on a date with someone she knew through work.

'He's been asking me out for ages,' she said, 'But he's a bit intense so I always said no, but I've agreed to go for a drink with him. Can I use you to be my excuse to leave if it gets weird?'

'Of course,' I said, ignoring the knife twist of jealousy in my stomach. 'Just text if you need me to call with an emergency.'

The text I was half-hoping for never came and when we met at the Tower the following weekend, I forced myself to ask how it had gone.

'Oh, it was fine,' she said. 'He's nice enough I guess. He's very driven and ambitious and he's an excellent journalist. He's wasted on a local paper really – he wants one of the nationals and he thinks he's got a shot with The Telegraph. Apparently, someone he knows works for them and reckons there's a job coming up soon.'

'So not a long-term prospect then?'

She shrugged.

'It's a bit early to be thinking about that – we've only been on a couple of dates, but it wouldn't necessarily be a problem. There'd be nothing to stop me moving down to London as well if I wanted to. I've no real ties here. I mean, my family are all local, but I could always visit.'

'I suppose so,' I said. 'Do you want to move to London though?'

'It's not something I've ever considered before, but I wouldn't be completely against the idea.'

'It's very different to life up here,' I told her. 'Everything is done at a much faster pace and the people aren't as friendly.'

'You're from down that way, aren't you? You're not exactly hostile.'

'It's not hostility, people just don't talk as freely down there. Mum knows more about our neighbours here after less than a decade than she did about our old neighbours after twice that time living next door to them. You might find it a culture shock, that's all I'm saying.'

I didn't inquire after any further dates – it was none of my business and I didn't want to pry. I had no choice in the matter when it came to Grace's birthday though. It fell on a Sunday, so rather than cancel our plans, she simply invited Danny and her brother to join us in the Tower.

They were already seated in the ballroom when I arrived and my first impression of Danny was not positive. He was good-looking – even as a man I could recognise that – but it was a kind of cruel handsomeness. He reminded me of a boy I went to school with who left a string of broken hearts behind him. It wasn't that he set out with the intention of hurting anyone, but he was so single-minded about what (or who) he wanted that he simply trampled over anyone who got in the way. They were almost accidental victims of his ambition – their hurt was uncalculated, but the wounds no lesser because of it. I reasoned with myself that just because Danny happened to physically resemble Alex Copeland, it didn't mean he was going to break Grace's heart. I accepted my own reasoning but it didn't make me warm to him any better.

'So, what got you into all this dancing then, Tommo?'

His tone was friendly and he was trying to show an overt interest in Grace's friends, but I'd met his type before; there was always a longer game. I resisted the urge to tell him my name was and had always been, Tom. Instead, I gritted my teeth and forced a smile.

'Actually, I first learnt with my wife, but it was Grace who persuaded me to take it up again and I'm very grateful she did.'

I directed a more genuine smile in her direction.

'Oh. Sorry. Yes, I remember Grace saying that now. What makes you do it though? It's a bit poncey, isn't it? No offence. Mate, but I mean, all the sequins and fake tan.' He shuddered. 'No, it's not for me.'

Grace squirmed in her chair and I gave her what I hoped was a reassuring glance.

'But you only wear them for competitions,' I said, standing up and twirling on the spot, showing off my plain trousers, shirt and tie. 'See? Not a sequin in sight. I left my sparkly jumpsuit at home today.' I leant forward and whispered loudly enough for Grace and Ashley to also hear. 'And I'm only wearing fake tan on the bits you can't see.'

There was a snort from Ashley, who knew my opinions on fake tan, which he quickly covered by finishing his drink, as his sister glared at him, albeit with her eyes dancing with suppressed amusement.

'I'm not saying there's anything wrong with it,' Danny said, trying to recover some ground, 'It's just not very manly, is it, all that twirling around? I know it's not very PC to say it, but dancing's for girls really.'

'Actually, I think you'll find male ballet dancers are significantly stronger and fitter than their footballing counterparts,' I smiled to show I wasn't being defensive. 'And Strictly has prompted a real resurgence in ballroom dancing. It's only relatively recently that dancing's been seen as a female domain. Back in the thirties and forties most self-respecting men could get around a dancefloor. In the fifties, Gene Kelly showed you could be the absolute epitome of masculinity and still be a sublime dancer. There was nothing feeble or feminine about him. If you look at the example of *Billy Elliot*, it's male insecurities that cause them to condemn what they can't do themselves as being somehow 'not masculine'. I'm not insecure about myself, so it doesn't worry me if other people judge.'

I stopped, unsure whether to push it further or not. Danny was Grace's boyfriend after all and I didn't want to upset her on her birthday, even if he was a complete tool.

'What do you think, Ash?' I said, deflecting attention to him. 'You're a dancer.'

'Oh, I agree,' he said. 'You're definitely all man.' He grinned at me but fell silent again.

I was prepared to let it rest there, but Danny wasn't done, seemingly determined to make his views on the subject even clearer. I wondered if he realised he wasn't doing himself any favours with Grace, or whether he genuinely expected her to simperingly agree with his clearly superior opinions.

'And what about the sex?'

'Well, it's usually frowned on to do it on the ballroom floor,' I said.

He glared at me. 'I meant all those people running off with their dancing partners. It doesn't make for a stable relationship if your girlfriend's dancing with another bloke, does it?'

I felt myself go pale at his insinuation and a chill ran through me. Was he going to insist Grace stopped dancing with me? Out of the corner of my eye, I saw Ashley sit straighter in his chair at the same moment as Grace's arm shot out to keep him in it. Danny was nothing like Alex

Copeland. Underneath all the bluster he was afraid. He felt threatened by me. I shared something with Grace that he never could and for some reason that worried him.

'Well, it's a bit like if you're with someone who goes all over the country for work. Someone like a journalist, I guess. It's only an issue if you don't trust your partner. And if you don't trust them, perhaps you should be questioning why you're together at all. If Grace truly loved someone, I doubt she'd give them up easily and certainly not for the sake of a short-lived fling.'

'Anyone want another drink?' Ashley said, getting to his feet. 'It's my round. Tom, can you give me a hand carrying them?'

I followed him to the bar.

'I don't like him,' he said as we waited to be served. 'I don't know what it is, but I don't trust him. It's like he calculates the worth of everyone – I don't mean financially; Grace hasn't got enough money for that – it's people's value to him I mean. How can they help him? How will they enhance his life?'

'Well don't we all do that to some extent? Why would you be friends with someone if they brought nothing to the relationship? You don't think you're being overprotective, do you? I understand why,' I said hastily, holding my hands up, 'And I don't blame you, but unless you know something specific about him, I'd leave it to Grace. You don't know anything, do you?' I was suddenly anxious and I shot a nervous glance back at the table.

'You'd love it if I did, wouldn't you?'

'Of course not,' I said too quickly. 'I want Grace to be with someone who makes her happy.'

'Well, that's not him,' Ashley said. 'Grace doesn't love him. I'm not even sure she particularly likes him, but she said she had to make an effort to meet someone so it might as well be the person who kept asking her out. Be honest Tom, you want Grace to be happy with you.'

I looked at him sharply.

'That's not going to happen. I've told her that.'

'I know,' he said, 'And I know all about Olivia and the kids. Don't worry, she didn't betray any confidences, but I know the situation you're in and I'll be honest, I think it's ridiculous. I understand wanting to protect your children, but if you wait until they're old enough to fully understand, you'll have wasted half your life. Grace is head over heels in love with you and it's obvious to anyone with a pair of eyes that you're in love with her. Why do you think Danny boy's been making such a prat of himself? He's showing off for her, trying to show how much better than you he is.'

This little speech rather took me by surprise. Knowing how Ash felt about Grace I'd have been less surprised if he'd told me to get out of her life completely and I told him so.

'Look, I agree the situation's not ideal, but you're a decent bloke and I know my sister and she'd rather have half your heart than the whole of someone else's. It's not necessarily what I'd choose for her, but you love who you love and no amount of wishing's going to change that.'

He shrugged and I didn't reply. I knew Grace had been attracted to me, but I didn't know she felt as deeply about me as I did about her. It didn't change how I felt about Olivia, but there was a world of difference – in my head – between indulging in a purely physical relationship and involving myself in something that potentially had a long term future. I'd thought that in letting Grace go I was doing her a favour, but if she was anything like as miserable as I'd been these past few weeks, I was only hurting her more. Suddenly I couldn't bear to pretend anymore and I made my excuses and left soon after.

'Tom, is everything all right?' Grace hurried after me and caught me by the arm.

I tried to pretend but felt the weight of my thoughts bearing down on me. 'No, not really. I'm not happy, Grace. I haven't been for a long time and I don't know what to do about it. It's not the depression – at least not wholly, the tablets are helping with that – it's this, this mess I've created.'

'Tom, you know I...' she trailed off and glanced uneasily back to where Danny and Ash sat watching us carefully.

'I'll be fine, Grace, honestly. Enjoy the rest of your birthday. I'll see you for our lesson next week, but then I'll have to miss a few as the kids have things on at school and I need to be there.'

'Oh.' Her face fell, but she immediately forced herself to smile. 'OK. Well text me the next date you can do and I'll phone Liz and sort it out before the lesson.'

'I will.'

I kissed her cheek and left the warmth of the ballroom behind me, heading out into the cold autumnal day. It was drizzling heavily and I reflected miserably that even the weather couldn't be bothered with positivity.

Our last lesson together was conducted with polite formality with Liz reminding us to keep practising our steps on our own until we were able to practise together again. As we were leaving, Grace caught hold of my hand.

'Just tell me one thing,' she said. 'Is this because of what Danny said?'

I stared at her. 'What? No, of course not!'

'So, you're not trying to be all noble and end our dancing partnership so I don't have to?'

I couldn't help laughing. 'For him? No.'

'You don't like him?' For some reason the idea seemed to please her.

'I don't dislike him,' I said carefully. 'I don't think he's good enough for you that's all. You deserve to be with someone to whom you're everything. With him you'd only ever be a part in his life, someone to be his support act.

You're too good to be a bit part player, you deserve the leading role.'

'What if I'd be happy with just being a part of someone's life?'

'Then it should be your choice to make, not theirs. If you're happy with him, it doesn't matter what I think.'

I kissed her cheek and hurried away before I could say something I might regret. I hadn't lied to her, I did have to attend performances and Parents' Evenings for the kids, but if I'd really wanted to, I could have rearranged our lesson. The truth was, I was beginning to doubt myself. I'd always believed it wasn't possible to love more than one person at a time. I'd laughed at the excuses of adulterers on TV shows who tried to convince their spouse they still loved them, despite an affair which suggested otherwise. Nevertheless, this was the position I now found myself in. I could no longer deny I was in love with Grace. My feelings towards Olivia were more complicated, but it was still love. The question remained though, what was I going to do about it?

'Tom, you'll never guess,' Grace sounded excited when she rang out of the blue one day. I turned down the Christmas music and paused in my present wrapping so I could hear her properly.

'I take it you've had some good news?'

'I passed my MA with a merit and I got the job!'

'Oh Grace! I'm so pleased for you. Congratulations. Which job is it?' I knew she'd applied for a couple over the last few weeks.

'It's only a junior post at *The Lancaster Guardian*, but at least it's in the right field.'

'That's really wonderful, I'm so proud of you. I tell you what – when are you free next? I'll take you out for dinner to celebrate.'

'How about tonight?'

'I'll have to check, but I'm sure it will be fine.'

It was. Mum was more than happy to babysit and for once, I beat Grace there and as she took her seat, her face lit up at the sight of the bottle of champagne chilling in its bucket.

'I believe the occasion calls for it,' I said, as the waiter poured her a glass. 'Although I was surprised you're not out celebrating with Danny.'

I'd not intended it to come out as a question, but she answered me anyway.

'You got in first. Anyway, he didn't think the job was worth celebrating. He thought I should have applied to one of the nationals or gone to the Gazette with him. He was cross I wouldn't let him speak to his boss, but I wanted to get a job on my own merits.'

'You don't want to owe him anything.'

'I knew *you'd* understand,' she said.

'Have you told him about Austin?' I asked as our meals arrived, wondering why I was trying to help Danny out of a mess of his own creation.

She shook her head. 'I told him I was divorced, but that's it.'

'Well, if you haven't told him about that, then how can you expect him to understand why it's so important to you to be independent?'

'Have I told you how annoying it is when you make me be reasonable?'

She laughed and I was struck again by how beautiful she was. For a moment I couldn't take my eyes off her.

'What?' she said, touching her mouth self-consciously. 'Have I got dinner all over my face?'

I shook my head. 'No, I was just...' I stopped. 'Actually, I was just thinking how pretty you look tonight.'

'You mean as opposed to the ugly mess I normally am?'

'That's not what I meant and you know it.'

She blushed.

The warm feeling that surrounded us persisted throughout the meal and I didn't want the evening to end.

'It's getting late,' Grace said, as she swallowed the last of her tiramisu. 'I probably ought to go. I don't want my boss to think I'm slacking now I'm leaving.'

I rang for a taxi and wrapped my coat round Grace as we shivered on the pavement waiting for it to arrive.

'I'll never understand why women don't wear sensible clothes,' I said. 'It's the beginning of December and yet you come out just wearing a thin jacket.'

'Well in my defence I wasn't expecting to be outside for any length of time,' she said. 'I didn't know the taxi was going to get stuck in traffic.'

When it finally arrived, I slid onto the back seat next to her and put my arms around her. Despite the added protection of my coat, her teeth were still chattering as she laid her head against my shoulder and closed her eyes.

'Sorry. I'm so tired,' she said, yawning.

'Don't worry, we'll drop you off first,' I said. 'You won't be long out of bed.'

'Would you like to come in for a drink before you go home?'

It was asked casually enough, but I could feel the weight of the question. It felt wrong to go into the flat when she was someone else's girlfriend, but I couldn't miss this opportunity to talk to her.

'I thought you were tired?'

'I am, but the least I can do after you took me out for dinner, is to offer you a cup of tea before sending you home.'

I smothered a laugh. 'Ah, the good old British cuppa. Fixer of all ills if you ask my mother.'

Grace unlocked her door and led me through to the kitchen.

'Do you mind if I put my pyjamas on?' she asked. 'The kettle's there,' she pointed when I shook my head.

I stared out of the kitchen window, watching her reflection when she re-entered the room in a pair of plaid pyjamas and a thick dressing gown.

'Did you change your mind about the tea?' she asked on feeling the side of the still cold kettle.

'I never wanted tea,' I told her, turning round to face her. 'I wanted to talk to you but I didn't want to do it in the restaurant.'

She was close enough to touch and I clenched my fists to stop myself pulling her towards me.

'Grace, I –'

'Shh.' She put her finger over my lips. 'Don't talk.'

She stood on tiptoe and kissed me gently. My hands slid inside her dressing gown, caressing the curves beneath her pyjamas. Time seemed to stop, but it was still too soon when she pulled away from me.

'Was that what you wanted?'

I nodded, then changed my mind and shook my head.

'Well, which is it?'

I couldn't blame her for sounding a little impatient.

'I didn't come in with the intention of kissing you, but I'm not sorry it happened. I simply wanted to talk to you about Danny.'

'About Danny?' She took another step back. 'Why him?'

'I wanted to know how serious you were about him.'

'Why?'

'Well, I was rather hoping the answer would be 'not very'.'

'Because?'

'Not to put too fine a point on it, I want you. No, that sounds wrong, I don't mean it like that. I just mean I want to be with you.'

'What about Olivia?'

'I still love her, I always will, but right now I'm standing in your kitchen asking... No... begging you to give me a chance. I'm not saying I have all the answers right now. Or that I have any answers at all for that matter. I don't know what the future holds and I don't know what I'm going to do, but what I do know is that I'm tired of fighting this. I want you in my life and not only as my dancing partner.'

She narrowed her eyes. 'How much wine did you have with dinner?'

'Grace, I've been agonising over this for months, this is not the product of a bottle of wine.'

'I'm just making sure,' she said gently. 'If I'm going to dump Danny tomorrow, I want to make sure I'm doing it for a good reason.'

'Shut up and kiss me,' I said, pulling her close again.

It was hard to leave her and go home on my own, but I couldn't stay out all night without having to offer some kind of explanation on my return. As it was, I couldn't hide it from my mum for much longer. She was already suspicious and I wasn't sure how she'd react when I eventually told her. After all, it wasn't what she'd done. After Dad there'd been no-one and I didn't think there ever would be.

As it turned out, when I told her I'd met someone else, she was more philosophical about it than I had anticipated.

'Does she make you happy?' was all she asked.

I nodded.

'Then I'll say no more about it,' she said. 'You've been unhappy for so long. You're my son and I love you, so why would I condemn something that makes you smile like that?' She patted my face. 'Tell me more when you're ready.'

After that it became easier to see Grace and I'd met her for lunch in Blackpool one day when my phone rang.

'It was the school,' I said, as I grabbed my coat. 'Elodie's had a fall in the playground and she's bumped her head quite badly so they want me to pick her up. Sorry.'

'Do you want me to come with you?'

'No, it's fine. Having accident-prone kids, you get used to doing this kind of emergency school run. I doubt it will be anything too serious, but Mum's at home if it's anything I can't handle. I'll call you later.'

I kissed her cheek and ran back to my car, driving as fast as I dared through the streets back to Poulton and the school. As I drove I did my best to ignore the little voice berating me for putting my love life above my daughter's welfare. *If you'd been at home you'd have been there by now.* I always met Grace in Blackpool or near her home in Cleveleys, because not everyone was as delightfully accepting and incurious as my mother. If we'd met in Poulton it was more likely I'd run into our neighbours and I didn't want to face the suspicious glances and the inevitable barrage of questions and knowing looks we'd get. If we were seen, someone would eventually let something slip in front of the wrong people and everything would have to come out and I wanted to do it in my own time.

Fortunately, Elodie's injuries were not serious and the bump on her forehead had begun to recede even before we got home. However, the realisation of the increasing difficulty of keeping the two halves of my life separate stayed with me. I knew sooner or later my two worlds were going to collide.

❧ V ❧

OLIVIA 2005-2009

I put the phone down and stared at Olivia. I felt numb. She put her arms around me and pulled my head down to her shoulder. After some time, she stood up and lifted my feet onto the sofa and covered me with a blanket. It wasn't until she pressed a cup of tea into my hands and it spilled onto the grey covering that I realised how violently I was shaking. How could Dad be dead? He was only fifty-six. And he was fit – heart attacks only happened to people of his age if they were overweight, didn't they? Dad was a runner. He ate healthily; there was no reason for him to have had a heart attack and certainly not one severe enough to kill him. It didn't make sense.

By the time I'd drunk the tea, Olivia had spoken to her boss and arranged to take a few days off and settled with my boss for my work to be re-distributed. Her prompt thinking meant we could set off straight away to be with Mum. She had a friend with her, but it was me she needed. I threw clothes into a bag while Olivia organised Theo and his requirements. Then Olivia re-packed the bag, this time with underwear in it and in less than an hour we were on the road and heading east.

'Tom, are you okay? I mean... I know you're not okay, obviously, but you've barely said a word. Talk to me, sweetheart, please. I want to help, but you're shutting me out.'

I turned to look at her. 'I'm not shutting you out, I just don't have anything to say at the moment.'

I returned to staring out of the window. It was dark and all I could see was my reflection in the glass, which added to my sense of disembodiment. It was as though all this was happening to someone else and I was a mere observer, detached from the emotion of it. The face in the window scowled back at me, taut lines of grief and anger stretched across it as though it was judging me for not displaying my feelings in the way it thought I should. *I can't show something I don't feel.* I was empty of everything, a Russian doll of a person.

My mind flitted from one notion to the next, unable to rest or focus for more than a few seconds, until eventually one notion emerged from the rest and solidified into a concrete idea. Mum. She had to come first in all of this. I'd lost my dad, but she'd lost her husband – her partner in everything for the last thirty-six years. My sense of loss had to be put to one side to be dealt with at a later date, once I had steered Mum through hers. I had to be strong for her. She and Dad had looked after me all my life, counselling me through its ups and downs and now it was my turn. I knew it's what Dad would have asked of me if he'd known what was going to happen.

'Where are we?' I asked.

'We've just joined the M25,' Olivia said, risking a quick glance at me.

'Do you need me to drive?'

'No, I'm fine. It's only about an hour now.'

'We'll need to start thinking about the funeral,' I said. 'I don't know how long it will take though. You might have to go back to work and then come back up for it.'

She gave me a strange look and seemed about to say something, then changed her mind.

'Don't worry about that now,' she said eventually. 'We've got time to sort out the practicalities later.'

'I just thought if we could start making some definite plans it's less for Mum to worry about.'

'And that's fine, but you've lost your dad as well.'

'I'm well aware of that.'

'I only meant that you and your mum need time together to talk about your dad, without worrying about the funeral.'

'There's too much to organise to simply leave it. I'll have time to think about everything later, once the funeral's over.'

'Tom, you have to make time! Your mum will need to be with you and –'

'Will you stop telling me what I should be doing and how I should be feeling! I know exactly what my responsibilities are and I intend to do everything Mum needs me to. I don't have time to think about myself at the moment.'

'Tom –'

'Leave it, Liv! I don't want to talk about it. I can't. It's no different to when you shut everyone out so leave me alone. I don't want to talk everything through. If I open that box I can't close it again and Mum doesn't need me falling apart on her.'

My reflection resumed glaring at me and my conscience pricked further when I heard the whisper of a sniff from the other side of the car. I turned and wiped the tears that were rolling down her cheek.

'I didn't mean to shout, darling, I'm sorry. I just can't do everything that needs doing if I start thinking about how I feel. I'm no use to Mum if I fall apart. I've got to be strong for her.'

'It wasn't you shouting at me that upset me,' Olivia said

quietly. Her voice was shaking but she attempted a smile. 'I was pushing you too much, I get that, but... you called me Liv.'

I thought back and realised she was right.

'I'm so sorry,' I said. 'I don't know what else to say.'

We fell into silence after that. I'd hurt her badly by using the name everyone else called her. Even when we'd argued in the past I hadn't done that. It would have seemed such a silly thing to anyone else if I'd tried to explain it, but I knew how special it was to both of us that I was the only person to use her given name. By using the abbreviation I'd relegated her to the ranks of an outsider in our relationship.

'Olivia, I really am sorry. I know you were only trying to help.'

'Don't push me away Tom, please. I can't bear it.'

I cursed myself for forgetting that she was almost as upset as I was. My parents had welcomed her into the family and given her the loving family life she'd craved. They may not have been her biological parents, but she'd said often enough that she loved them as much as if they were and I'd not even spared a thought for how she might be feeling. I laid a hand on her knee.

'I won't, I promise. I'll talk to you when I'm ready, but I'm here for you too. This isn't easy for either of us.'

She released the steering wheel just long enough to squeeze my hand and I knew I was forgiven.

Mum was in bed by the time we arrived. She was exhausted, her friend explained, so she'd sent her to bed with the promise that she'd wait at the house until we got there. I crept upstairs to check on her, half-expecting her to still be awake, but she lay under the duvet, purple shadowed eyes closed and her face pale. Her skin was pulled too tightly across the cheekbones, as though she felt the pain even in her sleep. The wedding photo that usually stood on her bedside table lay where it had fallen from her hand and

I quietly replaced it before kissing her gently on the forehead.

'I'm here now, Mum,' I whispered. 'Everything's going to be okay, I promise.'

The days that followed were filled by meetings with terribly sympathetic funeral directors, florists and the badly-named civil celebrant. All of them had seen grief hundreds of times already and not one of them truly understood it. How could they? They hadn't lost anyone. It was our family who was bereaved, us who had to find a way to continue without Dad's steady presence. Mum cried and patted my hand or played with Theo, whose presence soothed her for he had no understanding of events and simply smiled and giggled as normal. She was happy to leave all the decisions to us, insisting only on Gordon MacRae's version of *Stranger in Paradise*, accompanying Dad's coffin into the crematorium.

'It was one of your dad's favourites,' she reminded me more than once, 'And he always used to say Oklahoma reminded him of how I resisted his charms for so long and wouldn't admit I was in love with him. I know that song's not from Oklahoma, but *People Will Say We're In Love* is a bit jolly for a funeral and it's the same singer, so it will do.'

The service at the crematorium was brief, but the room was full. So many people wanted to pay their respects to Dad and at the wake it felt like an endless parade of people telling me how wonderful Dad had been. I listened politely until I felt as if the walls were closing in on me and my breath stuck in my throat. I didn't need to be told – I knew I'd been lucky with him. We had a good relationship and nothing had been left unsaid when he died. I was glad he'd met and loved Olivia and that he'd seen Theo born. Many people weren't that lucky, but even as I told myself all this I raged at the injustice of his death.

In the months that followed, Olivia and I progressed, at different rates, through Kübler-Ross' seven stages of grief, but

Mum stalled at depression and loneliness, turning away from well-meaning offers of support. She sold Dad's wine bar and even though it had only been a few months since Dad's death, her doctor agreed she wasn't coping very well. When we saw her after a gap of only a few weeks, even I could see how much weight she'd lost.

'I'm not hungry,' she said, when I challenged her on how little she was eating. 'I can't always be bothered to cook just for myself and I've not much appetite anyway.'

'Why don't you come down and stay with us for a couple of weeks?' Olivia suggested. 'It's the Easter holidays soon, why not come and spend it with us? Theo would love to see you and you'd be more than welcome.'

After Olivia repeatedly laid out all the reasons why it was a good idea, Mum agreed and duly arrived two weeks later.

'It's been lovely having you here,' I said at the end of her visit. 'Not only was it nice to see you and Theo's loved you being here, but I've got twice the amount of work done.'

'It was nice to feel useful,' Mum said, 'And Theo's such an angel, who wouldn't love looking after him?'

We hoped it would be the start of her spirits beginning to recover, but it soon became apparent this was a false hope.

'What are we going to do?' I asked Olivia, 'I've never felt so helpless.'

'When she was here, I was thinking that it was a shame she doesn't live closer. It's really good for Theo when she's here and looking after him gave her a purpose as well. Do you think we could persuade her to move down here?'

'It wouldn't solve the problem of her being lonely though, would it? She'd still be on her own most of the time.'

'Would she move in here?'

I shook my head.

'We don't have the room – I know we've got a spare room, but if you want more children it's going to be too small even for us soon enough. Besides which, I don't think she'd want to. She's too independent to want to live with us – she's still only in her fifties remember.'

The following day, Olivia came home her face flushed with excitement.

'What about if we moved? If we sold this place and your mum sold her house we could buy somewhere bigger with an annexe or two properties on one plot, or something like that anyway. We might have to move out of Exeter to do it, but you can work from anywhere and I'm sure I'd be able to find a job nearby. Your mum works in a school, so if she still wanted to work she could – there's schools everywhere. Why don't you ask her?'

I wasn't convinced Mum would be interested, but after an evening of listening to Olivia spell out all the advantages I agreed to ring her and ask. As I'd predicted, her initial response was an immediate refusal, but after a long conversation where I insisted she wouldn't be disrupting our lives and uprooting us, she eventually confessed that she quite liked the idea. Dad had left her financially secure so she could take early retirement if she wanted to. Her main anxiety was whether – now the possibility of an end to her loneliness had been dangled in front of her – it would be possible to find somewhere large enough to suit our purposes. Although she loved the idea of being close by, she was adamant that she wanted her own space – it was necessary for all of us, she said and we'd need at least five bedrooms if Olivia's desire for three children was to be fulfilled. On top of that we required either an annexe or separate building and that kind of living space was bound to be expensive.

'We could always look at places up north,' Olivia said one evening as I groaned my way through a list of properties. 'Houses are a lot cheaper up there.'

'I'm not moving to Manchester,' I said quickly.

'I'm not suggesting we move anywhere near my parents either,' she said, 'But there are some lovely places in

Lancashire and Yorkshire.' Her face lit up as a thought occurred to her. 'If we moved near Blackpool we could learn to ballroom dance. I haven't danced since I was a kid, but I'd love to give it a go. We could learn together.'

I held up a hand.

'Let's get the house sorted before you start signing us up for lessons.'

As usual however, she was right. House prices were significantly lower up there and as Mum was happy to consider anywhere, we spent a couple of weekends in Lancashire viewing different properties and finally found one that matched our requirements almost exactly. It was a beautiful red brick building with ornamental white gabling around the roof. The large garden had a one-storey, two bedroom apartment at the bottom of it and this was screened from the main house by a thick hedge which gave it a little privacy. The whole property was surrounded by six foot fences broken only by the iron entrance gates at the front and a double wooden gate at the back, which gave easy access to the annexe flat. It was perfect. Poulton was only a handful of miles from Blackpool, which suited Olivia's plans perfectly and it was only about half an hour's drive from the University of Lancaster, where she had got herself a job as head of the campus library. Just knowing the move was approaching had already made a visible difference to Mum and I prayed nothing would happen to halt the sale.

My worries were groundless and the sale went through as smoothly as any house sale ever does. It was a fraught time for all of us, with letters and phone calls going backwards and forwards between us, the solicitors, the vendors, our buyers and the various estate agents, but eventually we exchanged the various contracts and heaved a sigh of relief. The removal vans were booked and all that was left to do was pack our few remaining possessions and bid farewell to our house and our friends.

'I know we can come and visit, but it won't be the same as having you just round the corner,' Sophie said on our last evening. 'It will be weird not having the kids playing together like this.'

We looked over to where Theo and the thirteen month old Esther were fighting over a toy they both wanted to play with.

'Weird, but quieter I suspect,' Olivia laughed. 'At least until number two arrives anyway! And she can always come to the seaside for a holiday with Uncle Tom and Auntie Liv,' she continued, removing Theo's fingers from Spiderman's neck and handing him to Esther.

'No, Theo. Essie had him first. We have to share. You play with something else.'

Her voice was firm and Theo's face crumpled, but then he looked at his mother's stern expression and picked up Tickle Me Elmo instead.

'We'll be there so often you'll be sick of the sight of us,' Sophie said, laughing. 'You will come down and see us when baby's born though, won't you?'

'Try and stop us,' Olivia said. 'I'm hoping that by the time baby's here there'll be another one on the way.'

She didn't quite manage to conceal the note of envy in her voice. We were ready to start trying to provide Theo with a sibling but had agreed to put it on hold until we were settled in the new house. Given that Olivia had been so ill at the beginning of Theo's pregnancy we hadn't wanted to risk her being pregnant when we were moving. That Sophie had fallen pregnant so quickly this time after the difficulties of conceiving Essie, had been a wonderful surprise, but had made us long even more for another one of our own.

It took several months for us to make the new house feel like home and even then it felt strange hearing the harsher tones of our northern neighbours, rather than the soft Devonshire drawl we'd become accustomed to.

Olivia threw herself into her new job with typical enthusiasm, but it took Mum and I a bit longer to work out how we wanted to do things. I didn't want her to have Theo all day because the whole point of me working from home was so that I was with him. She however, wanted to help out as much as she could. We drew up a compromise that meant she had him one full day each week and then she'd take him for a few hours at a time across the rest of the week if my workload was particularly heavy. She also had him one evening a week so Olivia and I could go for a dancing lesson and then out for dinner or to the Tower Ballroom to practise what we'd learnt. Sunday was Olivia's day to have Theo to herself and she came home full of delight about the adventures they'd had. Theo was usually filthy and exhausted, but keen to tell me everything they'd done. It was Olivia's way of making sure that as well as spending time with me and with us together as a family, he also got her to himself on a regular basis.

'When he gets older I want him to be able to talk to either of us,' she explained, when I questioned the necessity of their day together. 'If I don't have those days with him then he'll always come to you by virtue of you being at home with him all the time. I don't want that – it's important he knows he can come to me as well.'

I still wasn't convinced of it being necessary, but as it gave me the chance to catch up on work uninterrupted or go to the cinema to see the films no-one else was interested in, I didn't object further.

On Valentine's Day, Olivia woke me unusually early and handed me a slim, gift-wrapped box.

'I know we said we'd do presents this evening,' she said, bouncing up and down on the bed, 'But I couldn't wait to give you this one.'

I slid a metal pencil case out of the bright red wrapping paper and frowned, uncertain why she was so excited about such a mundane gift.

'Open it, silly!' She clapped her hands together and laughed again.

Inside the tin was a positive pregnancy test.

'I found out yesterday and I've been dying to tell you ever since,' she said, 'But I thought it would be a nice present today. By October we'll have two children!'

I beamed at her. Another baby – a brother or sister for Theo. He'd be delighted when we told him: at two years old he'd recently started at a pre-school for one day a week and many of his friends already had a sibling, a fact of which he was most jealous.

'This one will never know my dad,' I said, an unexpected burst of sadness coming over me.

'Of course they will,' Olivia said. 'We'll make sure of it. They won't meet him, but they'll know all the stories.'

I smiled as I swung my legs out of bed. I still missed Dad, of course I did. We all did, but Mum had been so much better since we'd moved here. She wasn't exactly back to her old self – I didn't think she ever would be – but we got occasional glimpses of the old Mum. Then she'd remember about Dad and her face would shut down again. She was at least eating better now and a new baby to fuss over would undoubtedly help her.

Once again, Olivia spent the first few months experimenting with different ways to keep her nausea under control, but this time nothing seemed to work and eventually the doctor referred her to the hospital. She spent the next month attached to various drips that were alternately feeding her and pumping her full of drugs designed to keep the contents of the other drip inside her. We reassured Theo that Mummy and the baby were fine, but I worried for them. Olivia wasn't at her healthiest weight to begin with and she could ill afford to lose any more. To my relief, once she was discharged from the hospital, her appetite returned.

'Don't look so worried, Tom,' she said one day, noticing

me scrutinising her plate. 'I know I've been struggling again, but I have to be healthy for baby's sake. I'm being sensible, I promise. He or she comes before my issues. I've got it under control.'

I wasn't convinced but vowed to keep my observations more subtle in future. Her weight gain with Theo had been the thing that upset her most and she'd worked hard to lose it all as soon as he was born. I knew she found being pregnant difficult and I didn't want to become part of the problem by increasing her worries about it. However, she was carrying our child and he or she was our primary responsibility, not to mention that Theo needed his mum healthy as well. I wanted to be ready to step in if I had to. In her more rational moments, Olivia would absolutely have agreed that it was the right thing to do, but I knew from experience that pregnancy and rationality did not always make good bedfellows.

However, much to my relief, it didn't become necessary for me to intervene and our second child ceased to cause problems, growing exactly as all the charts said he should and – as I had learnt from my mistakes when Theo was born – when the time came for him to be born, the process was as uneventful as the journey to the hospital. My car had plenty of petrol in it and the staff at the Victoria Hospital, with some help from Olivia, calmly and efficiently delivered Alexander Nicholas Blythe into the world.

Within a couple of days, we were back home and remembering everything we had forgotten about life with a newborn. Although Olivia bore the brunt of it as she was feeding Xander herself, I did as much as nature (and my wife) allowed me to. We had been a little concerned how Theo would react to sharing us. After all, he'd got used to being the sole focus of our attention for almost three years, but our worries were unnecessary. He took to the role of big brother instantly, wanting to help feed and change Xander. He spent hours talking to him, trying to share his toys with him, until we explained gently that small babies couldn't play with toys in the same way he could, He'd have to wait until Xander was a bit bigger before they'd be able to play games together. We'd spent a lot of time ahead of the birth, talking to Theo about being a big brother and explaining that he had to look after Xander and set a good example for him. From the very beginning it was clear he was taking his role incredibly seriously.

We were so happy. Then when Xander was about eight months old, Olivia began to complain about feeling unwell.

'My back is killing me,' she said one evening, kicking off her slippers and stretching out on the sofa. 'I'm only twenty-nine for God's sake, but my joints feel like they belong to a ninety year old.'

'Flip onto your front,' I said, kneeling at the side of her. 'I'll give it a rub for you. Where does it hurt?'

She gestured to her lower back and I applied pressure to it.

'I can't feel any knots in the muscles,' I said. 'Have you been on your feet a lot today?'

'No more so than usual.'

Her groan was muffled by the cushion pressed into her face.

'I'd say maybe a new mattress, but we bought a new one when we moved in here, so it shouldn't need replacing yet and you've been fine with it up to now, haven't you?'

She nodded.

'How long has it been hurting?'

'Only a few weeks, but it's getting worse.'

'First thing tomorrow get yourself down to the doctor's. You might need some physio or something. They have an open surgery every morning, don't they?'

I knew she'd never agree to go at such short notice, but in pushing the issue I'd made sure she'd agree to make an appointment for the following week when I eventually suggested that as a compromise.

She came home from the surgery just before lunchtime on Monday and I knew from the fact she'd come home instead of heading straight to work that something was wrong.

'I'm pregnant.' She burst into tears.

'Are you sure?'

She glared at me.

'But you're still feeding Xander.' I was utterly bewildered. 'I didn't think you could get pregnant if you were still breast-feeding.'

'Well clearly you can!' She glared at me. 'We obviously weren't careful enough.'

I put my hand on top of hers.

'I wasn't doubting your word, I'm just confused. How do you feel about it?'

'Oh, I'm overjoyed,' she said. 'Can't you tell?'

'Look, I know the timing's not ideal, but you always said you wanted three by the time you were thirty. If this baby is born in... what would it be, March time? You're not thirty until July. I thought you'd be... well, if not happy, then at least... I don't know, not devastated.'

'Tom, I know I'm only feeding Xander at night now, but I'd at least have liked to have him fully weaned before I start thinking about getting ready to feed the next one! I'm not a bloody cow! I'm exhausted. Three babies in four years is a lot to put my body through. I'm not ready to do all this again.'

I forbore from pointing out that the timing of our children had been almost entirely her idea.

'So, what are you saying? You don't want this baby?'

I wasn't sure how I felt about that, or about how her answer might make me feel about her.

'I do want a baby, I just don't want it now,' she said after a few moments' consideration.

'You want...' I swallowed, willing myself to keep my voice light. 'You want an abortion?'

She burst into tears again.

'No! I don't know... oh, Tom!'

'Is that what's causing the back ache?' I needed to change the subject before I said something I might regret.

'I think so. The doctor said it probably was, but she wanted to run some other tests anyway, just to be sure. She said she'd ring with the results in a few days.' She wiped her eyes and sat up straighter. 'Look, I need to get to work and we both need time to think about this. We'll talk about it properly tonight when I get home.'

I couldn't believe she was going to work and leaving this unresolved. This wasn't a discussion about what to have for dinner or where to go on holiday. We were discussing whether or not to end out child's life!

'I don't need time to think, thank-you,' I said coldly. 'I love you and I love our children. All of them,' I emphasised, 'Born or unborn. I want this baby. I cannot believe you're even considering a termination.'

I turned and walked away so she wouldn't see I was shaking in case she thought it was because we'd argued. I couldn't understand how she could even contemplate killing our baby. She was the one who'd insisted she wanted three children. She was the one who wanted them all close together and now she saw another baby as an inconvenience? I heard the front door slam and Xander wailed in protest at being woken up so abruptly from his nap.

Picking him up out of his cot, I put him carefully in his highchair and fed him his lunch, my mind elsewhere.

'Sorry mate,' I said when he protested at having another spoon of pasta pushed at him. His little cheeks were like a hamster's. 'Was Daddy going too fast for you?'

I couldn't concentrate on any work for the rest of the afternoon and kept myself occupied with mundane household chores and playing with Xander until it was time to collect Theo from pre-school. I still hadn't calmed down when Olivia arrived home, but we put on a unified front of cold politeness until the boys were in bed.

'Do you think you have the right to tell me what I can or can't do with my body?'

Her question floored me for a moment. Of course I didn't, I wouldn't dream of it.

'No,' I said cautiously. 'But this isn't just about you, is it? We both helped make that baby and I think as the father I should get a say in what happens to it. You have to go through the pregnancy and the birth, but it's me who does the majority of the childcare afterwards.'

'You're right. To a point,' she said. 'But knowing what I went through last time, can you understand why I might have reservations about doing it all again?'

I nodded.

'Then why are we arguing about it? I never said I wanted an abortion, I just said I wasn't sure I wanted a baby now. You were the one who mentioned a termination. You're my husband, Tom, we're supposed to share our fears with each other, but when I tried to do that this afternoon you accused me of wanting to kill our child.'

I closed my eyes and replayed the conversation.

'You were scared.' I opened my eyes to see her nod. 'I'm so sorry. I was too and I lashed out because I thought you wanted to get rid of it. I didn't give you a chance to tell me what you meant, did I?'

It was an uneasy truce, but we were at least able to talk to each other. Olivia took some consolation from the fact she'd got so far without any sickness and we began to make tentative plans for a future with three children.

We assumed her pregnancy was the cause of the various aches and pains she felt, particularly as this pregnancy showed every sign of being very different to the first two. The aches and pains – which she hadn't experienced before – didn't go away, but neither did the hyperemesis gravidarum make a re-appearance. When the doctor's office rang however, it was only the surgery's receptionist, who asked Olivia to make an appointment to discuss the results.

'I'm worried,' Olivia said when she hung up. 'If there was nothing wrong she'd have given me the results over the phone. What if there's something wrong with the baby?'

'I'm sure it's nothing too serious,' I said. 'You know what it's like sometimes, they get you in over not very much. They have to be overly cautious to make sure they don't get sued or something.'

I could see I hadn't convinced her, but there was nothing we could do but wait for the day of the appointment. When it arrived, Olivia's anxiety had only grown worse.

'You'll come with me, won't you?'

'Of course,' I said. 'Whatever it is we'll face it together, but I'm sure there's nothing to worry about.'

The doctor was grave when we entered her consulting room and a little of Olivia's nerves infected me. I gripped her hand tightly.

'Mrs Blythe, thank-you for coming in.'

'Is there something wrong with the baby?' Olivia blurted out.

'No, no, baby is absolutely fine,' the doctor said. 'I'm afraid it's you we need to talk about. I asked you to take the tests because I wasn't happy to just write off some of the symptoms you described as simply pregnancy related issues. Unfortunately, the test results show that you have leukaemia.' She paused for a moment, while we stared at her. 'Now it can be treated, but obviously treatment is complicated by the fact you're pregnant.'

She continued to speak and I could see her lips moving but heard nothing over the buzzing in my ears. How could this be happening? I forced myself to focus on the doctor.

'We've caught it reasonably early, but if you want to

continue with the pregnancy, we'll have to consider chemotherapy.'

'Won't that harm the baby?' Olivia asked.

'It's a calculated risk,' the doctor said. She handed over a handful of leaflets. 'Have a read of this when you get home once you've had time to take it in. We find many patients forget most of what they're told at the first diagnosis, so make an appointment to come back and see me in a few days and we can talk through your options then.'

I followed Olivia out of the little room and back to the car, driving home automatically, thankful to arrive without incident as I couldn't recall the route we took or if we met any other vehicles. I could only hope I hadn't run any red lights – I knew there were several traffic lights between the surgery and our house, but I didn't remember the colour of the lights at a single one of them.

We were too shell-shocked to talk much that evening, but over the next few days we read the leaflets the doctor gave us and did our own research online. Some sites suggested a termination of the pregnancy and immediate treatment was the safest option, while others said that with chemotherapy and other drugs during the pregnancy, it was possible to wait until the baby was born before beginning to properly address the leukaemia. The one thing they all agreed on was that it was impossible to know for certain what effect chemotherapy might have on the baby. Leukaemia during pregnancy was relatively rare and understandably there wasn't enough evidence to give any firm guarantees.

'That settles it,' Olivia said, closing her laptop. 'I'm not having any treatment until the baby's born. I'm not risking him or her.'

'It's unlikely there'd be much risk, otherwise they wouldn't suggest it as an option,' I reasoned. 'Olivia, this is serious. Leukaemia isn't something you can beat just by deciding you will. Please be sensible about this. I don't want to lose you.'

'You won't.'

I hadn't gone as far as suggesting the most extreme of our options, but I'd have agreed if it was the path Olivia chose to take. I hated the idea, but not as much as I hated the idea of losing my wife and the mother of our boys.

'What about Theo and Xander?' I said. 'They need you too.'

'And I fully intend to be here for them,' she said. 'I have no intention of dying any time soon. We'll get through the next few months and then I promise I'll have any and all treatments I'm offered. But only once it's only my body that will be affected by them.'

I could have carried on with my pleas and appeals to her conscience, but it would only have led to arguments. I'd been with Olivia for more than a decade and I knew by now that once she'd made up her mind about something, it was futile trying to change it. I was keen not to add to her stress, having read it could be a contributory factor to cancer. As I had always done, I had to trust in her judgement and believe she was going to beat the illness just as she had overcome every previous obstacle in her life. We told my mum and Eoin and Sophie of course, but Olivia made us promise not to tell her parents unless it became absolutely necessary. Her relationship with them had improved over the years and to our surprise, Laura was still sticking to her graduation day resolution. As far as we knew she'd been clean since then and this fact helped to make some repairs to her relationship with her daughter, as well as allowing her to spend more time with her grandchildren. I was still cautious, but at least any hurt now caused was unintentional and born of thoughtlessness rather than the product of an addled and twisted mind. However, Olivia didn't want to give her mother an excuse to fall back into old habits and didn't think it was fair to tell her dad without also informing her mum, so decided to keep them both in the dark. I didn't agree with her on this either – I felt they had a right to know, but all the same I promised not to say anything.

'It's developing quicker than they expected,' Olivia told me on her return from the hospital, where she had been for one of her increasingly regular check-ups. 'I'm going to have to have a Caesarean and they want her out as soon as possible.'

Her tone was very matter of fact, but I could hear the fear lurking at the back of her voice.

'When?'

'Next week.'

I stared at her.

'But you're not due for another three weeks.'

'I know. At thirty-eight weeks she'll be classed as full-term though, which is why they're prepared to leave her in there for another week. If it was any longer they said they'd have kept me in today.'

'How long do you have to wait after the birth before they can start the treatment?'

'I don't. As soon as they've done the Caesarean, I can start taking the drugs. It just means I won't be able to breastfeed her.'

Elodie's birth was nothing like those of her brothers and as soon as all the necessary tests had been done on her, she was handed to me and we were escorted out of the operating theatre. My daughter lay in my arms and already I knew she'd be able to wrap me round her little finger, but half my mind was still in the theatre with Olivia who was, in her own way, just as helpless and vulnerable as her new-born daughter.

Having Elodie to myself so soon after her birth was a unique experience. Although I'd held both boys almost immediately after they were born, Olivia had been with me and it was something we shared. This time our new baby was completely mine to watch over and I revelled in her tiny hands and feet and the sweet, milky smell of her. This was the baby Olivia had fought so hard to protect and she was perfect in every way. I kissed her gently, taking care not to wake her.

'Elodie Beatrice Blythe, you are a very special and very lucky girl,' I told her. 'Mummy loves you so much she risked her life to keep you safe. But it will be okay. Mummy's strong and she's going to fight this.' A tear fell onto her blanket and was absorbed into the soft wool. 'We have to be good for her though, don't we? So, you'll have to put up with Daddy looking after you for a while, just until Mummy gets better. Will that be okay?'

She made a soft mewling noise in her sleep and her nose twitched.

'I'll take that as a "yes",' I whispered and kissed her again. 'Good girl.'

It was a gruelling few months that followed, but we got through them. I persuaded Olivia to tell her parents when she started her treatment and I promised to keep them updated while she recovered. Mum increased her help with the children and between us we endeavoured to keep the boys' routines as normal as possible. Xander and Elodie were too young to understand, but at four, Theo was old enough to pick up on the atmosphere in the house and needed reassurance that while Mummy was poorly, she was going to be all right.

Much to my relief, I had spoken nothing but the truth to him and although Olivia would have to continue going for regular check-ups, the chemotherapy had worked and she was given the all-clear.

GRACE

The weeks of December disappeared with increasing speed and although I continued to feel myself being pulled in two different directions, conversely I also felt more settled about the whole affair. Grace continued to demand no more than I was prepared to give and I grew more confident in both our love and my ability to move past my guilt. Consequently, as Christmas approached I was able to think about the festive season in a more positive way than I'd thought would be possible.

I took the children shopping to buy presents for Olivia and in the end we settled on a small resin figurine of a mother surrounded by three children.

'It's us, see?' Xander said, 'So Mummy will know we love her.'

The male figure was conspicuous by his absence, so I added a stone angel to the basket as my contribution.

As we headed for the nearest till, we passed through the jewellery section. The artificial brightness made me blink – all the lights seemed to be set to maximum brightness and directed in such a way as to ensure the greatest possible reflection off the glass cabinets full of temptingly sparkling stones. Even at only four years old, Elodie was already captivated by their luminescent twinkling. As she got older and even more susceptible to their charms, I could foresee an expensive future for myself.

I usually tried to hurry through the ostentatious displays, knowing how long it could take to extract Elodie from within them, but that day I was content to linger, keeping a watchful eye on her while talking to the boys, who had no interest in diamonds and resented any time spent in their presence. A silver chain with a single tear drop diamond hanging from it caught my eye. The label proclaimed it to be white gold rather than silver and although it wasn't cheap, it wasn't as eye-wateringly expensive as I'd expected it to be. Before I'd had a chance to second guess my decision, I was handing over my credit card in exchange for an exquisitely wrapped gift box.

Thankfully the children were too young to question such an unusual purchase, for it was far from the style of their mother's jewellery. Their firm belief that Father Christmas brought their gifts on Christmas Eve also saved me from answering any difficult questions which might otherwise have arisen.

Grace was spending Christmas with her parents and brother, so we exchanged gifts on the final day of the school term, as it was the last occasion where it would be possible for me to see her until after the New Year.

'Oh Tom, it's beautiful,' she said, as I fastened the narrow chain around her throat. 'I've never owned anything so lovely before.'

I kissed the curve between her neck and shoulder and slid my arms around her.

'It's not as beautiful as the woman wearing it.'

'So cheesy,' she laughed, but turned around and kissed me anyway.

'Do you like your watch?' she asked after some little time.

'I do.' I returned her kiss with several of my own. 'How did you know I needed a new one?'

'Noticing things is my superpower,' she teased. 'Not particularly heroic, I admit, but jolly useful all the same.'

We laughed and I leant back against the sofa.

'I'm sorry I can't see you over Christmas,' I said, teasing her curls gently.

'I understand. Christmas is family time. Maybe next year we'll celebrate it together.'

'Mmhmm.'

I resumed kissing her.

Olivia and I always went full tilt at the Christmas celebrations. I loved the crisp coldness of winter anyway and Christmas was just an added bonus. Since we'd had the children we'd made sure the season was as magical for them as it could possibly be. Last year's festive season had been quite muted, due only in part to my Fluoxetine induced numbness – I wasn't the only one who hadn't felt much like celebrating – and I was determined this year would see a return to our normal festivities.

At the beginning of December, we'd opened the big box of decorations and festooned the tree with them, decorating picture frames with tinsel and hanging Santas with springy legs from the window catches. As the youngest, Elodie was allowed to put the fairy on top of the tree and I lifted her up so she could balance it, at a drunken angle, on the topmost branch. From her lofty perch the Fairy Queen coolly surveyed her domain, ensuring the requisite amount of Christmas cheer was in evidence.

The fairy herself was something of a relic, bordering almost on bearing the lofty title of 'antique'. Bought in the early 1970s she wore a pale blue feathered dress and her round pink face was topped by a cloud of golden hair and a silver crown. Or at least, so had been the case when she was first purchased. Forty odd years later, she was looking rather more bedraggled and had already survived one attempt to retire her. A year or two before Dad died, having grimaced at the gaps in her dress, the matted hair and lopsided crown, Mum had bought a rather more tasteful – but in my opinion at least, far more soulless – silver star, in an attempt to modernise their decorations. Over the years, the mix of glittery salt-dough trains, poorly coloured cardboard baubles and the rather rude looking paper candle of my childhood, had given way to monochrome shop bought decorations in sophisticated shades of silver and white. The fairy was the last remnant of the trees I remembered and I had been aghast at the final indignity visited upon her when I discovered her upside down in the bin. I rescued her and set her to watch over our tree, fondly imagining that it must have been like a reunion of old friends for her as most of the decorations we had were either the self-same ones my parents had replaced, or – in later years – ones of a similar ilk created by our own children.

The Christmas meal itself was always on a grand scale and every year Mum insisted on cooking it, taking over our kitchen to do so when we moved house. Olivia and I would occasionally be permitted to help with some menial tasks like peeling the potatoes or bringing in the turkey from where it had been hanging from a crook lock in the garage. But mostly, Mum flew around the kitchen stirring, basting and occasionally sipping a Gin and Tonic, happy that everything was organised for the feast.

The presents, although welcome, were almost an afterthought to the day. Once the children arrived they were opened at speed before breakfast, but then were often forgotten in the muddle of eating and playing games that followed. It was tiring, it was noisy, it was messy, but when we eventually dragged ourselves up the stairs to bed at the end of the day, it was always with a smile.

This year, in contrast to the disaster of last year, things were back to normal. Mum excelled herself with the turkey and all the trimmings and the children kept up a non-stop commentary throughout the day. It felt odd not seeing Grace though. We texted and I managed a quick phone call while the children were opening their stockings, but it startled me to realise how much I missed her. Almost without me realising it, daily contact with her had become an embedded part of my day and a rushed and whispered phone conversation while hiding in my study, just wasn't the same. I of all people, was painfully aware that nothing lasts forever and it was beginning to feel as though I might be wasting whatever precious time I might be granted with Grace.

Consequently, in that empty space between Christmas and New Year, when everything feels a little bit dull, I decided I needed to make some kind of commitment to Grace. Unfortunately, it was easier to make an intellectual decision than to take the physical step of acting upon it. For one thing, I wasn't due to see her other than via Skype until January and the kind of action I had in mind was one that required us to be in the same room. I was frustrated in more ways than one and the days dragged interminably.

Those few days were always slightly dismal even under normal circumstances. After any kind of excitement, it was natural to experience a sense of anti-climax, but when almost an entire month has been spent building up to one day and then suddenly it's all over, it's equally natural for the resultant rebound of emotion to be correspondingly great. New Year always induced in me a sense of melancholia anyway, as I – along with a large percentage of the population – balanced my account of the year. My list of achievements this year was depressingly low. The children were all doing well at school, my client list was looking healthy and of course, I had Grace, but on the debit side, I was still taking the anti-depressants and I was, if anything, even more torn between the two women I loved than I had been six months previously. My recent behaviour was not something that filled me with pride on anyone's account and yet at the same time I could not wholly regret it and my newfound determination to move things forward with Grace gave me hope that I was getting closer to making a decision about the direction my future would take.

When I next saw Grace I couldn't find the words to tell her what I had been thinking about all over the Christmas period. Words fought each other to be said, but I rejected them all without hesitation – too trite, too blunt, too rude. I decided that actions would probably speak louder than words and I did my best to demonstrate what I was feeling. Even more than twenty years after losing my virginity, sex was still something I wasn't comfortable discussing and although I knew it was what I wanted, I was making an assumption that Grace shared my desires. I needed to make sure that assumption was correct before I went much further. I tried not to consider that I might not be any good at it. I didn't have a huge bank of experience to draw on and although Olivia had never complained and I knew how to satisfy her, I had no idea if the same applied to all women and I didn't really want to be thinking about Olivia. It was disrespectful to both her and Grace – if we were going to do this, I had to be totally focused on the woman I was actually with.

'Tom, are you okay? You don't seem like you're really here today.'

I looked at Grace blankly. 'I'm sorry. I wasn't.'

'Do you want to stop?'

'No.'

The force of my denial shocked us both. Me because it was so vehemently genuine and Grace presumably because of the volume at which it was delivered.

'Could we...' I glanced towards the open door of her living room, unable to vocalise what I was suggesting.

She looked at me for a few moments before replying. 'Are you sure? If we do this, it's not something you can ever take back.'

'I know,' I said quietly, 'But I think I'm ready.'

She held my gaze for a long time, then slowly nodded. 'If you're sure?'

I wasn't. I didn't know if I would ever be. I was, however, sensible enough to realise that the longer I put it off, the more difficult it would be when the time finally came. Doubling the number of people I'd slept with was a big deal, but the fact Grace recognised that made me more confident I was making the right choice. I kissed her again, then let her lead me silently along the corridor to her bedroom.

In the minutes that followed, I didn't think of Olivia once and afterwards it was this more than anything else that filled me with guilt. I had been so caught up in the passion and excitement of sex with Grace that I hadn't given a moment's thought to my wife. *I've had sex with someone else. It's no longer just Olivia and me. What have I done?*

The words of condemnation jostled for supremacy. Cheat. Liar. *You said there'd never be anyone else for you.* It wasn't my voice I heard; it was Olivia's. *You said you'd love me forever.*

I will, I pleaded. *I do. But things have changed. I love Grace as well.* The words swirled around inside me, filling me with angry accusations. Words of scorn poured through every vein, every artery. Harsh remonstrations rose through me, blocking my airway. *I can't breathe.*

'Tom? Tom? Darling? Please talk to me. You're scaring me now.'

Something wet splashed on my bare shoulder and I flinched.

'Tom, can you hear me?'

'Grace?'

I turned my head as far as I was able to, for hers rested on my shoulder. She had moulded herself around my back, a thin sheet the only thing separating us. My body reacted viscerally to that realisation, but I ignored it.

'Why are you crying?'

She sat back on her heels, the sheet clutched to her as though for protection.

'Oh God. Did I hurt you?'

'No! Oh darling, no. It was wonderful, but then you just seemed to black out. You were conscious but you couldn't breathe. I haven't seen you have an attack like that since that first day in the Tower.'

The day the organist had played *Unforgettable*. And yet I had forgotten her. Only for a moment, but the length of time didn't matter. The fact itself was more than enough to condemn me in my own eyes

'I don't remember.'

'You've been sat there for half an hour not saying anything, not even moving. I don't think you could even hear me talking to you.'

'I couldn't,' I said. 'All I could hear was Olivia's voice berating me for betraying her. She was angry, Grace. So very angry.'

For the first time, I saw a flicker of impatience cross her face before she smoothed out her expression.

'You haven't betrayed anyone. This was meant to be, Tom. We were meant to be. I knew it that day in the garden and I'm even more convinced of it now. Why do you think I invited you to come dancing with us? Why do you think I carried on calling you even when you didn't answer the phone? We love each other and that's all that matters.'

I smiled weakly and nodded. What else could I do? I was in no position to argue.

Over the next few weeks, I continued to meet Grace at her flat rather than for lunch and on a few occasions, sneaked her into the house when no-one else was around. Having sex with another woman in the marital bed was another hurdle for my conscience to overcome, but I did and with fewer pangs of remorse than I might have expected. Without any conscious thought from me, I was committing myself more and more fully to Grace. My future was clearly with her now and it was simply a case of when I would make that verbal commitment which would confirm what we already knew.

The children were the biggest stumbling block for me to face. Telling them I'd fallen in love with someone else and introducing Grace to them was going to be one of the hardest things I'd ever done. I didn't know if the children were ready. I didn't know if they would ever be.

VI
OLIVIA 2013-2014

We'd celebrated Elodie's third birthday the previous week and Olivia arrived home from her hospital appointment as I was tidying up the pile of toys Elodie had received at her party and insisted on playing with every day since. Mum was out in the garden where she'd taken the kids to play so I could restore some order to the living room and when I saw Olivia's face I had to resist the urge to run out there myself and seek shelter with the innocent.

She was red and blotchy and had clearly spent the entire drive home in tears. I gathered her into my arms. I knew what had happened and I didn't want to hear it said out loud, but knew I needed to understand what we were dealing with. I'd wanted to go to the appointment with her, but she'd insisted on going alone.

'How long?'

'A few months maybe. If I'm lucky.'

We'd known the news wasn't going to be good, but it was so much worse than we'd expected. I took her coat off and made her sit next to me on the sofa where I could keep my arms around her.

'Isn't there anything they can do? Chemo like last time. That got rid of it before, didn't it? Can't they just do that again?'

She'd kept it at bay for two years. How could it have come back so viciously? There had to be something they could do. There had to be.

She shook her head. 'It's too far gone. Anything they can do will only help manage the pain and prolong the inevitable.'

'How do we tell the kids?'

'Together. Like always.'

I couldn't stop the tears then. That one word. She was right. We'd done everything together for the last fifteen years. Our names went together – Tom and Olivia. Except there was going to be no 'and' anymore. It would just be 'Tom'. All the occasions where I'd thought about us celebrating distant anniversaries and watching our grandchildren run around us, came back to taunt me. That vision of the future no longer existed and the memory of it mocked me for taking it for granted.

Clutching each other we headed out to the garden and called the children over, my mum hovering at a distance, knowing what our actions meant. Theo understood what we were trying to tell them. Xander barely grasped what we said but knew enough to make him cry. Elodie only knew we were all very serious, which made her sad, but she had no real concept of what death was. I pulled Theo into my arms and he stood stiffly while I tried to cuddle him.

'It's okay to cry, kid,' I whispered in his ear. 'You don't have to be brave about this.'

I could see the conflict in his face, but he shook his head stubbornly and pulled away from me. I watched as he walked to his brother and sister and held his arms out to them and my heart broke all over again as he comforted them. He was his mother's boy through and through and I'd never been prouder of him.

Olivia was determined to make the most of the time she had left and filled our diaries with daytrips and mini-breaks, heedless of her own need to rest. It became a kind of frenzy and I could see her disappearing before my eyes, but the frailer she became physically, the stronger her spirit was.

The summer months brought the Olympic Games to London and as we'd managed to get tickets for several events we headed south for a few days. Olivia was growing increasingly weak and I suggested offering our tickets to someone else, but she wouldn't hear of it.

'It's the biggest event in the country for years,' she said, 'And a once in a lifetime experience to be a part of it. I want you and the kids to remember doing things like this with me. We're going and that's that.'

When we arrived at the Olympic Stadium, already draped in our flags, the atmosphere was electric. The walk from Stratford station was slow, but everywhere we looked there was a sea of red, white and blue, with the flags of other countries dotted among the Union Jacks. Despite the alcohol that was flowing freely there was no trouble and every face we saw was wreathed in smiles.

Olivia and the children enthusiastically entered into the joy of the occasion and shouted and cheered their way through the athletics programme, along with the rest of the stadium. My face smiled and my arm waved the flag it held, but I felt as though I was watching everything from somewhere deep inside myself. The entire country was celebrating the exploits of Greg Rutherford, Jessica Ennis and Mo Farrah, caught up in the spirit of the Olympics, but I wanted to stand up and scream. I wanted to rage at them – how dare they celebrate when my life was falling apart? How could they be so cheerful when my wife was dying? Why was life continuing as though nothing had changed?

I looked across the row of seats to where Olivia bounced up and down, shouting encouragement to the athletes far below and urging the children to do the same. For that moment, her pain and their fear of a future without her was forgotten, so caught up were they in the events unfolding in the arena. If this was to be our last adventure as a family, then we had to make it a good one, one the children would remember for the rest of their lives. I took a picture of the four of them on a bridge overlooking the Park and then one of the Games Makers offered to take one of all five of us. We beamed at the camera as though we hadn't a care in the world.

By sheer force of will, Olivia remained at home and we planned Theo's seventh birthday party from her bed. Eoin and Sophie came up as usual with Essie and Oliver and stayed overnight to say a quieter farewell to Olivia. A few days later, my beautiful wife – my Olivia – fell asleep in my arms, her face free from the deep lines of pain for the first time in months.

GRACE

'Tom!'

Grace's call echoed across the shop from the doorway. I handed over my card to pay for the flowers, then hustled the children outside.

'I thought it was you,' she said. 'I'm just on my way to do an interview. Do you fancy meeting for lunch later?'

'I'm sorry, we can't,' I said. 'We have plans today.'

She frowned and bit her lip, then smiled at the children. 'You must be Theo, Xander and Elodie.'

The children looked blankly at her and nodded.

'Kids, this is Grace. She's the lady I dance with sometimes,' I added to cover the awkward silence that followed my first sentence.

Grace stiffened as the children continued to stare blankly at her.

'Well, I must dash, or I'll be late,' she said eventually. 'Tom, I'll see you tomorrow maybe?'

Maybe? She knew we were meant to be going dancing as usual.

'Of course.'

She hurried off and I stared after her, not moving until Theo tugged my arm.

'Daddy, why was that lady cross with you?'

'What made you think she was cross?' I asked, too surprised even to deny the accusation.

'She had those little lines on her forehead that Mummy used to get when she was trying not to shout,' he said.

'She wasn't angry, she was sad,' Xander said. His class had been learning about emotions that week and he relished any opportunity to tell me what they'd learnt. 'I know that because she was crying when she walked off.'

I looked thoughtfully at them.

'You're probably right,' I said. 'I'll have to try and make it up to her when I see her tomorrow.'

'Can we come with you?' Elodie asked. 'She was pretty.'

'Not tomorrow,' I said, 'But I could ask if she'd like to come for dinner next week if you'd like?'

We went to the cemetery to take the flowers to Olivia's grave and the children told her everything they'd done at school since our last visit. We didn't have a set time to go and see her, as I never wanted the children to feel obliged to go and they were always given the option of staying at home with Nanny. However, their counsellors had suggested visiting her grave might be a useful exercise to help them cope and as I'd found it helpful myself, I'd agreed to give it a go and we usually ended up going about once a month. On one of my recent solo visits, I'd noticed that although the artificial flowers I'd bought from the stall in Fleetwood still looked bright and cheerful, the figurines we'd bought at Christmas were beginning to look a little weather-beaten after three months exposed to the elements, so on this occasion we'd brought wipes to try and clean them up a bit. These visits to Olivia's grave never felt solemn or morbid in any way, especially when Elodie, who had just discovered ‘knock-knock’ jokes, decided to perform her entire repertoire for us.

‘I’m sure Mummy would have loved them. I thought they were hilarious,’ I reassured her when she sulked, having failed to elicit even the hint of a laugh from her brothers.

‘She would. I’m the best at telling jokes, aren’t I Daddy?’

I smiled and ruffled her hair.

When we got home I found I had a text from Grace asking me to come to the flat the next day rather than meeting her at the Tower. I didn’t mind, although it did cross my mind that perhaps the children had been right and I’d somehow upset her. If I had, I wasn’t sure how, but I was happy to apologise if that was what was needed.

When she opened the door to let me in, her face was strained and her eyes red.

‘What’s happened?’ I asked, immediately concerned.

I tried to take her in my arms but she stepped back out of reach.

‘Sit down,’ she said and perched on the edge of a chair across the room from me.

‘Grace, you’re really worrying me now. What is it? What’s wrong?’

‘I want you to tell me in very simple words, how you feel about me.’

‘You know how I feel about you. I love you.’

‘Do I know? You’ve never told me that. Not in so many words. It’s been hinted at, but never actually said. I’d have taken that though. It would have been enough.’

‘Would have?’ Her use of the past tense alarmed me.

‘Yesterday when I saw you and the kids, I thought it would be a perfect opportunity to meet them, to let them start getting to know me a little bit. I thought that was what you wanted.’

‘It is!’

She held her hand up sharply.

'Tom, they didn't even know my name! You haven't mentioned me to them at all. We've known each other for a year and your children don't know I exist. Can you imagine how that made me feel? You told me you wanted me in your life, that you wanted me to be a part of your family one day and now I discover it's all lies – you've no intention of moving on. I'm starting to think you enjoy being miserable.

I've been so patient with you. I've waited, I've given you space, I've understood that you needed time to come to terms with being a widower. I'd probably have been prepared to wait a lot longer to hear you say "I love you" because I knew you were special and I believed you had feelings for me; that you wanted to be with me and all I had to do was wait until you were ready to fall in love again. But yesterday really opened my eyes to how stupid I've been. You're not serious about me, you never have been. What was I to you? Someone to keep hanging around to witness your martyrdom? A convenient way to relieve the frustrations of celibacy? All you're interested in is Olivia.

I never wanted to replace her or compete with her. How could I? She was perfect. But Tom, your perfect wife is dead. This imperfect woman right here just wanted to be loved and like an idiot I lapped up every crumb you threw my way and tried not to take it personally every time you had a panic attack because it wasn't Olivia you were with. But I can't do it anymore. I can't compete with a ghost and I'm not going to try from now on. You're a decent man and I hope you find someone who can make you happy, but I don't think that person's me.'

She sat stiffly in her chair, the tears in her eyes being contained by sheer force of will.

'I'd like you to leave now,' she said.

My legs moved without any command from me and propelled me over to her. I pulled her up out of the chair.

'I wish I could say you were wrong about everything,' I

said, 'But you're not. I'm not fully over Olivia's death – it's only been eighteen months after all – and I have avoided mentioning you to the children. It wasn't because I didn't care about you, but if I'm honest, I suppose I didn't want them to think I'd forgotten their mother so quickly. That was a mistake and it was unfair on you and for that I apologise unreservedly. You are wrong about one thing though. I love you beyond anything you can imagine. I've only felt this way once before and sleeping with you was not a step I took lightly. I love you more than you will ever know.'

I lowered my face to hers and kissed her. It was gentle and sad, but I held nothing back, allowing her to see how I felt, to feel the despair running through me and she clung to me in return. I held her for another moment, then let her go and let myself out of her flat, wiping the tears from my eyes as I went. For the second time, I pretended I didn't hear the sobs from her living room. It wasn't that I wasn't prepared to fight for her – I'd have fought anyone else who tried to come between us, but I couldn't fight Grace herself. If she didn't want to be with me, it would be unfair of me to try to change her mind. She'd had enough of being told what to do by her first husband. I had to set her free if that was what she wanted, no matter what it cost me.

My resolution to do this, however, was sorely tested a few weeks later when I passed by a café and happened to see her at a table with Danny. They were deep in conversation so I was able to pass by unobserved, but I couldn't help noticing he was holding her hand across the table. It took all my self-control not to march inside and rip her hand out of his. It was no use pretending even to myself that I wasn't jealous. Grace had been mine since the first moment I laid eyes on her, but it had taken losing her to make me realise I loved her just as much as I had loved Olivia. Grace was just as wonderful and unique as my wife had been and now I'd lost them both.

That evening, I was surprised to hear the doorbell ring and see an agitated Ashley on camera at the gates of the house. I buzzed him in and opened the door as he came up the drive.

'Wow,' he said as he stepped over the threshold. 'I reckoned Grace was exaggerating about this place, but it's huge!'

'Not that it's not pleasant to see you and not that I don't love people admiring my house, but why are you here? Is Grace okay?'

He scowled at me.

'No Grace is not okay,' he said. 'Oh, she's not physically hurt if that's what you mean. As for why I'm here, I should have thought that was fairly obvious. I'm here to stop you and that stupidly stubborn sister of mine making the most colossal mistake of your lives.'

'You're going to have to be more specific,' I said.

'Danny asked her to meet him today and he told her he's got a new job down in London. He gets to choose his own assistant and he's asked her to take the job and move down there with him.'

'God, he didn't waste much time to start sniffing round her again, did he? Has she given him an answer yet?'

'She's asked him to let her think about it overnight. She has to let him know tomorrow evening. If you don't do something you're going to lose her for good. She loves you and I know you love her, but you have to convince her of that.'

'And how exactly do you propose I do that? She doesn't want to know,' I said. 'I told her I loved her and she told me it was too late, that she was tired of trying to compete with Olivia's memory.'

'Then convince her otherwise,' he said. 'Show her that she's not competing. She's different, but just as loved.'

'I can't tell her what to do. I won't. She had enough of that from Austin. She's made her choice and I'm trying to respect it, even if it's killing me to do it.'

'I'm not suggesting you force her into anything you idiot! I'm telling you that she loves you as much as you love her but you're going to lose her if you don't make it clear that you want to be with her.' He sighed, his shoulders slumping. 'Look mate, I think the pair of you belong together, but ultimately it's your life to screw up. If you want to be all noble and lose it all, that's up to you. But it's also up to me to tell you you're an idiot if you do. Just talk to her.

But whatever you decide to do, you need to do it quick. Make a decision once and for all, Tom. Do you love my sister enough to stop feeling like you're cheating on Olivia? If you don't, then let her go to London and make a life there. But if you do, then for God's sake make her understand that. Which is it going to be?'

VII
OLIVIA 2014

The day of Olivia's funeral was unreasonably sunny. The stark, unforgiving brightness of the sun seemed to mock our feelings, demanding to know how we could fail to be happy on the beautiful day it had gifted us. I was merely grateful it gave me an excuse to hide my eyes beneath dark glasses. From behind their lenses I could observe without being spied upon myself.

How is he coping? Does he look sad enough? Is he too sad – is that level of grief normal?

As if my face could ever convey how I felt about Olivia – even Branagh and Olivier at their finest would have struggled to do that emotion justice with a mere expression.

I had thought losing my dad was hard, but it was nothing compared to the loss of my wife. I woke each morning expecting the evidence of my grief to be somehow carved upon my skin for the world to see, but the face that stared back at me from within the mirror was still recognisably my own. A little thinner perhaps, a few lines that were deeper than before maybe, but still very definitely the face of Tom

Blythe and yet it didn't feel familiar. I felt old and tired, but outwardly none of this showed. I was much as I had always been.

Olivia and I had spoken in the last few days about whether or not the children should come to her funeral. We didn't want to overburden them, but knew they needed to be able to say their own goodbyes to her and we decided, contrary to much of the advice we were given, to give them the choice. Theo immediately declared his intention to go and always happy to follow where his brother led, Xander said the same. Not wanting to be left out – even of something she didn't truly understand – Elodie joined the boys in the car with me to follow the hearse that bore Olivia's coffin to the crematorium. All three of them were wearing outfits Olivia had helped me to choose – we'd planned the funeral together, in the same way we had everything else in our marriage. Olivia insisted it was because she wanted to make sure she got a decent send-off and that we played music she liked.

'I want to go out singing,' she said, 'And I can't do that if I leave the choice to you. You'll give me all the modern stuff and I don't want that. I'm going for Hollywood glamour. I'm not suggesting you dance down the aisle of the chapel, but I certainly don't want it to be all doom and gloom.'

Despite the best efforts of the weather, I couldn't manage to raise a smile with which to say goodbye to Olivia. I mumbled my way through the songs she'd chosen and focused instead on the children. Not only were they Olivia's legacy, but they were now my sole responsibility and I had to attend to their needs before my own.

The only thing I had done for myself in the service was the choice of song for the end. Olivia had introduced me to the music of Nat 'King' Cole, and now he sang my feelings to her as the curtains closed in front of her coffin. Nat was right. Olivia was 'unforgettable'. She was the most wonderful person I'd ever known and I hadn't believed my luck when she said she loved me too.

As we left the chapel I pulled the children in close, taking comfort in seeing Olivia in their faces. While I had them she would never truly be gone from my life. Eoin had said that in his eulogy I thought. I'd found it hard to focus on what he was saying, but I remembered him mentioning the children and how much Olivia loved her family.

When he'd asked me if there was anything specific I wanted him to say, I told him all the things he already knew about our early time together, but he hadn't known how I'd fallen for her the first moment I saw her. He didn't know how a smile from her made me feel like I was floating through life; that one look was all it had taken for me to know that I wanted her to become my wife. There was safety in our partnership – she made me want to be a better version of myself and stopped me doing stupid things. I kept her anxieties at bay and understood when she was irrational; never letting her feel less than loved just as she was in that moment.

Adam, Lisa and Laura sat together in the row behind us and through the haze of my own grief I heard their whispered support for each other and for us and I couldn't help but think how proud Olivia would be if she could see them. I was grateful they'd mended their relationship both with her and with each other. They were going to need that mutual support in the coming months. A part of me wouldn't have blamed Laura if she'd relapsed in the face of her daughter's death, but her sombre demeanour held no suggestion of it and again, I felt a tiny burst of pride on Olivia's behalf.

The garden outside the chapel was overflowing with flowers. There were wreaths from the family and sprays of blooms from friends and work colleagues, which as per Olivia's instructions, once the funeral was over, would be pulled apart and delivered to the local hospice. Even some of the parents of the children's friends turned up to pay their respects and with offers of help should we require it. They were all well-meant and appreciated, but I was beginning to suffocate. It was all too much and the words on the condolence cards blurred. My head swam and I pulled at my tie, trying to ease its constricting pressure on my throat. Black spots danced in front of my eyes and my feet were rooted to the spot. Thankfully, Eoin and Sophie had taken charge of the children for a moment while I looked at the flowers and I stood alone, head bowed, throat tightening, wondering if I was going to pass out.

'Dad will look after her you know.'

Mum's voice was barely above a whisper. The words seemed to stick in her throat, but the arm she hooked around me kept me upright. I didn't know if I believed in any kind of afterlife, but in that moment it was a comfort to think they were together, gently teasing each other and laughing, just as they had done in life. Whether it was true or not, the image was enough to allow me to regain control of myself and return to the children.

I wouldn't have got through the weeks that followed without Mum. She took care of the kids and did her best to look after me, but no matter how hard she tried, it was as much as I could do to motivate myself to get out of bed and begin each day. I got the children washed, dressed and fed, but when it came to myself it was too difficult to think about eating. It was enough that the children were okay. I listened to them, talked to them, held them when they cried and soothed them after their nightmares, but I felt nothing beyond that. It was as though every emotion had been trapped in the coffin with Olivia and I no longer had access to them. In many respects it was better that way. Not feeling anything made it easier to function my way through each day.

For the first time perhaps, I felt I understood what Mum experienced after Dad died and why she had found it so difficult to carry on with her life. I also finally got what Olivia had tried to explain to me about her anorexia. When her world had spiralled out of control, what she put in her mouth was the only area she could impose some order upon, so she focused on that. For me, the simple routine of the morning and the school run were the only things I could do with any ease. I had promised Olivia I would do everything in my power to keep things as normal as possible for the children and this I did rigidly. Every piece of homework was handed in on time for the boys, Elodie continued full-time at pre-school and at home we continued with our Saturday days out, the only difference now being that Sunday was spent with Nanny instead of Mummy.

'Here.'

I took the envelope Mum held out, thinking it was some post I'd missed, but the handwriting on the envelope was Olivia's.

'Olivia left it with me in case it was needed,' Mum said in response to my raised eyebrows. 'I think it's needed.'

She swept the children out of the house with her, leaving the envelope burning my fingers. I opened it with shaking hands.

Dearest Tom,

I very much hope you will never read this, but I know you my darling and I fear you will need to at some point after I'm gone. We've always been honest with each other and I'm here to tell you you're an idiot. I know you – you're likely to take my entirely reasonable request to keep the children's lives as normal as possible and take it the nth degree. My darling, I only meant that I wanted you to make this as easy as possible for them. (Not that I didn't think you would, but I needed to hear you say it) If I know you, you will have buried all your own grief deep within yourself and you will keep it hidden until you can successfully pretend you have dealt with it and are moving on. How can I know this, I hear you ask? Because I'm your wife and I *know you better than you know yourself... and also because I watched you do exactly the same thing when your dad died. All your energy went into supporting your mum and there was nothing left for you. You can't take everyone else's grief onto yourself – they have to bear their own share of it and you have to take care of yourself. I'm beyond sorry to be putting you through this and wish I could be there to support you, as you've supported me on so many occasions. But then I guess if I was there you wouldn't need my support because you wouldn't be missing me so terribly. It would be so much easier to tell you this in person but talking makes me tired and I know if I tried to make you listen now, you would dismiss my concern with that airy wave of your hand that so infuriates me. You can't fix everyone, Tom, as much as you want to and you can't even begin to try if you are broken yourself.*

Life will go on my darling, even without me and yours must continue too, for your own sake, not just the children's. I'm enclosing a poem that I hope will bring you some comfort and I can only hope that you listen to what I'm trying to say to you. Your life did not end when mine did. It's okay to be sad and it's okay to think about others, but you must think about yourself as well. I love you so very much and you must promise me to be well.

Your
Olivia

I turned my attention to the second sheet of paper, scrubbing at my face with the back of my hand to stop the closely written words jumping around on the page.

Remember (you know how much I love Christina Rossetti)

Remember me when I am gone away,

Gone far away into the silent land;
When you can no more hold me by the hand,
Nor I half turn to go yet turning stay.
Remember me when no more day by day
You tell me of our future that you plann'd:
Only remember me; you understand
It will be late to counsel then or pray.
Yet if you should forget me for a while
And afterwards remember, do not grieve:
For if the darkness and corruption leave
A vestige of the thoughts that once I had,
Better by far you should forget and smile
Than that you should remember and be sad.

The corners of my mouth lifted very slightly. Even after her death Olivia was still trying to take care of me and I loved her all the more for it. Leaving a note for Mum, I drove to the cemetery to talk to my wife.

'As usual, you're right,' I told her as I tidied the flowers on her headstone. 'I haven't been at my best, much as I hate to admit it. It's hard though – I don't like getting upset in front of other people and everyone is being so kind still. If I let myself feel, I'll cry every time someone says hello to me. Everything feels wrong these days. I've no-one to share my Kit-Kats with anymore.' My voice broke and I forced a laugh, 'Well, the kids are doing their best to help with that problem anyway. Seriously though, I know you're right, but I'm not ready yet. I will listen to you, I promise, but I want to hang onto you for a bit longer. I'm not ready to let you go yet.' I touched my wedding ring. 'The vows say "until death do us part" but even that doesn't really end a marriage, does is? You don't stop loving someone simply because they're not around anymore.'

I stopped and let the tears pour down my face, taking

great gulping breaths. I couldn't do this. I wasn't strong enough without Olivia to lean on.

Now you're just being silly. Her voice came to me as if carried on the wind. *You're so much stronger than you realise. You don't know what a difference you made to me and you'll do the same for our children now. They'll never know what it's like to have a parent they can't rely on. You're a good man, Tom Blythe. I love you and I believe in you and I trust you to raise our children for both of us.*

It was an echo of the conversation we'd had the night she died, but I heard it as though for the first time. Olivia had faith in me and I'd never betray that trust. I kissed my fingers and touched them to the top of the cold marble.

'I'll come back and see you soon, sweetheart.'

That evening, Mum favoured me with her unvarnished opinion as well.

'It's not enough that you're taking care of the children. You've got to look after yourself – you'll be no good to them or anyone else if you don't.'

Although I hadn't shared Olivia's letter with her, she knew my wife well enough to guess at the contents and she hadn't hesitated to let me know she agreed wholeheartedly with Olivia. I needed to begin the process of 'getting over' her death. To start actually living my life again.

I realised she was correct as I observed the children over the next few days. For a boy of his age, Theo was too quiet and far too serious. He'd also begun to fuss over Xander and Elodie much as a parent would. However, it was a phone call from the school informing me that Theo had punched another pupil which finally prompted me to action. I suppressed my initial anger at his behaviour, trying to reason as Olivia would have done, that it was so out of character there must be more to it than I'd been told. When I spoke to her, his teacher had also recognised that and requested I let her know if I extracted any further detail from Theo, who had apparently sat in mute misery ever since the incident. When I arrived to pick him up, he still didn't speak, but threw himself, sobbing, into my arms.

'What happened, kiddo?' I asked him later that evening after the other two were in bed. As he sat on my knee in his Star Wars pyjamas and dressing gown it suddenly struck me, in spite of his growing maturity, he was still very young. His face took on a pinched expression.

'Come on love,' I said. 'I know there must have been something. You don't even punch your own brother, let alone another child. What happened?'

He shook his head and tears brimmed in his eyes.

'Are you scared to tell me?'

He nodded. That worried me. He'd never worried about telling me things in the past, even on the rare occasion he'd been seriously naughty. Had I really changed so much in the months since Olivia's death?

'You don't need to be scared of Daddy, Theo. I promise I won't get cross.'

'I'm not scared of you,' he stated, his eyes wide. 'I just don't want to upset you.'

'Okay. I promise I won't be upset. Tell me, please.'

I cuddled him into me and he hid his face in my jumper.

'I was talking to Freddie about the different colours of lightsabres,' he said, 'And Nat came over and he said I was talking rubbish. He said his mum told him you could only get lightsabres in blue, green and red. I said that in that case his mum was silly then because everyone knows that Mace Windu's was purple. He said...' he gulped, 'He said, "Well at least I've still got a mum, yours is dead" and that's when I hit him.'

He was rigid in my arms and I took a deep breath, willing myself to stay calm. I didn't understand how anyone, even a child, could be so cruel and the thought of the pain he'd caused my gentle boy was more than I could deal with. I moved Theo back so he could see my face.

'What you did was wrong, Theo, you know that. However, that said, I understand completely why you hit him. You know I can't condone it and Mum wouldn't have done either, but I do understand. I'll talk to your teacher tomorrow and let her know what happened. If there's a punishment, you'll just have to take it on the chin, but I'm not going to say anything more about it.'

He relaxed and cuddled up to me again. I wrapped my arms tightly around him until his breathing became deeper and I realised he'd fallen asleep, worn out by the emotion of the day. I knew how he felt.

I'd arranged counselling for all three of the children so they could talk to an adult without worrying about upsetting them and Theo was the one who was the angriest with Olivia and, to some extent with me, for allowing it to happen. He might look like his mother, but there was a lot of me in his character and what I'd half-guessed at, his counsellor had confirmed: he felt responsible for Xander and Elodie. He was trying to be strong for them, but she was gradually getting him to accept that ultimately, they were my responsibility not his and he was allowed to be sad and think about himself.

It was in the lead up to Elodie's fourth birthday that I hit my lowest point since Mum had given me Olivia's letter. After reading that I'd tried to focus on the future but as spring approached and new life appeared everywhere, it only emphasised my sense of loss. Light was returning after the dark cold of the winter months, but I felt as though I was still stranded in that season.

Meeting Grace was like seeing a single shaft of sunlight in a dark forest. It reminded me that it still existed, even if I was choosing to ignore it. Intellectually, I knew Olivia was dead, but in my heart she was still at the very centre of who I was. I was at war with myself, understanding that on one level

I was doing nothing wrong: I was a widower contemplating a new relationship, but on another level I was unable to silence the part of me that insisted I was betraying my wife.

I tried to stay away from Grace – after all, it had only been five months since Olivia's death when I first met her – but I kept returning to her. It seemed I was always destined to fall in love at first sight, but unlike with Olivia, this time it was complicated. I didn't want to admit I was in love with Grace and I had the children to consider, plus she wasn't really looking for a relationship and neither was I. I told myself we were only friends and friendship was not infidelity. I had nothing to feel guilty about and yet the self-reproach persisted.

As the months went on, I found a way to live with my conscience but still couldn't reconcile my behaviour with how I felt someone in my situation should behave. However, Ashley's visit had made me realise I was risking everything if I didn't sort myself out. As always when I was troubled, I went to Olivia's grave to talk it over with her.

'I think I've fallen in love with her,' I said, then reconsidered the statement. 'No, I don't think it, I know it. I love her and I don't know what to do about it. I'll never forget you or stop loving you – nor would I want to – but I don't want to not be with Grace either. It would be good for the kids to have a mother figure in their lives aside from Mum, especially as Elodie gets older, but I don't know what to do for the best. I wish you were here to advise me, but if you were, I wouldn't need the advice, would I? I suppose in a way, I'm simply asking your permission. I think you'd have liked Grace. She's less fiery than you, but just as strong in her own way. She's had her own issues to deal with so she won't take nonsense from the kids any more than you would have done. She'll never replace you for them or me, but you're not here. All the same, I wouldn't like you to think I'd forgotten you. And before you say anything, I know you'd never think that and

I'm talking nonsense, but better that I talk nonsense to you than anyone else. You at least, understand me.'

When I returned home, Mum was waiting for me.

'Feeling any better?'

'Not really. Talking things through with Olivia normally helps me straighten things out in my mind, but in this case I'm not sure she's the right person to talk to.'

'Is Grace?'

'Good God, no! I've hurt her enough already by not being able to properly commit to her. I daren't talk to her until I've made a decision. She has the opportunity to make a fresh start away from all this mess and I have to be sure of what I want before I speak to her. It wouldn't be fair otherwise.'

'Here.'

She held out another letter with Olivia's writing on the envelope.

'Did she give you a letter for every eventuality?' I asked, feeling unaccountably cross that my behaviour was so predictable.

'Not quite. Just ones where she thought you might need a little push in the right direction.'

I slit the top of the envelope and with a feeling of déja-vu, pulled out two sheets of paper.

Dearest darling Tom,

If you're reading this then you've fallen in love with a woman your mum thinks I would approve of and you're dithering about what to do. I don't like to think too much of this – I want you to be happy, but I'm only human and I can't help a tiny spark of jealousy at the thought of you loving someone else – so I will keep this note brief and say only this.

If you truly love her and the only thing stopping you declaring it is some misguided sense of loyalty to me, then for goodness' sake, put the poor woman out of her misery and tell her. You dawdle so dread-

fully with things like this (remember how I had to prompt you to our first kiss?) and try to use your head because listening to your heart scares you. I had to nudge you along the road to matrimony with me, but she may not be as confident of your love as I was and you might lose her to someone else if you don't tell her how you feel. Oh, and don't use the kids as an excuse. If you love her then I'm sure they will as well. Just do it, Tom!

I love you. Be happy
Olivia

P.S. You know I like a poem, so here's another one for you. Take note of what it says.

Let Me Go – Christina Rossetti

When I come to the end of the road
And the sun has set for me
I want no rites in a gloom filled room
Why cry for a soul set free?
Miss me a little, but not for long
And not with your head bowed low
Remember the love that once we shared
Miss me, but let me go.
For this is a journey we all must take
And each must go alone.
It's all part of the master plan
A step on the road to home.
When you are lonely and sick at heart
Go the friends we know.

Laugh at all the things we used to do
Miss me, but let me go.
When I am dead my dearest
Sing no sad songs for me
Plant thou no roses at my head
Nor shady cypress tree
Be the green grass above me
With showers and dewdrops wet
And if thou wilt remember
And if thou wilt, forget.
I shall not see the shadows,
I shall not fear the rain;
I shall not hear the nightingale
Sing on as if in pain;
And dreaming through the twilight
That doth not rise nor set,
Haply I may remember,
And haply may forget.

Wiping yet more tears away, I slid the paper back into the envelope, picked up my phone and tapped on Grace's name.

'It's me. Can we talk?'

GRACE

'What do you want, Tom?' Grace sounded tired.

'I told you, I want to talk.'

'Haven't we said all there is to say?'

'You might have done, but I haven't. Can you come over?'

'Now?'

'Yes now. You have to give Danny an answer by this evening and I don't want you to do that without hearing me out first.'

'You want me to come to your house?'

'Yes. What's so difficult to understand about that?'

'Nothing. It's just... it's Saturday. The kids will be there.'

'No, they won't. I've asked Mum if she'll keep an eye on them for me. Just while we talk,' I added hastily, anxious for there to be no misunderstanding this time. 'Once we've done that, they'll come back and you can meet them properly. If you want to, that is.'

'I'll be there in half an hour,' she said and the phone went dead.

I'd spent all the previous night rehearsing what I planned

to say to her, but when she was actually sitting in my living room, my mind went blank. I stared at her. I couldn't help it. It felt so right having her openly in the house and for a mad moment I considered bolting the doors and refusing to let her leave.

'Well?' she prompted. 'You dragged me out here. What was so important it couldn't wait?'

I took a deep breath. 'First of all,' I said, 'I'm not asking you to turn down the job. If it's your dream job, you should absolutely do it. If, when I've said my piece, you still want to talk to me, we can work something out so you can still accept it. Secondly, I have no expectations of you at all. Thirdly, although the possibility of you moving away is admittedly the prompt for me to speak to you about this now, it's absolutely not the only reason. I've wanted to say this to you ever since that Sunday, but I didn't think you wanted to hear it and I was trying to do the right thing by you.

Last night, Ashley told me I was being an idiot. He also said you did want to hear what I have to say, you just didn't know you did, or at least, didn't want me to know you did and then I got very confused about whether I was doing the right thing for the wrong reasons or the wrong thing for the right reasons. So, in the end, I decided to lay it all out in front of you and see what you said.'

'About what?'

'Didn't I say?'

'No.'

She sounded exasperated but I thought I could detect a faint air of amusement in her eye.

'Oh. Well, put simply, it's this. I love you. I've loved you for almost a year whether I wanted to admit it at the time or not. I wasn't comparing you to Olivia, I never have, but I also wasn't being fair to you. It felt like we were having an affair because Olivia didn't feel dead to me. I loved her so much I didn't want to accept she was gone. It was stupid of me and I don't know why it took me so long to do something about it, but last night I talked to Olivia. I told her all about you and then Mum gave me a letter she'd left for me. When I read it, I realised what a colossal fool I'd been. Here.'

I handed her Olivia's letter. She read it then looked up at me. There was no hint of the smile I'd hoped to see.

'So, you're telling me that after months of you dithering, we can be together now because you got permission from your dead wife? Jesus, Tom.'

'No, it's not like that! Please Grace, try to understand. It's not about my being given permission. It's about being freed to not feel guilty that I'm still alive. It's about understanding that my life didn't end with hers and that's okay. All this time I've been feeling that I'm an awful person for wanting to move on with my life. If I loved her as much as I claimed, how could I even be thinking about falling in love with someone else, let alone actually doing it? I never expected to meet anyone after Olivia died. I thought that was it, I'd had my chance at happiness and it was gone, so to meet someone less than six months after her funeral and instantly connect with them, made me question who I was. It made me examine every part of my character and I got lost in the process. Olivia's letter only made me realise it was all right to take the path out. You were the light that was guiding me through it, I just didn't want to see it. I am begging you to give me another chance. I promise I will not let you down this time and I will do whatever it takes to show you how important you are to me.'

'How do I know you won't say this now and then change your mind again in another week?'

'Now who's not listening? I'm not going anywhere. Grace, I'm not talking about a casual relationship here. If you want commitment, I'll marry you as soon as we can book a registrar. If you want to redecorate the entire house, that's fine, although you might have a fight with the children if you touch their rooms! If you want me to move house, we'll move and choose somewhere together. What do you want from me?'

'I've always fancied a winter wedding,' she said. 'Do you think we could organise one by Christmas?'

'We'll find a way,' I said, pulling her towards me and kissing her soundly. 'Consider yourself engaged.'

'Can I let you into a secret?' Grace whispered in my ear. 'I turned the job down this morning. It wasn't my dream job and I wasn't quite ready to give up on you altogether.'

'So, I didn't need to make that speech? You could have said!'

'Oh, you needed to make it,' she laughed. 'Even if you know something, it's always nice to be told.'

'Duly noted,' I said, smiling. Then I pulled her towards the back door. 'Come and meet the family.'

The children were cautious, but welcoming and I knew from the smile on Mum's face she'd guessed what was happening and had prepared the kids for our news.

'I'm not trying to replace your mum,' Grace said quietly, 'But I'll do my best to make her proud by looking after you and your dad for her. Is that alright with you?'

I wasn't naïve enough to believe that there wouldn't be bumps ahead of us, but we'd made a good start and I was confident our family would soon knit together. Grace was a natural with the children and they loved her for it. If she'd tried to be artificially friendly, they'd have spotted it and instantly hated her. By being herself, she won them over to her side and I had a feeling it wouldn't be too long before they were joining forces to gang up on me and tease me. The laughter was back in our home.

DECEMBER 2014

Grace laid her bouquet at the foot of the headstone.

'Here you are, Olivia,' she whispered. 'Your family will be okay, I promise. I'll take good care of them for you, but I can't promise I won't need to come and ask your advice from time to time.'

She stepped back and watched as I touched my fingers to my lips and pressed them against the marble. I took Grace's hand in mine and together we made our way back to the wedding car, which was waiting to take us to the hotel where our family and friends were gathered waiting for us. I looked back at the grave.

'Goodbye sweetheart.'

ACKNOWLEDGMENTS

There are so many people who helped to bring this book to life. I hope I haven't missed anyone out, but if I have, please accept both my apologies and my thanks. Without the support of these people, *Unforgettable* would not exist in the form it does today:

Tim, Shirley and Tracy, who read the various early drafts and gave me feedback on them.

Danny, my Open University tutor, who encouraged me to believe in myself as a writer.

Dini and Jenny, who gave me a hefty (and metaphorical) kick up the bum whenever I had a wobble about my writing.

My wonderful editor, Jane, whose notes were invaluable.

The fantastic Sam, who designed my cover.

Jo, for her help making a last minute addition to my author biography.

Ed and Debbie, for their insights into the world of competitive ballroom dancing

Moyra, for her guidance with the medical aspects.

All the university friends who prompted my memories of life in Exeter in the late '90s.

Lastly, my boys – James, Henry and Arthur, without whom my life would be dull. It's only because of their love and support that I'm able to write as I do.

ALSO BY R.E. LOTEN

FOLLY (AVONSTOW BOOK ONE)

1917

Avonstow is at war, but it's a friendly invasion that forces deeply held secrets to emerge. The arrival of the Australian engineers upsets the equilibrium of the wartime village, while the commander of the village's naval base is convinced a spy is lurking in their midst. The consequences are far greater than anyone might have imagined.

1995

Ellie Whitemore travels to Avonstow after her great-uncle's body is discovered on the salt marshes near the town. She sets about unravelling her family's past and finds that their fortunes are inextricably linked with those of the town itself. But there is always a price to pay when secrets are unearthed.

THE MERMAID (AVONSTOW BOOK TWO)

World War Two.

Headstrong. Impetuous. Brave. Frankie has been called all of them. Her loved ones are doing their bit for the war effort and she is determined not to be left behind. Then she meets Mac and everything changes.

But war has a habit of interfering with the best-laid plans and Frankie finds herself caught in a dangerous game where the stakes are high.

2017

There are secrets in Hannah's life that she cannot bring herself to share with anyone, but no matter how deeply they are buried, they always find a way to resurface.

Avonstow is united in trying to save their Lido from closure, but will

Hannah find her place in the quiet community or will she once again have to run from the mistakes of her past?

As Frankie begins to share the untold story of her wartime exploits, there are lessons Hannah can learn.

But perhaps some things are best left alone.

AS HENRIETTA EDWARDS

MAX, THE BRIGHTLINGSEA CAT

LILIBET THE LOBSTER

THE COURTS SERIES

THE REIGN OF THE WINTER KING (THE COURTS BOOK ONE)

Everyone knows the stories of Robin Hood and King Arthur.

Everyone knows they're just legends.

But what if everyone is wrong?

While Sam, Henry and Arthur think they're going to spend their summer holiday with Uncle Alan, their adventurous relative has other plans. The Silver Arrow has gone missing, and Robin has been kidnapped.

The race is on to find the arrow and rescue Robin, before others beat them to it. Who can be trusted? One wrong move and disaster is sure to follow!

This series is perfect for fans of Susan Cooper's 'The Dark Is Rising' series.